MW00782143

A Season in London

A Season in London

Elizabeth Johns
Heather B. Moore
Rebecca Connolly

Mirror Press

Copyright © 2017 Mirror Press
Print edition
All rights reserved

No part of this book may be reproduced in any form whatsoever without
prior written permission of the publisher, except in the case of brief passages
embodied in critical reviews and articles. These novels are works of fiction.
The characters, names, incidents, places, and dialog are products of the
authors' imaginations and are not to be construed as real.

Interior Design by Cora Johnson
Edited by Jennie Stevens and Lisa Shepherd
Cover design by Rachael Anderson
Cover Photo Credit: Richard Jenkins Photography

Published by Mirror Press, LLC

ISBN-13: 978-1-947152-25-0
ISBN-10: 1-947152-25-4

Other Timeless Regency Collections

Table of Contents

Poor Relations

By Elizabeth Johns

One

"This is my cousin, Emma Standrich," Lady Jane Wetherby said for the hundredth time that evening.

"Also known as the poor relation," Emma muttered to herself in tandem with the greeting as she made a curtsy in her pale pink ball gown, second hand from Jane's first Season and not the most flattering colour for Emma's dark hair and fair complexion.

A gentleman was bowing before her, and her breath caught in her throat as he actually stopped and looked down at her with a piercing stare. His eyes were the palest shade of grey, and his hair was a light shade of brown. He was wearing a red regimental tunic adorned with gold braid and white breeches covering his well-formed legs. He presented a picture of strength and command.

"Will you honour me with a dance, Miss Standrich?"

Emma stood speechless as the unexpected invitation caught her by surprise. Had he heard her and was now taking pity on her?

A sly nudge in the foot from Jane brought her back to the present.

"I would be delighted . . . sir." She had forgotten his name!

"Shelton," the man repeated. He had a particular, penetrating look in his eye. "Is the first set spoken for?"

"No, sir."

"Until then," was all he said as he bowed and walked away.

Emma was elated and mortified at the same time.

"Rumour has it he has no fortune. 'Tis such a pity," Jane said as she watched the soldier's departure with obvious appreciation.

"Is that Colonel Shelton?"

"In the flesh. Mama will be the talk of the town for securing him at her ball."

Emma ignored everything past the affirmation of this being the very man of whom she had heard tell for years. She had hoped to find him, but she had not expected it so soon, nor at a ball—the very man she had come to London to see.

His face was more handsome than she had imagined, despite the harsh countenance and thin purple scar running across his cheek.

"Do not stare, Emma. It is gauche."

How could she not stare? This was the man her brother had served under and idolized before he died. His letters had been full of nothing but Shelton. Emma had to hold back a tear as she thought of her older brother, Christopher, for whom she had just put off her mourning clothes. He had been sent away early as Papa had many mouths to feed, and he had subsequently died too young—not long after Papa.

"Come, Emma, the dancing is about to begin."

Emma felt her cousin seize her wrist, leading her towards the ballroom, and suddenly she wanted to escape. She did not belong here, and everyone would know it.

"What if there are whispers?" Emma asked, trying to resist the summons.

"No, Emma. You promised you would be here with me tonight."

"I do not belong in there, Jane."

"Your birth is as good as mine, if you please." Jane held out her arm and linked it with Emma's.

"But my fortune is not."

"Then enjoy your time here and do not worry about having to see any of these people again."

Jane's mother rushed up from behind them as the doors were closed and the music began to play.

"You must find a husband this Season, Emma," Aunt Tilda said quietly as they made their way from the entry hall to the ballroom. "But be warned, for there is only one thing a fortune hunter wants with a pretty face."

"My position as governess to Lady Malvern is already arranged, Aunt."

"That is easily mended with a letter." Her aunt waved her hand dismissively. "You will never succeed as a governess. You will be sent home as soon as you arrive, once the mistress sees your face. I told your mother how it would be."

"I have little choice, Aunt. Without Father or Christopher to provide for us, I must have an income."

"This is neither the time nor the place to discuss it. I will find you a husband this Season, but stay away from him." Aunt Tilda nodded her head towards the door that Colonel Shelton had walked through.

"She has already consented to the opening quadrille with him," Jane pointed out.

Her aunt sighed. "I suppose you must dance with him then, but only once. Make it plain to him that you are uninterested, though I am not sure why he is singling out a young miss. It is not at all like him."

"Am I to be rude?" Emma asked.

"No, no. Never be rude. You will not have learned the subtleties in the country, but do not elaborate when he asks you questions. Only answer as little as necessary. Do not encourage him with your eyes."

"I will do my best." Emma endeavoured to sound reassuring.

"I know you will, my dear." Her aunt placed her hand on her arm. "If only things were not so desperate! Forgive me, I must attend to my guests now." She opened her fan and flitted it before rushing away.

Emma and Jane watched her move toward Lady Crofton with her arms stretched forward in welcome.

"Mother is right, you know," Jane said. "You will not succeed as a governess."

"I can and I will because I have to," Emma replied, infusing her voice with fierce determination.

"You mistake me, Emma. It is not your abilities we speak of but the wandering eyes and hands of men. It is a known fact."

Emma shuddered. "Nevertheless, I cannot refuse two hundred pounds per annum when my mother and siblings will go hungry," she explained.

"Oh, that certainly means the master is horrid—or the children are—if they offered you such a sum! Here comes my first partner," Jane said. "Do not fret. We shall find you a husband!"

Emma blew out a frustrated breath. Things were not so simple as finding a husband.

"Ominous words, to be sure," a deep voice said from behind her.

Emma started.

"I apologise. That was badly done. I came to claim my

4

dance and overheard," Colonel Shelton said as he held out his hand.

Emma did not know how to respond to such ill manners, so she inclined her head in a cool nod.

He let out a harsh laugh. "I am to be punished for my uncouth ways, no doubt."

He led her to the dance floor, and they took their places across from one another in the set. Emma kept hoping the floor would open up and swallow her, or someone would yell "fire" to save her from this predicament. She was out of her depth conversationally, in age, and experience. She knew none of those deceptive arts her aunt had referred to. In her country village, they spoke plainly. But she dared not alienate this man as she desperately wanted to ask him about her brother—how his last days had been and whether he had been happy? Had he been brave? Had he ever spoken of her? Why had he been killed? She had to muster some courage.

The quadrille progressed with relative smoothness and she was thankful her feet had recalled the steps while her mind had been elsewhere.

"Very well," he said, after a stretch of painful silence, "I believe I can recall from my youth how to carry on an insipid conversation. I must say, however, I expected more from a sister of Christopher Standrich."

She shot him an angry look.

"Excellent. I am glad to know there is warm life in there."

"You amuse yourself in insulting me, sir."

"I do nothing of the sort," he retorted.

The movements of the set then separated them, and she was left to ponder his reasons for dancing with her.

He spoke first when they came back together. "Has my reputation already been so polluted to your innocent ears?"

"I may have heard some things, yes."

"I see. May I presume this is your first Season in London?"

"I am visiting my aunt before journeying north to a new position." Why had she said that to him?

He showed no signs of hearing her. "And how is the family in Devon?"

"They were in good health when I left them, thank you."

The movements of the dance saved her from furthering the uncomfortable conversation until they were reunited at the end.

"I trust your aunt will warn you against me, Miss Standrich. There is likely some truth in rumours. I would like to say, however, you will always find a friend in me. Do remember that."

"Thank you," she said awkwardly as he walked her back to her aunt.

"Miss Standrich? Your brother . . ." He paused, perhaps to compose himself. "There was no finer man nor officer than he."

Her eyes filled with tears, but she nodded as he bowed swiftly and walked away.

"That was rather abrupt. What did he say?" Jane asked quietly. From nowhere, it seemed, she had appeared beside her.

"I do not wish to speak of it now. Please take me somewhere away from here before I make a scene."

"Before you make *more* of a scene," her cousin corrected. "The entire ballroom was attentive to your every move and gesture. It will be the mystery discussed at every morning visit on the morrow," Jane said, as she whisked her cousin through the servants' door to a private room, away from prying eyes and ears.

"I beg your pardon, Cousin? Why would anyone care about the poor relation?"

"Because no one knows who you are, and Shelton neither attends society events, nor dances with anyone. It is quite delicious. I mean, it would be, if it were not my cousin involved," Jane clarified quickly.

Emma sighed as she walked toward the ivory silk settee and sat down. "A further instance of London sophistication I do not own."

Jane patted her cousin's arm. "I must return to my next partner. Do not stay in here too long, because now every man will be vying for a dance with you."

Emma shook her head and wiped her eyes as her cousin left the room. Her emotions were in turmoil. She truly had no idea of Shelton's reputation other than the idol-worship stories her brother had told. Her stomach was in a flutter when she was near the colonel. He exuded masculinity, strength, and danger. She would have to quiz her aunt and cousin for information later. She needed to know. She could not stay away from this man until she had found out more about Christopher and why there were suspicions surrounding his death.

Emma took a deep breath and checked her face in the glass. She was relieved to find her eyes were not red and her cheeks were not splotched. She returned to the ballroom feeling more composed. It was indeed as her cousin had said. Her hand was requested for dances for the remainder of the evening.

Two

Emma arose the next day and followed a pleasant floral aroma all the way to the morning room. The scene that greeted her, of flower arrangements covering every available surface, astounded her. She knew Jane was a desirable catch on the marriage mart, but she was still astonished to see such adoration. Emma bent over to smell some yellow roses, and her gaze stopped on a card addressed to Miss Standrich.

"For me?"

She tentatively reached out, took the card, and opened it.

To the belle of the ball
Yours, etc,
Bragg

"There must be some mistake," she mused aloud.

Lord Bragg, she remembered then, was the handsome older gentleman she had danced the Cotillion with. As she stood admiring the yellow roses, the butler entered with another delivery.

"Good morning, Jensen."

"Good morning, Miss Standrich. You certainly made an

impression last evening. I do not know if the house can hold many more flowers. I think you may have more than Lady Jane. There are so many, my lady has requested some be moved from the drawing room into here to make room for callers. She is expecting a house full."

"More than Lady Jane?" Emma said to herself in confusion. She looked around, and sure enough, there were several addressed to her from those gentlemen with whom she had danced. She walked in a daze to the drawing room and found a similar sight greeting her.

"Good morning, my dear," her aunt said pleasantly.

"Good morning, Aunt."

"Oh, Emma," she declared at once, "you cannot wear your country work clothes today! Do go and change into the sprigged muslin!"

"I was saving it for a special occasion."

"This is a special occasion! You shall have many callers from last night, and you must make your best impression. It is not unheard of to be proposed to after two or three encounters," Aunt Tilda explained.

Emma fancied her simple country dress; it was her favourite, and she rather thought she looked nice in it.

"Do not look at me as though I drowned your kitten," her aunt chided. "You do not understand what this means!" Aunt Tilda held out her arms and spun around amongst the flowers.

Emma stared at her aunt and shook her head.

"It means you will find a husband! I have no doubts about Jane, with her figure and fortune, but I did not realise it would be so simple to match you. Now *do* go and change before the visitors start arriving. I will send Smitty to help you dress."

"Yes, Aunt," Emma said, bobbing a dutiful curtsy.

Emma walked back to her room with a sinking feeling in her stomach. What could this be about? She was no fool. Her face may be passably pretty, but she was virtually penniless. Was it simply because Shelton had danced with her? She had heard tell of such things in letters from her cousin. London ways were strange. However, she did not wish to be the latest curiosity. She removed from her bandbox the last note she had received from Christopher and fingered it gingerly before opening it and reading again the lines which most disturbed her.

I am to deliver an urgent missive to F tomorrow for S. Take heart, S believes this will be over soon and I may return home.

But Christopher had been found dead the next day—apparently shot from his horse—with little explanation as to why he had died outside of battle.

She hoped she would be able to find answers and some measure of understanding during her short time in London. Once she removed to Durham, she had little hope of discovering anything about that fateful last day of his life.

Aunt Tilda may be opposed to Colonel Shelton, but Emma must find a way to speak to him.

Smitty helped her dress, and her stomach gave a twinge of nerves at the thought of seeing the colonel again. Her aunt thought of marriage, but Emma knew none of the gentlemen would want to wed her when she had nothing to offer in exchange. There was no place for romance where she was going, and she would stay mindful of it. Just a few short years ago, her daydreams had been filled with handsome suitors, a Season, and her future family. How quickly things changed.

The maid spent more time tending to Emma for the prospective visitors than she had spent altogether when readying herself for the ball, and she had to admit she did look much more elegant and smart in the new dress her aunt had given her. She felt more confident blending in with the current fashion, though she hated to think what the fine sprigged muslin with a beautiful floral pattern had cost. The maid finished tying the knot on the matching blue ribbons in her hair and declared her ready to receive callers.

Emma rushed back downstairs in the hopes of finding out more about Shelton's reputation from Jane. But when she arrived, there were already a few guests, including Jane's hopeful beau, the Viscount Lofton, and two of his cronies, who were also soldiers. She paused as she heard voices.

"I was surprised to see Shelton show his face at your ball last night."

"Indeed, it was quite the triumph," Aunt Tilda said.

"Perhaps, but I would caution your niece, since he seems to have singled her out," Lofton remarked as he stroked his whiskers.

Aunt Tilda raised a condescending eyebrow. "I think there can be little harm in dancing one set at a ball, Lofton."

"No need to take offence, ma'am. I am only looking out for your niece and dear Jane, of course. He has gained quite a reputation for being dangerous, but that is not for tender ears."

"I understand there are rumours about him, but until substantiated, I will reserve judgement, sir. He was my nephew's commanding officer, and I suspect he was merely showing my niece a kindness."

"Bravo, Aunt!" Emma whispered, listening unashamedly just outside the door.

"Your prudence does you justice, Lady Wetherby. I hope my wariness will prove to be unfounded."

Emma could no longer risk eavesdropping, though she wanted no part in toad-eating Viscount Lofton. He made her skin crawl, but her dearest Jane wanted to marry him and saw good in him, so she would attempt to do the same. She entered the drawing room, and the men rose to their feet.

"Ah, there is Emma now. I believe you were all introduced last evening?"

"Indeed," the viscount said as he performed a slight bow. "May I offer my condolences on the loss of Lieutenant Standrich. He was a fine young man who was unfortunate in his commander."

Before anyone could reply to this defamation, the door opened, and Jensen announced Colonel Shelton.

"Good day, Lady Wetherby, Lady Jane, Miss Standrich," Colonel Shelton said upon entering the room. "Lofton, I believe we could find a better place to discuss my leadership than Lady Wetherby's drawing room."

Lofton's ears burned red at being caught in the act of maligning Shelton. Emma thought the colonel could have called Lofton out for such words.

"I cannot stay, unfortunately," Shelton continued, "but I came to ask Miss Standrich if she would honour me with a drive this afternoon?"

Emma was caught unawares. She really did not wish to be alone with Shelton, but she was so angry with the viscount, she wanted to spite him.

"I would be delighted, Colonel Shelton, if my aunt has no objection."

Aunt Tilda, whose constitution did not agree with confrontation, quickly assented.

"Excellent. I shall call for you around four." He bowed with a curt click of his heels and marched through the door.

An uncomfortable silence followed his exit.

"I apologise. It is regrettable you had to witness such a scene," Lofton said. "Please use caution, Miss Standrich. My only concern is for your safety."

"Consider me duly warned, my lord," she replied, trying her hardest to appear civil.

"I cannot guess what he is about. I thought he knew better than to dangle after a young miss," Lofton said haughtily.

"Perhaps he recognises the charm of Miss Standrich, as do I," another young man said—quite handsomely, Emma thought.

"Of course. Please pardon my words, Miss Standrich. I meant no offence to your obvious charms. He is not suitable for London drawing rooms, in my opinion," Lofton replied, further adding insult to injury.

"I knew his dear mother, and he will be welcome in my house whenever he chooses, Lofton, unless you wish to go into further detail?" Lady Wetherby said, clearly trying to put an end to the slanderous insinuations about Shelton.

"Yes, Lofton," one of the other gentlemen agreed. "Best leave your grievances with Shelton to the club or the battlefield."

Emma wished Lofton would leave. His posturing had spoiled the mood of the morning, and if he continued, she feared her aunt would forbid her to see Shelton.

"We must take our leave now. Thank you for the lovely ball last evening, Lady Wetherby. Lady Jane, may I also drive you in the park this afternoon?"

Lady Jane dutifully looked at her mother, who gave a proud nod.

"I shall call for you at the usual time," he said with an arrogant air as he took a pinch of snuff and snapped the lid of his snuffbox closed. He brushed back a brown curl from his brow and adjusted his sleeves.

"I shall be ready," Jane assured him, though he paid little regard as he and his friends took their leave.

"That was most unfortunate!" Aunt Tilda exclaimed. "I wonder, what could it all mean?"

"I do not know," Jane said. "I was afraid someone would slap a glove in the other's face!"

"Is Colonel Shelton's reputation limited to the battle-field?" Emma queried.

Lady Wetherby wrinkled her brow in deep thought. "I suppose it must be. He has always had a mysterious manner about him, but he has been a soldier so long, it is difficult to remember." She held up her finger as a memory struck her. "There was some incident a few years ago, involving Shelton, his brother, and someone else. I cannot recall the details or who the third party was, but it resulted in him being disinher-ited."

"But he is still accepted in society? It makes little sense," Jane reasoned.

"It was kept very quiet, and considered a private matter. Of course he is accepted—he is a Shelton. It is he who chooses to ignore society, so it is a positive coup if he attends any-thing."

"Then why is he someone I should be kept away from?" Emma asked.

"Because the rumour is he has no money and he is too handsome for temptation!" her aunt said, as if stating the obvious.

Emma could see her aunt's point, but her brother had always had nothing but praise for his commander, and she desperately needed information from him. She was more certain than ever that something foul had happened to Christopher, and she might not have many chances left to speak with the colonel.

Colin could have stayed, but he did not wish to put himself in Lofton's presence unnecessarily—especially not after he happened upon him maligning his name to an attentive drawing room. How he wished this dreadful ordeal would be over, and, if all went well, he would never hear the name Lofton again.

Had the brother and father not died in a horrific accident, one in which the circumstances had been most suspicious, Melvyn would not now be Lofton. And yet, he had chosen to stay in the army instead of returning to run his estate. Not that it was unusual to have peers in the army, but Melvyn had never been one to sully his fingers if there was an easier way to obtain his object. Melvyn had always been fond of gambling, and an officer's pay would hardly afford a heavy habit—which was why Colin was overly suspicious of everything Lofton did. While Melvyn might not be in his regiment any longer, he was in Colin's division and thus he knew almost every move the viscount made.

There were also many unanswered questions where Christopher Standrich was concerned, and he owed it to the Standrich family to see them resolved. He had not counted on the sister's involvement, however. It would seem Lofton was courting the heiress cousin, and it was too convenient for Colin's comfort. Emma Standrich was no simpering miss, and had a sharp eye. Colin was tempted to warn her, but he did not want her to be in danger as well. He felt an unusual wave of protectiveness for this girl who he barely knew.

He went straight from the Wetherby house to Whitehall. Something had to be done quickly if Lady Jane was the next intended victim. He asked to see his superior and was shown into an anteroom while the clerk enquired if his lordship was available. Less than five minutes passed before he was shown to an office at the end of a long, dim corridor. In contrast, the office was spacious, flooded with daylight from a large window and furnished for taste as well as function.

"Thank you for seeing me, sir," he said, bowing.

"What has you troubled, Shelton?" The elder man looked at him over his spectacles.

"It appears Lofton is intent on courting Lady Jane."

"Yes, yes. Along with half a dozen other suitors." He waved his hand dismissively.

"But you, of all people, know what he is capable of!" Colin protested.

"I am hardly in a position to tell a Peer of the Realm to decamp when I have no proof of his nefarious activities. What I do have are some very serious theories and accusations based on seeing the body of a smuggler some years prior and the untimely death of his father and brother, God rest their souls."

"And what of the leaked information? Is treason not enough to give you pause?"

"You know very well we have not been able to pin it directly on him. I will say he is very clever, and there are a number of coincidences where he is concerned."

"I beg of you to use caution, then. You may not know him as I do, but it will eventually all come out, and you do not want your name—or your daughter—anywhere near that man."

"Thus far he has done nothing more than ask to call on her. I will do my best to refrain from any further private audiences with him."

"Thank you, sir. I can ask for no more." Colin turned to leave, but paused with his arm stretched towards the handle.

"It would be quite the *coup de grâce* for him to secure your daughter."

Colin turned to see a proud father's smile.

"But for her inheritance or to force the Crown into a pardon?"

Colin gave a curt nod and left, feeling guilty for the frown he left on his superior's face.

Three

Emma straightened her bonnet for the fifth time while she waited for Shelton to call. She still had no idea what she should ask him or if she should tell him what Christopher had written. She could not allow any wrong-doing to be attributed to her brother without proof.

Jensen finally sent a footman to tell her the colonel had arrived. She walked hurriedly down the stairs to meet him, hoping to avoid another quarrel with Viscount Lofton.

"Good afternoon, Colonel Shelton," she greeted him, as she reached the bottom step.

"Good afternoon, Miss Standrich. I brought my phaeton. I trust you are not afraid of heights?"

"No, sir. I have always rather fancied a ride in one, thank you."

He helped her climb into the lofty conveyance. He had a lovely pair of high-stepping greys harnessed to it, and he evidently noticed her admiring them, for when he joined her on the seat, he asked, "Do you know horses well, Miss Standrich? Your brother was an excellent judge of horse flesh."

She shook her head. "I know only what Christopher taught me, which was very little."

"He chose this pair for me. They are the finest horses I

have ever owned—not to be disloyal to my trusted battle steed." He pulled into the street and managed the team with ease through the traffic.

"But those are a different type of horse altogether, are they not?"

"Yes." He paused, and the silence alerted her to the nearness of this large man, and she was acutely uncomfortable. She had never been this close to a man, and she could feel her hands perspiring inside her gloves. She must force herself to be bold.

"Colonel Shelton, about my brother . . . Could you please tell me why he died that day? It makes little sense to me."

"I am very sorry for your loss, Miss Standrich. He was a fine soldier, but soldiers die all the time, even when they are not fighting a big, glorious battle." His voice held a hint of sarcasm, and he kept his gaze on the horses as they neared the gate to the park.

"How did he die? And why was his discharge not listed as honourable?"

Colonel Shelton pursed his lips and then exhaled audibly. "His death is still under investigation. I am not certain we should be speaking of this. What good will come of it? It will not bring him back to either of us."

"Please," she whispered. "I need to know."

He drove through the crowds before answering. He slowed the phaeton to a walk, drew the horses over to the side of the path, and thence to a stop. He turned slightly to look at her. "You need only know that Christopher did nothing wrong."

"It is not enough," she said, staring down at her gloved hands.

He looked away for some time, in silence. "This shall go no further, do you understand?"

"Yes," she said breathlessly. Her hands trembled.

He considered her, his expression so piercing she could almost feel it, and then gave a slight nod before looking away again. "I sent him to deliver a message to"—he paused—"never mind to whom. I sent him with a message, and he must have been intercepted or delivered it to the wrong person. At least, I deduce such because the intended person never received the message."

"So my brother has taken the blame for the wrong outcome of this message," she surmised.

"Yes. It is my hope that I am able to clear his name while I am here. There is suspicion of a spy, and some have bandied about the theory that Christopher was on his side."

"Christopher, a spy? Never!" she said, her voice raised in disgust.

"Hush, woman!" he commanded harshly, and she could feel the presence he must have with his men on the field. "I apologise for speaking roughly, but there is still danger until the spy is discovered. I did not suspect any imminent threat when I sent Christopher away with the message. And I should not have mentioned so much. The less you know, the safer you are."

"Do you know who the spy is?" she asked.

"I have a very good idea, but I must have solid proof. I had no intention of revealing any of this to you. My only intention was to see if you were in need. Your brother had requested to sell his commission so he could return to care for the family."

Emma had to brush a tear away from her eye and hoped he did not notice.

"We will manage."

"But you are taking on a position to care for them, are you not?"

"My mouth runs away with me sometimes. I wish I had not said anything."

"Will you allow me to help you? I promised your brother I would give assistance if ever there was a need."

"It would not be proper, Colonel Shelton. You are very kind," she said, barely masking her offence. Next, would he wish to show her a quaint little cottage—where he happened to keep his mistresses?

"I can see by the look on your face you mistake me."

Emma's cheeks flushed pink. She felt the warmth of it.

"You may have heard my brother and I had a disagreement many years ago, and I was disinherited."

"I did hear something of that nature," she confessed.

"I do not have a grand estate or title as my brother has, but I am not without means. I inherited property from my mother and a more than modest cottage to accompany it. I am rarely ever in England, as my duties take me abroad most of the time. In effect, Miss Standrich, I am offering you my name and income so you may provide for your family."

"Do you mean . . ."

"I mean I am asking you to be my wife."

"While I am flattered, I am sure, I do not understand, Colonel Shelton. Why would you do such a thing?"

"I have no need of it, and you do," he stated simply.

"I see," she said as she struggled for words. Then she noticed another vehicle approaching.

"You need not answer me today," Shelton added. "Think about it."

"Here comes Jane with Lord Lofton," Emma replied.

"Devil take it," she heard Shelton whisper under his breath.

"Miss Standrich, Colonel Shelton," Lord Lofton said as he pulled his vehicle next to theirs.

Jane sat prettily next to the viscount and must have noticed the look on Emma's face. "Cousin, is something amiss?"

"No, no. I assure you I am quite well. We were only speaking of Christopher."

"Such a tragedy," the viscount said, clicking his tongue.

"If you will excuse us, I have kept the horses standing for too long," Shelton said loudly. "Enjoy your outing, Lady Jane, Lofton." He tipped his hat to them and flicked the whip.

Shelton and Emma rode in silence throughout the remainder of the drive back to the town residence, a journey which left Emma in complete confusion.

"I will call on you tomorrow," he said sternly as he handed her down from the conveyance.

She nodded and answered distractedly as she attempted to sort her thoughts. "Thank you for the drive."

"Emma, Emma, Emma!" Jane exclaimed breathlessly as she burst through the door to her cousin's room some time later.

"What has happened, Jane?" Emma asked worriedly. She sat up on her bed, where she had been staring at the canopy while trying to sort out her thoughts.

"Oh, so much," she exclaimed, "but I want to hear what happened with you first. You looked very upset, and I want to know what Shelton said to you."

"I still do not know quite what he said. I am bewildered."

"Then tell me what you can remember," her cousin urged. She untied her bonnet and kicked off her kid half-boots before she joined her cousin on the bed.

"Well, first, we discussed Christopher."

"Did you tell him about the letter?"

"No, but I did ask him about the circumstance of Christopher's death not being during action and his discharge."

"And?"

"He was rather evasive, really. He said many soldiers die away from the battlefield," Emma responded, recalling Shelton's words of warning and quickly omitting certain details.

"That is most unkind in him," Jane said, frowning. "I wanted to know who the mysterious 'F' was."

"He did not want to discuss much and said it was for my safety, so perhaps you had best not discuss it either, other than with me."

"Very well," she agreed. She looked a little worried.

"Then he offered me his name and his income to support my family."

"Well *that* was very handsome of him!"

"Was it?" Emma asked doubtfully.

"Of course it was! Now you will not have to work," Jane pointed out.

"I know very little about him other than from Christopher's letters, and his reputation concerns me."

"Oh, pish! If he will never be home and is willing to provide for you, then I say it sounds a match made in heaven."

"Maybe," she said warily.

"I take it you did not answer him?"

"No. He told me to think on it and he would call tomorrow."

"A quandary, indeed, for you. I know what I would say."

"I wish I could speak with my mother," Emma mused.

"My mother would be happy to help," Jane suggested.

"Enough of me. What of your news?" Emma asked, diverting her cousin's attention from the unwelcome idea.

Jane's face was transformed by a huge smile. She leaned forward and whispered, "Melvyn has asked me to marry him!"

"Is this not good news? Why are we whispering?" Emma asked.

"Because he wants to marry before he returns to the Continent," Jane replied sadly.

"When does he leave?"

"In less than a month."

Emma was thoughtful as she calculated in her mind. "Which will not allow time for the banns to be called, since you missed this Sunday and they must be called three times."

"Precisely. So we must go to Scotland," Jane whispered.

"No, Jane, you must not," Emma insisted. "You must speak to my aunt about this. It is not a poor match, so I am certain she would be willing to help rather than have her daughter elope. Perhaps you could obtain a special license."

Jane shook her head. "Mama and Papa said no. Mama wants a grand wedding and time to prepare for it."

"You have already asked?"

"Yes." She dropped her head in her hands and began to weep.

"Can Lofton not obtain the special license?"

"It seems not. He would not explain. He said it is impossible for he is away for a few days."

"Why cannot you wait until he returns again?" Emma did not understand the hurry. Jane would not be penniless without the marriage.

"Mama and Papa do not even want it announced until he returns. What if he were to die in battle?" she argued.

Emma had no answer to that, since her brother had

recently died. "How do you propose to pull it off? Does Lofton have a plan?"

"When Mama and Papa go to Grandmama's for a day, we can stay behind. It will give us more than a day's head start. We will leave detailed letters and beg them not to stop us."

"I cannot like it, Jane. If your parents do not support this, in the end there will be a huge scandal. I cannot believe Lofton would suggest it!"

"My parents abhor scandal, so they will go along with it. They do not oppose Lofton, only a hasty marriage. Will you help me, Emma?" Jane pleaded.

"If you are certain this is what you want, I will not stand in your way."

Jane threw her arms around Emma in excitement, but Emma could only just keep herself from becoming ill.

Four

Emma had decisions to make. She had spoken with her aunt about Shelton, and any hint of ineligibility vanished from her aunt's mind at hearing the word *offer*. Her uncle only stated Shelton had spoken with him and had proposed a handsome settlement—much more than he would have suspected the man even owned.

At this juncture, Emma suspected her mother would give her the same advice as her aunt and uncle if she found a man willing to take her with no dowry. She needed someone who could help her think through life beyond the vows. Her brother was no longer an option, and her aunt and cousin were little help. Would relying on her brother's opinion be enough to erase her doubts caused by the viscount? It seemed to Emma as though the viscount's objections were related to the army or perhaps some other offence to his masculine egotism, which she could easily dispense with.

Shelton's estate, Newton Park, was in Dorsetshire, only a day's travel from her mother and younger siblings; her brother's education would be provided for, and her sister would have a dowry. It seemed too good to be true, and perhaps it was—not to mention being a lifelong decision. She supposed, as long as it provided for her family and she was not abused, the decision should be easy. She laughed to herself. It was not so different a decision from the one she had made to become a governess. However, she could always walk away from a post; she could not from a marriage.

Emma had no romantic feelings for Shelton, although she could acknowledge he was handsome. What if her feelings were to change? What if his expectations changed? Her uncle had assured her the funds for her family would be placed in a separate account upon the marriage and could not be tampered with. And that was what settled her decision.

As she dressed, she felt at peace having decided, and that was as much reassurance as she could give herself. She wished she felt such hope for her cousin.

Colonel Shelton was waiting for her alone when she entered the parlour. It was a pleasant room, cheery with afternoon sun, but it felt smaller with him as the centrepiece.

"Good afternoon, sir."

"Miss Standrich." He bowed.

"Shall we sit down?" She waved her hand to a chair, and he followed. "Sir, I have decided to accept your generous offer. I am still uncertain as to why, but it eases my mind greatly. Thank you."

She was convinced a sigh of relief passed through him, and she grew more perplexed.

"I do trust you will find yourself content. I must return shortly to the Continent, so I have taken some liberties with arrangements. My uncle happens to be an archbishop—and my godfather—and was kind enough to sign a special license for us."

"Your uncle is the archbishop?" Emma desperately wanted to question him about Lofton, but she held her tongue.

"Convenient, is it not?" He smiled slightly for the first time, and she at once thought she had best guard her heart.

"When shall the happy event take place, then?" she asked.

"The day after tomorrow, if you agree. Unfortunately, it will not allow time for your family to travel here, but I will make arrangements for them to travel to Dorsetshire soon after."

"You are very kind, sir."

"Please do not ever call me kind again," he said stiffly, surprising her. "I have your aunt's permission to take you out for the day to do some shopping."

"To do some shopping?"

He nodded. "I would like you to select some items for Newton Park. You will be happier there if it feels like your own. It still boasts the furnishings from several generations past."

"If that is your wish," she agreed.

He escorted her out to a carriage and four and handed her inside.

"I hear your cousin is being courted by Lofton."

"I suppose so, yes," she said warily. "Nothing has been settled."

"Your uncle mentioned Lofton had spoken to him during our discussion of settlements."

"I wish I could feel happier for her," she confessed. "Do you know Lord Lofton well, sir?"

"I do." He sat quietly for a moment. "I would not wish the match for a daughter of mine."

"Is that from personal feeling or professional?"

"Both," he said candidly. "He appears a good match to society because he is titled and looks well in uniform, but I do not trust him by my side in battle. And I should not say such things without being willing to provide facts to substantiate them."

"It was quite obvious to me that there was no love lost between the two of you. I promise to keep your feelings to myself, however, unless you can tell me something I should discuss with my uncle. I have sworn secrecy to my cousin, but if she is in danger, I will breach my word for such knowledge that would do her harm."

"There is nothing I am at liberty to disclose at this juncture. I hope the situation will be resolved before such an event takes place, and my suspicions will be proved unfounded."

"Very well. I only hope she will not act hastily."

The carriage slowed, stopping before a shop on Bond Street, and he helped her to alight. What a strange sensation it all was. She was to be married in two days' time to a complete stranger, and now she was to select colours for a house she had never seen—a house which would become her own with the union.

Emma never could have imagined selecting fabrics with her father. Shelton was surprisingly engaged and opinionated as he held up a fabric for her perusal.

"Primrose?" Emma questioned. She had never considered the colour for a sofa or curtains—only for gowns.

"I do believe it is my new favourite colour."

Emma glanced down at her gown and realized his meaning and looked away to hide her blush. Was he flirting with her? She never would have taken him for a tease.

"Perhaps the colour would be more appropriate for my dressing room."

"I believe I prefer a blue for my bedchamber," she said, running her fingers over an azure fabric.

"Then blue you shall have. Now I believe we only have one room remaining."

"There is yet another room?" She was astonished, for they had already selected colours for four rooms. He was not acting as though his home were a simple cottage.

"Why, yes, the parlour. Would you fancy a coquelicot, perhaps? I can envision you in a field of poppies."

"Thank you, sir. It is my favourite flower. I think it would look lovely in a parlour."

"This was much easier than it would have been with my mother. You seem a sensible woman, Miss Standrich."

"Poverty has a way of making one wise."

He barked an appreciative laugh. "I would that I could prescribe it for some of my officers."

"Including Lofton?"

"Especially Lofton," he snapped.

His face took on a scowl, and she wished she had not mentioned it. She vastly preferred the pleasant side of Shelton. She suspected he did not reveal it often.

"My cousin," she started and then paused. Was it breaking her word to reveal Jane's plan to her betrothed?

"Lady Jane?" he prodded, his tone neutral.

"Yes. I fear for her."

"Wait." He ushered her out to the carriage, where many of their purchases were being loaded. When the door was closed and they were alone, he asked, "What is your fear for Lady Jane?"

"I gave my word," she whispered. He nodded understanding. "Lofton is trying to coax her into eloping."

"Whatever the devil for? I know he is up to something. I just wish I could pin him on it."

"Is it he you suspect to be a spy?" she asked daringly.

He hesitated before answering. "Yes and no. He is clever, but I suspect not clever enough to manipulate entire armies. I cannot make the connection work, nor discover the mastermind. There is a piece missing."

"Perhaps you underestimate him."

He gave a slight nod of his head. "I hope we may discover the piece before your cousin is irrevocably linked to him."

"Whatever can I do? Should I go to my uncle?"

"Not yet, but beg her to delay. We must think of something."

"I will try," she whispered.

"Do not worry, Emma. I will do my best to see this through. I intend to clear Christopher's name as well." Hearing him use her given name almost made her forget why they were drawn together in the first place.

"Thank you, sir."

"I think it is time you called me Colin when we are alone."

"I will try," she said with a slight smile.

"I may not be a model husband, but I will never hurt you, Emma."

He looked deep into her eyes, and reaching up, stroked a stray hair back from her face. Her stomach fluttered at his touch. He took her face in his hands and placed a tender kiss on her lips.

She felt so many conflicting emotions—not the least of which was a growing attraction to her future husband. She did not think him capable of murder. She felt he was genuine, and she knew somehow he would never purposely harm her. It was the unintentional hurt she was less certain of.

Emma walked through the garden, pondering how she might possibly find a way to delay Jane's elopement without betraying her to her parents. She also wondered what she might do to help Shelton discover the piece of the puzzle he sought in order to solve the mystery of the spy.

"Very little," she said out loud, feeling hopeless. She knew nothing other than Christopher's mission to deliver the missive to "F." It was not as if she could query every soldier she met or call upon the war office and browse through the files.

She let out an exasperated sigh. There was little time to discover either before her wedding and leaving London. At least she could seek out Jane to see if she could discover any new plans from her.

"Jane," Emma offered by way of greeting when she joined her cousin in the shared sitting room between their bedrooms. "Why the sad face?"

"Our plans have been delayed. Melvyn had some business to attend to and will be away for a fortnight."

"What kind of business?" Emma somehow restrained herself from dancing in jubilee.

Jane waved her hand dismissively "You know, business."

"I suppose he must have estate duties to attend to when he is home."

"Yes, yes, but it will ruin everything!"

"Why did you not go there on the way to Scotland?"

Jane frowned. "I wish I had thought of it!" She began to cry.

"No matter," Emma said as she sat next to her cousin and comforted her. "It is for the best. You do not wish to elope, Jane."

"I don't?"

"No, dear. The news would certainly leak out through servants or someone seeing you en route. Your marriage would forever be tainted or, at the very least, whispered about."

"I suppose you are right." Jane gave a sad sigh.

"I promise you, the romance of it would wear quickly. And if it failed, no one else would have you."

"No one?" she squeaked. Jane looked at her askance, as though she had not considered this.

"Besides, you are far too beautiful not to have a grand London wedding. I have always pictured you in a beautiful lace gown, walking down the aisle to a large crowd in the rectory, with flowers lining the pews."

"You have?" Jane asked thoughtfully.

"I have, though I will not have the opportunity to do so myself. It would mean a great deal if you would stand up with me tomorrow," Emma said.

"Of course," her cousin answered sweetly. She seemed genuinely happy for Emma. "I only wish Melvyn and Shelton were cordial."

"I know. It must be something from the army or long ago. It does seem deeper than mere dislike."

"Yes. Can you believe Melvyn thinks Shelton is responsible for Christopher's death?"

"I beg your pardon? He said so?"

Jane looked guilty, but she nodded.

"I see. Did he say anything else about Christopher?"

"Only that the poor boy had been brainwashed by Shelton and had been used as his pawn," she said distractedly, fidgeting with some of her golden curls.

"How can I know the truth?" Emma demanded, throwing her hands up in frustration and pacing the room. "Shelton says similar things of Lofton. I fear one of us is going to attach ourselves to a snake."

"Now, Emma, do not exaggerate. These men are commanders in the army. They are not about to do anything monstrous. They are gentlemen! I am sure it is nothing more than prideful boasts or jealousy."

"Perhaps. However, my brother died, and I do not wish to marry the person responsible, if that is the case!" she exclaimed.

"Even if he were responsible in name, it does not seem he were guilty in intention. He seems to wish to do right by the Standrich family."

Emma sat down and sighed with annoyance. "I suppose so. However, my principles will not feed the mouths of my family. If only we could discover who 'F' is, perhaps I could put Christopher's death behind me."

"Do you think my father could be of help? Certainly he could narrow down the field. He is involved with the war office to some extent."

"He is? I was unaware of that. Do you think he would be willing to enquire for me?"

"Christopher was his nephew," Jane pointed out.

"I suppose it cannot hurt to ask."

"Why can you not ask Shelton who the missive was written to?"

"I suppose I could." She pondered the notion. "But how can I know which of them to trust?" Her instinct told her not to trust Lofton, but she did not want to hurt Jane unless she had proof.

"Let us ask Father first, then," Jane said. Rising, she walked to her father's study with Emma trailing behind.

After Emma had explained her suspicions to Lord Wetherby, he sat for some time contemplating the situation.

"Why are you only now telling me this, Emma? The greater the time elapsed after an event, the harder it is to discover the truth."

"I thought you would think me silly. I had hoped to

determine something on my own. But Shelton affirmed my suspicions with his own and told me to be aware of the danger."

"I agree. This is certainly not business for a young lady to be involved in. I will look into this situation myself. It never did sit right with me that Christopher was killed running a simple message to another officer, and then some have tried to blame him for giving away our movements to the French."

"He would never be so careless," Emma swiftly defended her sibling.

"Nor traitorous," her uncle added. "Unless perhaps he was the poor pawn of someone he trusted so deeply not to question. This is much deeper than I could have imagined. Emma, you need to distance yourself from this and feign ignorance. Jane, you do not discuss it outside this room, do you understand me?"

"Of course, Papa."

"I made a list of all of the officers I am aware of whose names begin with F," Emma said. "But I know little about any troop movements or who would have been in a position to receive such a message." She handed him a paper with the names Faircloth, Felton, Fletcher, Fawkes, Frey, and Fuller written on it—all men Christopher had written about over the years.

"You would not, no. And if you ask any questions, word may get back to the wrong people."

"Yes, ladies should not know about these things," Jane added unhelpfully.

"I will call on your betrothed to see if I may be of assistance to him," Lord Wetherby said to Emma.

"Thank you, Uncle. And please do be careful, yourself."

"There is one advantage to people assuming you are a lazy lord. No one suspects I know anything about anything!" He chuckled.

Emma had thought much the same thing herself, but she would be most grateful if he proved her wrong in this instance. There happened to be the minor detail of her marrying Shelton in the morning. If only she had the luxury of better knowing the man she was to marry.

Five

The next morning felt much like any other day as Emma dressed for the wedding ceremony. It did not feel like any of those wedding days she had sometimes dreamed of; her closest family was not present, and she had no joy or expectations of this union. Her aunt had presented her with a beautiful puce-coloured gown, trimmed with pearls and dark maroon ribbons, and Smitty had curled her dark hair to frame her face.

In the empty chapel at St. George's, her uncle escorted her to her betrothed's side. Jane and an unknown man were standing with Shelton, who was looking stern.

The reverend performed the ceremony without any embellishment, and both bride and groom recited their vows without hesitation. Emma supposed each of them had resigned themselves to the union.

After the registers were signed, Shelton's man quickly disappeared. Perhaps he had no one to stand up for him and had asked a stranger. Perhaps it was his batman? She had little time to ponder as she was ushered into the carriage to return to her aunt and uncle's home for a small wedding breakfast.

Emma sat across from this handsome stranger, not feeling any different but trying to convince herself her name was now Shelton.

"I wish this had been the wedding of your dreams, Emma. I cannot change it, but I do want you to know what a beautiful bride you are."

Emma blushed and struggled with the compliment. She managed a soft, "Thank you," which was followed by a few moments of self-conscious silence. Shelton did not appear to notice.

"Where is Lofton? I had heard Jane say he was out of town. Not that I am disappointed, mind you," Shelton asked as he sat next to her in the carriage.

"He told Jane he had business in the north."

"In the north? That makes no sense. His estates are in the east, adjoining my brother's, in fact. What could he be about?" Shelton muttered, seemingly to himself.

"Perhaps he did not go anywhere at all. Could it be a diversion?"

He looked at her as if she were a celebrated wit. "Indeed, it could. My contacts said nothing at all to me of any movement."

"You are having him watched?" she asked with astonishment.

"I am not having him watched. But yes, he is being watched. I had several visits this morning concerning Lofton. You did not heed my advice to be silent," he gently chided.

"You refer to my uncle."

"And your cousin, Jane."

"Surely you do not suspect Jane?"

"No, but I do not trust her ability to hold her tongue around Lofton. He has a way of manipulating a person into saying things they did not intend."

"I had told her of Christopher's letter long before I met you."

"Christopher's letter?" He looked at her, incredulous. "What did he write? I must know at once," he insisted.

"Would you prefer to see it before the breakfast or after?"

He let out a sigh of exasperation. "After. My apologies, my bride. We will have to delay our trip to Dorsetshire for a few days, I am afraid."

"I think it best as well, sir. I would prefer to remain with Jane until this is resolved, or at least until Lofton is cleared."

"Perhaps you will glean some information about Lofton's whereabouts if she receives word from him."

"Shall I continue to stay at my uncle's house, then?" she asked with a blush. They had not spoken of their living arrangements after the marriage.

"Yes, yes, of course, I had planned on leaving for Dorsetshire, not taking you to my rooms."

She tried not to look as relieved as she felt. She needed more time to come to terms with her sudden change in name and all it entailed.

Her aunt's cook had prepared a lovely breakfast for them to include kippers, bacon, sausages, potatoes, kidneys, and fresh rolls, followed by a plumb cake, but it seemed no different from any other meal—certainly not her wedding celebration. It was not how it should have been.

"I would like to take a look at the letter before I go," Shelton leaned over and said to her as the family was rising from the table.

"Of course. Please follow me."

They went into the hall, and both felt the awkwardness of the situation.

"Shall I wait for you in the parlour?" Shelton asked.

"Do you think it private enough? There is a small sitting room adjoining my bedchamber, if you prefer."

"I suppose that would be wiser. Lead the way."

She retrieved the bandbox, which held her precious letters—all those she had received since their uncle had purchased Christopher a commission.

"He was a dutiful brother, was he not?" Shelton remarked as she pulled out the thick packet of correspondence.

"Yes, he was," Emma said softly. "Most of them were full of stories about you," she told him as she sorted through the letters, searching for the one she wanted. "Here it is."

She handed over the last letter—the one she treasured most.

"If you would prefer to point out the necessary part?" he asked. She was touched by his consideration.

"If you wish." She leaned across his arm to find the appropriate part, and a tantalizing waft of sandalwood assailed her nostrils. She almost forgot about the letter.

I am to deliver an urgent missive to F tomorrow for S. Take heart, S believes this will be over soon and I may return home.

Shelton read and reread the fateful line.

"The devil!"

"Does it help?" she asked, removing the paper from his hand to preserve it, since he appeared in imminent danger of crumpling it within his fist.

"It only confirms he delivered my message to the wrong person, or he was intercepted and a note was planted on him to throw us off the trail."

She whimpered at the mention of her brother's demise. "What note?"

"Forgive me. That was heartless of me to speak so callously. A note was found on your brother's body—not the one I wrote."

He tentatively reached out a hand to her.

"I must go now and let my contacts know of this."

She nodded and with a small, perfunctory bow, he left her alone.

"Be careful," she whispered.

Six

Jane was rather glum after her cousin had been married by special license earlier in the day. She considered the matter as she was out for her daily walk with her maid. How had Colonel Shelton been able to obtain one when Lofton could not?

"Lady Jane!" She heard a man's voice hiss from behind the shrubbery.

"Lofton?" she asked in confusion.

"Yes, come quickly!" he said quietly.

"But—my maid!" she protested.

"Send her away so you can speak to me for a few moments."

Jane agreed and told Sally to wait for her near the fountains by the garden. Sally objected to leaving her mistress unattended, but went reluctantly as Jane returned to the path behind the hedge.

"Whatever are you doing in Hyde Park when you told me you were going north?" she chastised.

"My plans changed. Is it not good news?" he said. He sidled up to her and placed his arm around her waist, making her nervous.

"I suppose it is, but I confess myself to be cross. Colonel

Shelton was able to obtain a special license," she said, puffing out her lower lip in a pout.

Lofton scoffed. "Yes, he would have. I hope your cousin does not live to regret her choice."

"One could argue she had little choice. I applaud him for taking care of his lieutenant's family. Why do you and Shelton dislike each other so?" She looked up at him and tried to push him back to create some distance between them.

"I have good reason, Jane. I know him better than most. We were essentially raised together, did you know?"

She shook her head.

"He will do anything to get what he wants. He even tried to run away with my sister and steal her from his own brother!"

"I had not heard. What a horrid thing to do! Poor Emma," Jane said, though she had seen nothing but generosity from Colonel Shelton.

"Indeed. Now you may begin to understand the sort of man he is. I pray your cousin will know none of it." He pulled her back to him and planted a rough kiss on her lips.

"I still do not understand. Why must we run away?" she asked. Twisting, she pulled out of his hold and tossed her head. "As if we were ashamed or had done something improper!"

"Jane, dearest," he said, taking her hands in his and drawing her back to him. "You said yourself your parents wanted to wait for a grand wedding, and my duty to the Crown will not allow me to wait much longer."

"But the scandal, Melvyn. It would so distress my parents, and I cannot bear to hurt them."

He pulled her into a passionate kiss, and she began to grow worried he would not stop.

"Melvyn!" She pushed him away again.

"You must speak to them. I cannot resist your charms much longer, dear Jane. Perhaps, if we put a notice in the papers, it would seem less scandalous. Certainly everyone would understand I must return to my duties with the army."

Jane sighed. "I will speak to my parents again."

"There's a good girl," Lofton said as he brushed her cheek with his fingertips. "Have your maid bring a note to my man. And Jane, do not tell anyone I am still in town."

"But . . ." She attempted to question him, but he sneaked away without another word. She was cross and felt none of her previous joy. She walked back to her maid with many heavy questions on her heart.

Jane entered the sitting room, removing her gloves and bonnet as she walked.

"Emma, I did not expect to find you here!" she exclaimed.

"Yes, we decided it best to remain in London for a few days," Emma replied. "Where have you been?"

"Oh . . ." She hesitated. "For a walk in the park. I confess I am glad you are still here," she hurried on.

"Has something happened?"

"Yes, but I was told not to speak of it. I wish I knew what to do."

"You may tell me," Emma said gently, rising and taking her cousin's hands. "However, if I think you to be in danger, I will go to my aunt and uncle."

"It is Lofton. He is still in London," Jane blurted out.

"Why ever did he tell you he was leaving, then?" Emma asked, wrinkling her nose.

"He said his plans changed, but he begged me not to tell anyone he was here. I do not understand. He asked me to speak with Papa and Mama again about publishing notices in the papers."

"He thinks it will force their hand?"

"Mayhap," Jane said with a frown. "He still thinks we should marry before he leaves. He thinks society will understand a quick wedding, given the circumstances."

"I believe he is correct in that assumption," Emma agreed, however little she wanted to encourage this match.

"Would you believe he told me he could not obtain a special license because of a family disagreement with the bishop?"

"The bishop is Colin's uncle and godfather," Emma informed her.

"Is he? Melvyn did tell me he was Shelton's neighbour and grew up playing with the brothers. He also proceeded to blacken your new husband's name."

"Pray tell," Emma said with growing interest.

"He said your husband was disinherited because he tried to steal his brother's wife, who happens to be Lofton's sister."

Emma sank down into her chair. "No, I do not believe it."

"I would think it would be easy to ascertain whether it was true or not. Grandmama is an inveterate gossip. She is bound to know."

"I suspect I am the only fool who was unaware of it."

"Melvyn shall be gone soon."

"Not soon enough, if what you say is true."

"Therein lies my quandary," Jane said. "I do not know that I fully trust Melvyn. It is a feeling I have inside."

"I understand. I always trust my instincts to guide me. Although now I am less certain."

"I think perhaps we should find out more information."

"And I think your father is to be trusted. He would never hold you to Lofton if he suspected anything amiss."

"My parents did discourage a hasty nuptial; in fact, they forbade it. They do not even wish for an announcement until he returns and sells out."

"Wise, indeed. Yet you say Lofton wishes to place an announcement? What is to stop him from doing so?"

"He seemed urgent about it. My vanity would like to believe it is simply from his eagerness to be my husband."

"Oh, Jane. I do hope it is." She reached over and squeezed her cousin's hand. "However, your prudence now will possibly prevent you from a disastrous marriage."

"Will it? Or will it make me undesirable for any future matches?"

"Not if we play our hand well. Lofton may be vindicated. It may be that I was the imprudent one. I will never forgive myself if I have married my brother's murderer."

"Father, we must disturb you once again," Jane said, entering her father's study unannounced and without checking if Emma was behind her.

"You never disturb me, Jane. Has something new occurred?" he asked, removing his spectacles and setting them carefully on the mahogany desk.

"I suppose it has," she said hesitantly.

"I know that look, daughter. You had best tell your papa everything."

Jane proceeded to tell her father about Lofton's supposed

journey north, accosting her in the park, his not wanting anyone to know he was in London, and his desire to place an immediate announcement in the papers. She carefully omitted the possibility of elopement, Emma noticed.

"I see," her father said distractedly. Getting to his feet, he walked to the window. Lighting his pipe, he stood there smoking and staring outside, deep in thought.

"Uncle, may I also add that Viscount Lofton was intent on maligning my husband to her?" Emma put in from where she was standing just inside the door.

"Is this true, Jane?" he asked, looking up at his daughter.

"Yes, Papa, it is true."

"I cannot condone his ungentlemanly behaviour, Jane. Under no circumstances are the notices to go in the papers. There is no official betrothal. He only asked for permission to pay his addresses to you. We have discussed no settlements. Do you understand?"

Emma saw the astonishment show on her cousin's face.

"But I thought . . ." Jane protested half-heartedly.

"I am certain you did, dearest," her father said gently. "And I take responsibility for it. However, with a fortune such as yours, there have been several men request to pay their addresses. I confess, I had hoped for more from Lofton, since he is the first one to have taken your fancy. I do believe, in light of what you have said, we should exercise caution. I have also spoken at length with Colonel Shelton, and until the circumstances surrounding Christopher's death are resolved, I will refuse to give your hand or your fortune to Lofton. Do I make myself clear?"

Jane nodded. The tears were streaming down her face, and Emma noticed the struggle Jane had to keep her lips from quivering. Her father rarely spoke harshly to her.

"I am sorry, dearest, but after you begged to be married

by special license the other day, I was under the suspicion you might act rashly."

"But—But Emma was," Jane objected through her tears.

"The circumstances were entirely different!" he declared. "Colonel Shelton behaved honourably by marrying Emma and supporting Christopher's family. There is nothing honourable in Lord Lofton's rushed courtship and efforts to persuade you into a hasty marriage!"

"But he has a respected title and estates," she argued in obvious disbelief. "What else was I to suppose, other than that he is an excellent match?"

"I know this is difficult to understand, Jane. It does appear to be a grand match, but he has not been forthright about his income or encumbrances. The circumstances are not clear, and we must therefore step back and be prudent."

"But he could be killed in battle!" she pleaded.

"Would I wish a widowhood upon you in your youth? If his estates are not in good order, you could find your entire fortune gone with nothing to provide for you. Is that what you would wish?"

"No, Papa," she whispered. She clearly could not control her sobs; her breathing was rapid and ragged.

Emma came over to her and placed her arms around her. Jane leaned on her cousin's shoulder.

"Jane, I must have your word you will do nothing rash," Lord Wetherby said. "It would be most painful, but I will not release your fortune to Lofton until I can be certain the offer is honourable, and I do not consider elopement to be honourable. Do I make myself clear?"

With a brief nod of her head, she pulled back from Emma's embrace and ran, sobbing, from the room.

Emma and her uncle looked across the room at each other. Incomprehension was etched upon his kindly face.

"This is my fault, Emma. I should never have let it go so far. In view of all your husband has told me and also my preliminary investigations, Lofton worries me."

"I, too, have reservations, Uncle. I must speak with my husband, however, and ask him to explain the accusations against him."

"I would not do so yet, Emma," he advised. "There is a dangerous game afoot, and I would let it play out before I made judgements that could alter any chance for a happy marriage."

She sighed. "Yes, Uncle."

However, she reflected, if she saw her husband at the moment, she might tear him limb from limb.

"Do you join us at Lady Easton's charity ball tonight?" he asked as she turned to take her leave.

"We have not spoken about it."

"Your husband shall be staying here as well. I suggested it to him when I comprehended why you could not remove to Dorsetshire immediately."

"You are very kind, Uncle."

At the very least, she had enough warning to master her anger before she saw her husband again.

***

"Is your husband not to join us?" Lady Wetherby asked as they stood in the entrance hall that evening, donning their shawls in readiness for the journey to the ball.

"I have not seen nor spoken to him since just after the breakfast."

"How strange," Jane mused.

"Can it be any stranger than attending a ball on my wedding night?" Emma asked sardonically.

"I suppose not. Are you to be announced as Mrs. Shelton?"

"I could not tell you. I wish he were here to advise me. He did not say to keep it a secret."

"Let us go, ladies. I left Shelton a note, should he wish to join us," Lord Wetherby announced on joining them in the entrance hall. "We were late discussing business matters." He stepped over to where Jensen was waiting with his hat and walking stick.

Emma did not wish to attend a ball this evening. She would much rather spend her limited time in London solving the puzzle of Christopher's death.

They drove the short distance to Lord Easton's town residence and were greeted by their hosts, a lovely couple who had devoted their lives to helping the less fortunate.

Jane was surrounded by admirers soon after they entered the ballroom. Emma was also engaged for several of the dances. She tried not to worry too much about her husband's whereabouts, but it would have been nice to dance with him on their wedding day.

"Forgive me for my tardiness, wife. May I have the next dance?" a deep voice said softly into her ear.

She turned and forced herself to smile at him. "Yes, you may."

He led her to the floor for a waltz, and she was captivated by his nearness and his scent, causing the questions she wished to ask him stayed, unuttered, on her tongue.

"Have you made any discoveries?" she finally managed to ask when she became used to the pattern of the dance.

"A few, but not enough, I am afraid. I was late because I was speaking with Lord Wetherby again. He was good enough to apprise me of Lofton's actions."

"Horrible, is it not? I fear he is using dear Jane for her fortune."

"There, I suspect you are correct. He has long had

encumbrances on his estate, and his gambling habit has only worsened the situation. My suspicion is his activities began as a need for funds," he said quietly.

"It disgusts me that one could be so desperate for funds as to betray one's country. Heaven forbid he take on some useful employment or sell property."

"You know it is not done, Emma. However, one need not turn to treason, either," he whispered in her ear. His warm breath sent shivers up her spine.

This was the first time she had waltzed with anyone other than her younger sister, and she was unused to the nearness of this stranger, her husband, and the new, unfamiliar sensations she felt around him. He exuded warmth, strength, and something she could not define. It caused her heart to race when her hands were in his.

"If Lofton is so desperate for funds," Shelton said darkly, "I fear what he might do to Jane."

"Do you think he would try to take her from here?" Emma began to look around for her cousin.

"The doors are being watched. It is not without risk, however."

"My aunt and uncle are aware?"

"Your uncle certainly is. As for your aunt, I could not say."

As the waltz ended, Shelton led Emma to her aunt.

"You make a very handsome couple." Aunt Tilda beamed. "Especially in your regimentals, Colonel Shelton."

"Thank you, ma'am. Do you know where we might find Lady Jane?"

"How kind of you to wish to dance with your new cousin," she exclaimed. "I believe she went to the retiring room."

"Which way?" Emma asked nervously.

"'Tis over near the fountain. She went that way before the last set." She pointed towards the door on the far side of the ballroom. "Why do you ask?"

Ignoring her question, Shelton took Emma's elbow in a firm grasp and hurried her across the room through the crush of people.

"I do not believe Jane would go with him," Emma gasped as they manoeuvred hastily through the crowd.

"I do not believe he would allow that to bother him," Shelton answered. "But it does not mean he has taken her simply because we do not see her, either."

They reached the door of the retiring room; Emma went inside but found no Jane. She came back out and shook her head worriedly.

"She is not there, but I found her reticule," she said, holding up Jane's small bag. Its strap was torn.

Shelton looked around. Following his gaze, Emma saw a pair of glass-paned doors nearby leading to the garden.

Her husband headed towards them as he spoke.

"Go for your uncle. I will alert the teams outside."

Suddenly, any anger Emma felt toward Shelton vanished. He so clearly feared for Jane's safety. She attempted to smile and walk calmly towards the card room, where her uncle had repaired on arrival. When he looked up and saw her, he quickly excused himself, causing the other men at the table to grumble.

"What is it, Emma?" he whispered as he led her from the room.

"The worst, I fear. Jane is missing."

"You are certain? Could she simply be in the retiring room?"

Emma shook her head. "She is not in the ballroom, either. She would not simply have wandered outside alone."

"No, indeed. Does your husband know?"

She quickly nodded. "He sent me to you; he has already gone after them."

"Please inform your aunt that I will need to leave early, but I shall send the carriage back for her. Please do not worry her unnecessarily."

"Of course, Uncle."

Emma did as she was told, but she could not remain idle at a ball while Jane was possibly in trouble. She found her uncle waiting at the top of the steps at the same moment his carriage was brought round to him.

"May I join you? I must try to help."

"Every instinct warns me that I should tell you to stay and comfort your aunt. However, if Jane is found, she will need someone to accompany her."

"Do you know which way my husband was to go? Is there any chance to catch up with him?" Emma asked as they climbed in and sat opposite each other in the coach.

"I suspect there is no other way but north."

"If it is the only place to force her into marriage, then I agree."

"Do you think she went willingly, Emma?" he asked worriedly. "Was I too harsh earlier?"

"I do not, Uncle. She was hurt, but I believe more by the knowledge that he was seeking her fortune rather than her."

"Indeed. He had best hope I never find him," he said worriedly as he directed the coachman to return them to the Wetherby mansion.

Emma was surprised to find Shelton there when they arrived. She wondered if perhaps he had come to gather supplies and his horse, for he appeared ready to leave when the conveyance pulled up to the house.

"Wetherby," he said. "I have sent men northward and southward after them. I shall see if there are any messages and send word back for you to follow in the carriage."

"Shall I not go with you?" Emma asked.

"I do not wish to put you in danger, as well."

"We cannot risk word spreading!" Lord Wetherby protested.

Shelton glanced at Emma, then reluctantly agreed. "Very well, when I have word of their direction. I do not trust Lofton to do the expected thing. Gather a bag for yourself and Lady Jane and be ready with the carriage."

He took her hands briefly and gave her a meaningful look. "Until later."

"Be safe," she whispered.

He let go of her hands and mounted the chestnut gelding before tipping his hat and trotting away. She watched him disappear to the echoes of hooves clicking on the cobblestones. She had to admit that her husband seemed sensible and capable. She did trust him, she found.

It was two hours before they received word from Shelton. Her uncle grabbed the missive and tore it open as fast as he could while Emma watched with anticipation.

Lord Wetherby,

My prayer is this note finds you with Lady Jane safely tucked in her bed at home. I have not seen her, but I have word of Lofton. Lofton has not taken the northern road, but has headed east. His estates are to the east, and I suspect he has taken her there in hopes of forcing your hand. Please follow in the carriage at once. I have taken the liberty of sending a message to my uncle, the Archbishop, to provide a license if it is your desire. In the meantime, I vow to do everything I can to maintain Lady Jane's honour.

Yours, etc,

Shelton

"Would that were the case," Lord Wetherby said. "It appears Lofton has done the worst."

"No, Uncle, let us not assume the worst. Perhaps we may salvage the situation. Shelton is close behind and we shall be shortly."

"Yes, let us make haste," he said and began a frenzied stir to leave, gathering papers and stuffing them into a leather bag. He paused and turned to a cabinet where his pistols were kept. He pulled them out, his hands visibly shaking as he checked them before slipping them into the case.

Seven

"How dare you kidnap me!" Jane exclaimed, the carriage swaying dangerously as they sped away from the ball. "How much did you pay my maid to lure me away? If you think this will convince me to elope with you, you are quite mistaken."

"You are now compromised, Jane. It will be all over London by morning. You and your parents will have little choice."

"You are wrong. I would rather live quietly in the country as a spinster than have my name attached to yours."

Lofton struck her across the face with the back of his hand. "Silence!" he commanded.

Her hand flew to her lip and came away dripping with blood. Her whole jaw throbbed.

"You will be lucky if I let you live. I vastly preferred you as an insipid, bird-witted miss to this shrew."

"My father will never release my funds to you."

"In exchange for your life?" He laughed menacingly.

"And you expect to walk away unscathed? They are already suspicious of you. They will know exactly who kidnapped me."

Jane realised as she said the words that she had misspoken. She should have guarded her tongue and played the widgeon he thought her.

"Who is onto me?" He sneered in her face. He was close enough she could smell the acridness of cigar on his breath.

She remained silent, though her heart was thumping with fear. Should she placate him now? Or was it too late?

"Tell me, woman, or I will throw you from the carriage!"

"I do not have a name. I heard rumours," she replied, wishing her accustomed quick thinking would not fail her at this moment when she was in desperate need of it.

"Tell me what you heard," he growled.

"I heard them speaking behind me at the ball. Your absence was noted by one man, and another remarked upon your debts and that you were hiding from them," she said coolly, hoping to pacify him.

He visibly relaxed the scowl on his face and leaned back against the squab.

"Indeed. It is true I have some debts from my father."

"Debts worth killing me over?"

"You will remain silent. I want no more words from you. I will decide what to do with you later, but now I must think."

"May I at least know where you are taking me?"

"Scotland, of course," he said smugly. An unpleasant sneer twisted his mouth.

Jane felt her lip swelling and decided her best course of action was to remain quiet, as commanded. She knew they had not taken the Great North Road, yet was certain they had headed eastward. What was he truly about if he did not intend to marry her?

The look in his eyes had changed, and it was frightening. It was as if she were looking at another person. She had had no idea Lofton was crazed. She could imagine him killing Christopher without a second thought.

He stared out of the window for several minutes before pulling some papers from his coat. She desperately wanted to look at them, but she tried to feign sleep. She settled into the corner as far from him as she could and lowered her lashes. He fingered the letters and beat them against his knee, but the dim light from the lantern inside the carriage was insufficient for her to discern the writing. She waited what felt like an eternity before his head lolled sideways against the gold padded wall, and a few minutes later, she heard him snoring softly. How he could sleep at such a time baffled her. She moved her head slightly, squinting to see the address on the letter.

Falteroy.

This must be the F her cousin had spoken of. Heavens above, Lofton had killed Christopher! He had the letter in his hand, which had been intended for Falteroy! Was he so arrogant he would keep a trophy?

She began to shake with fear and desperately wanted to cry. She had to calm herself before he woke. She took deep breaths and tried to think how she could escape from this situation. Her first inclination was to jump from the carriage, but it was rolling along too fast and he would catch her if she were not mortally injured in any case. She looked about the equipage, wondering where he kept his pistols.

When the snoring stopped moments later, she was afraid to look at him.

"You know, Jane, I do think it would be best if we married after all. There really is no other way to make us both look admirable." He laughed. "I could walk away, of course, and society would shun you. But I am feeling generous and will allow you to become a viscountess if we can forget this incident ever happened. If only you had used your influence over your father."

She nodded and tried to quell the rising nausea she felt, but she was terrified. She could not look this monster in the eye.

"There's a good girl. We should be at our first stop very soon, and we can start afresh on the morrow, and you will behave in a manner more befitting a viscountess, will you not?"

Emma awoke again when they pulled into the posting inn for yet another change of horses. Dawn had already broken. They must, therefore, have been travelling for over six hours. Emma wondered where in the east they were going, but her uncle had chosen to ride ahead and she was unable to ask questions as she wished. She peered around the curtain to try to determine their whereabouts. She saw the man who had stood up with Shelton at their wedding conversing behind a large maple tree with her uncle. She could not recall his name, but she thought he was probably a relative, for he shared the pale grey eyes and strong nose of her husband. He must be party to the scheme to capture the spy as well, she decided.

She sat back against the squabs, rubbing her neck. She had not travelled by carriage often, but she was thankful for the luxury of her uncle's equipage, as they had driven at a clipping pace throughout the night. There was a small knock on the door closest to her. She looked out to see who sought admittance.

"Enter," she said.

The man from the wedding climbed into the carriage, and a servant handed him a tray with some fresh rolls and tea.

"Good morning. Do you remember me?" he asked kindly.

"You were at the wedding," she replied.

He nodded. "So you know I am a friend." He set the tray down next to her on the bench. "You should eat. I do not know how the rest of the day will transpire. You will need sustenance. Lofton can be unpredictable." He tapped on the roof of the carriage, and Emma held onto the tray as they lurched forward.

"You are to go with me? Where is my uncle?" She still did not know his name.

"Your uncle is riding ahead to Lofton's estate, where we believe he has taken Lady Jane."

"I do not understand, but it is as Colin suspected," she said with a frown.

"Very likely so. Your uncle will try to negotiate with Lofton. We will wait nearby for word."

"Where is my husband?"

The man was clearly debating how much to say to her. She could see the indecision on his face. She decided to drink her tea while he deliberated. When nothing further from him seemed to be forthcoming, she selected a roll, despite no inclination to hunger, and nibbled on it. Having finished her repast, she placed her cup back on the tray. Emma did feel quite refreshed after the sustenance. Finally, she looked back at the man seated across from her. He was watching her with some amusement; his eyes twinkled in a mischievous fashion, the skin crinkling at the corners.

"I beg your pardon," Emma said. "I did not mean to be rude. Would you like a cup?"

He laughed. "No, I had my fill at the inn whilst awaiting your arrival. You are quite unlike other women I have met."

"I accept the compliment," she replied saucily. "Are you going to answer my question now?"

"Colin is waiting at Lofton's estate. The plan is for him to help Lady Jane escape while your uncle is speaking to the viscount."

She swallowed the exclamation she wished to expel. "I see," she said calmly instead. "And he is familiar with the estate because he was there frequently as a boy."

"Precisely."

"So we wait."

"Indeed. We wait."

Mindlessly, Emma selected another roll from the tray and took a bite. She tasted very little as she thought through what her husband must be dealing with and the fear her cousin must be feeling. While she had little idea of what might have happened to Jane during the night, she shuddered in unconscious dread as dark possibilities rolled through her mind. The viscount was little more than a beast from the fields, after all.

"You need not worry for your husband. He is very capable."

"I have seen it already. I was thinking more of Lofton's unpredictability and what he might have done to Jane."

"Has Colin told you much of Lofton?" he asked.

"He has said very little, in truth. I sensed it, and some of what Jane related yesterday confirmed me in my belief."

The carriage pulled to a stop some half an hour later, and the man opened the door. "You may wait in here or out there, if you wish."

"I would be happy to stretch my legs, if you think it safe."

"It had better be safe," he said, scanning the scene around

them. She joined him in surveying the beautiful landscape of mostly flat, grassy fields. There was a hint of sea air in the warm breeze. She would have enjoyed it greatly—if only her cousin and husband were not with that dangerous man.

"Is this Lofton's estate or does it belong to my husband's family?"

"You are standing on Shelton land, and beyond that rise is Lofton's property. We wait here for a signal."

"Do you not think Lofton will expect my husband? He knows we are very close."

"He might, but I suspect his interest lies more in Wetherby's fortune than his daughter."

"Yes, I would hope for much better for Jane."

"What of yourself?" he surprised her by asking.

"I believe it is too late or too premature to be asking me such a question."

"I beg your pardon. It was unconscionably rude of me to ask."

"You are concerned for Colin. I understand. I hope to be a good wife. I was to be a governess, did you know?"

"I do not pity him." He smiled at her, and she blushed.

"Forgive me—are you married?"

"I was. I lost my wife in childbirth."

"I am very sorry. Now it is I who am rude."

"Do not be. It was the logical next question. I have a beautiful daughter. You may greet your new niece after we have rescued Lady Jane."

"You are Colin's brother?" she asked in astonishment.

"In the flesh." He took off his hat and bowed. "I am Falteroy, William Shelton. My brother intentionally did not introduce us at the wedding to protect you and Lady Jane. He was concerned she would mention my presence to Lofton."

"You are helping Colin?"

A long, low whistle sounded across the hill. Falteroy held up a finger to his lips as he tilted his head. "I believe that was my signal. Stay here until I return."

He returned a loud whistle, and a groom on a horse came galloping to him. The servant jumped down and assisted Falteroy into the saddle. He was quickly mounted and away, jumping over a stone wall before she could comprehend all he had said.

Eight

Jane sat on the floor of the bedroom she had been locked in, her legs curled up to her chest, rocking back and forth as she had done as a child. She had heard the sounds of a rider arrive. She desperately wished it to be her father, yet she feared he was likely headed north.

Although she had been offered nourishment in the form of some cold meat, she had been unable to contemplate a single bite. She had not slept either. Fear of what her future might hold churned and roiled in her stomach, keeping her wide awake and unwilling to broach so much as a morsel.

She had toyed with jumping from the balcony of her room, but she was not certain she would live through the fall when she had looked down from the window over the garden. She did not wish to die, but she would rather that than be shackled to Lofton for life. How she wished she had a dagger, so she could thrust it into him!

"How dare he! How dare he!" she muttered fiercely to herself, the anger beginning to smother some of her fear.

She pushed up from the floor and listened. It seemed an age since the horse had clattered up the drive. Perhaps the rider was not, after all, her father. Did he know where to come? Would they ever find her? She wandered over to an

67

ornate looking glass and grimaced at her reflection. Who would want her now? Her face was swollen, her cut lip was black and crusted with blood, and her hair was in total disarray. She resembled a prize-fighter.

"Lady Jane?"

The deep voice came from behind her. She spun around to see a gentleman in riding attire standing before her in front of the window.

"Who are you? How did you get in here?" She had not heard a sound until he spoke.

"I was at your cousin's wedding," he said calmly as he removed his hat.

"Ah, yes. I do not believe we were introduced." She was acting as if she was at an afternoon tea party, though she did relax somewhat.

"I am Colonel Shelton's brother. Please come with me. We do not have time for small talk."

"Where are you taking me?"

"Too many questions, my dearest. Would you rather stay here and take your chances with your host?"

"No, but how do I know I may trust you?"

"It is me or Lofton, whom you already know to be un-scrupulous and dangerous."

He held out his hand, and she took it. It was warm, strong, and sure. A cautionary finger to his lips, he led her onto the balcony, where he had tied a rope to the balustrade. He swung himself over the side and held out his hand for her.

"I am to climb down?" she whispered.

"If you prefer, but I had planned to hold you."

She paused for a moment, then nodded. She was terrified of heights and prayed she was not leaving this prison for a worse fate.

She climbed over the balustrade and felt his arm wrap

around her, holding her tight against his muscled body while, with the rope twisted between his boots, he used his free hand to control their descent. As soon as their feet hit the ground, he grabbed her hand and they flew across a sweep of lawn at a run. She was soon gasping for breath and struggling to keep pace with his long stride.

"Wait! Please!"

For perhaps ten seconds, he slowed. Without warning, he bent and gathered her into his arms again before hastening on. Time seemed to lose meaning until she found herself sitting on an enormous bay horse. Her escort jumped up behind her and urged the great beast into a gallop. Trees, hedges, and streams all flashed by. He took a wall with incredible speed, and she had to close her eyes.

At last, he slowed down, and she could breathe again. She turned to look at him and was shocked by the awareness she felt from being near him—his breath on her neck, the stubble on his face, his light grey eyes piercing into hers.

"If Colin has not killed Lofton, he will answer to me," he said as he gently fingered the skin around her swollen, bruised lip.

She looked away, disconcerted by the heat rising within her.

"Am I to know where we are going?"

"To your cousin, and then to my house."

"Emma? Emma is here?" she asked with relief.

"Emma has been with you the entire time," he instructed.

"Yes, of course she has. I am very grateful to you, sir."

He drew the horse to a halt beside a coach and four, which waited in the lane on the other side of a crooked gate. Helped from the saddle by her escort, Jane saw Emma descend from the vehicle. Without a word, she ran into her cousin's arms.

"Write the note, Wetherby, or your precious daughter dies with her name slandered!" Lofton commanded as he held the sharp tip of a dagger to Wetherby's throat.

Colin could not wait much longer for his brother to return. He gripped his pistol tightly in anticipation. He vastly preferred to have William as support, but he was growing concerned Lofton would lose control and slit Wetherby's throat.

At last, he saw his brother's face appear at the window of the study behind Lofton. William nodded. Colin returned the nod from his post behind the curtains and saw his brother move away before he pulled the trigger.

The dagger flew out of Lofton's hand, and he grabbed his wounded arm. At the same moment, William leaped through the terrace doors into the room and pinned the viscount to the wall.

Wheezing stertorously, Lord Wetherby sank into a chair and grasped his neck. Having ascertained the earl was not badly harmed, Colin went to his brother's aid and to see how severely Lofton's arm was damaged. Considered a crack shot by his fellow officers, Colin had aimed merely to scratch. Fortunately, the pistol had fired true, and he had succeeded. He did not want Lofton to die easily. Colin untied his neck cloth and wrapped the wound as William continued to hold him.

"What is the meaning of this?" Lofton bellowed.

"We could ask you the same," William replied. "Or is it common practice for you to hold an earl at knife point? Or to kidnap his daughter?"

"She came willingly," Lofton said coolly.

Breathing more easily and having recovered some of his composure, Wetherby rose to his feet. "Your game is finished, Lofton. We have evidence of your treason and proof you committed the murder of Lieutenant Standrich." He looked to Colin, who pulled the incriminating evidence from his pocket and threw it on the desk.

"I admit to nothing," Lofton sneered.

"You wish to be tried in front of your peers?" Wetherby asked.

"There is nothing to try me for. You are fools if you believe it will even make it to a hearing."

"You are suffering from delusions," William said. "In addition to a high-ranking colonel, you have two peers, who are in direct service to the Crown, willing to testify against you."

"If you persist with this absurdity, allow me to remove to the Continent and live out my days in exile," Lofton suggested. He seemed remarkably calm.

"I might have considered such an arrangement if you had not chosen to play me for a fool and threaten my daughter's life," Wetherby exclaimed.

"Very well. I concede that was a poor move on my part. Challenge me to a duel and settle this the gentlemanly way— if you have the stomach for it!"

"You are no gentleman." Wetherby pulled back his shoulders and stalked across the worn carpet until he stood almost nose-to-nose with the viscount. Withdrawing a tan leather riding glove from his pocket, he slapped Lofton across the face and, seconds later, planted a punch on his nose worthy of a Corinthian at Jackson's Saloon.

"I believe a confession in writing will suit the purpose," Colin suggested before the two men became embroiled in a vulgar brawl. He wanted unadulterated proof to clear Lieutenant Standrich's name.

"Ah, yes, a timely reminder, Colonel. I get ahead of myself," Wetherby said, rubbing his hand, yet looking somewhat pleased with himself. Lofton's nose was already swelling, and blood was running down his face, dripping scarlet on his crumpled neck cloth.

William shoved Lofton roughly into the armchair behind the heavy library table, continuing to hold the viscount's hands behind his back.

Colin aimed the gun at Lofton. "I am only here for motivation," he remarked, lifting the muzzle in a deliberately threatening manner.

Wetherby placed the pen in Lofton's hand and directed it towards the paper the blackguard had been attempting to force him to write on.

"What would you have me write, my esteemed comrade?" he asked, his voice laced with sarcasm.

"The truth. Nothing more, nothing less," Colin answered in clipped tones.

"I am not certain the truth is necessary. What is it you require in order to clear your puppy-faced lieutenant's name?"

Without warning, William snapped Lofton's head back. "Start writing, now!" he growled.

A flicker of pain passed across the viscount's bloodied visage, but he merely laughed, a sound of bitter contempt.

"Is that any way to treat a brother-in-law?" he asked, with a haughty curl of his lip.

"You are no brother of mine," William retorted.

Arrogant to the last, Lofton raised a supercilious eyebrow but began to write, nevertheless. His hand travelled back and forth across the page for perhaps four or five minutes. When he had finished, he held it up for Colin to view.

"I trust this will suffice, Colonel Shelton?" His tone and demeanour mocked them all.

Colin tore the paper from the man's hand. It was more detailed and painful to read than he would ever admit in front of Lofton, who, he did not doubt for a second, had embellished the report for his benefit. Colin refused to give him the satisfaction of showing emotion.

"How do you wish to proceed?" William asked Lord Wetherby.

"Grant me one request," Lofton interceded before the earl could answer. "I wish you would recount this enchanting tale to my niece when she is old enough to understand why she has no more living relatives on her mother's side."

Such sentiments might have aided his defence had he not spoken with such disdain, Colin thought with disgust. He was undoubtedly about to be handed over for trial.

"I do believe that is the first honourable statement I have ever heard from your lips. Whether or not it is truly for my daughter's sake or for yours, I refuse to ponder," William said.

Wetherby coughed and lifted an imperious hand. "Very well. If you gentlemen will kindly leave me your pistols and wait outside, I would like a private word with the viscount."

"Is that wise? Are you certain you wish to remain in the room alone with him?" William asked.

"No, but I do not trust him not to run away. He is a Peer of the Realm and, as such, deserves the chance to make amends."

Making no secret of their reluctance, Colin and William did as directed by their superior.

"I abhor the fact he is allowed to take the honourable course," Colin said.

"I agree, but consider Evangeline. And Lady Jane," William countered.

"And even Emma. I could not ask her to suffer the notoriety a trial would bring. Nonetheless, he does not deserve the coward's way out."

There was a chilling silence from within the room, and then came the hideous, deafening report of a gun being discharged. Colin flinched. The sound never got any easier to bear. He glanced at William and read the same response in his expression.

"Do you think he . . .?" Colin began to ask, but William held up his hand.

"I think it better not to know," he said, quietly opening the door. The body of Viscount Lofton lay slumped across the desk, a pool of blood seeping in gruesome avowal. One arm hung limply towards the floor and on the carpet, inches from his fingers, lay the empty pistol. Lord Wetherby stood before the fireplace, his back to the room and his head bowed, his very posture one of horror and sorrow.

Nine

When the men finally returned to the Shelton estate and entered the house, Emma and Jane immediately ran to them. Jane threw her arms around her father, who was still visibly shaken. Emma felt the urge to do the same to her husband, but she held back. She did walk over to him, and he reached out his hand towards her. She put her palm in his and looked up at him.

"Lofton is dead," Colin said softly.

"Why do I not feel more relieved?" Emma said sadly.

"There was no happy ending to this situation. Now two men are dead."

"How did it happen? Are any of you hurt?" Jane asked. She pulled back to inspect her father and then the other men.

"We are all unharmed," Lord Wetherby said quietly. I think it best if we not discuss Lofton's death. Shelton, Falteroy, and I will deal with the authorities."

"What of Christopher?" Emma asked.

"Lofton signed a confession before he died," Colin answered.

"Thank heavens." Emma sighed. A great burden lifted from her heart.

"I believe I would like to rest, if you can spare a room, Falteroy," Lord Wetherby remarked. He looked exhausted.

"Yes, of course. Everyone is welcome. I will call the housekeeper to show you to your chambers and order baths."

Jane and her uncle both accepted the offer of a room and bath. When they had been shown out, Colin turned to her.

"Would you like to rest, as well?"

"I do not think I could. I was able to sleep a little in the carriage. You must be exhausted, however. I doubt you slept."

"I did not, but I could not sleep now. Would you walk with me?" he asked, holding out his arm to her.

She laid her fingers on his arm, and he led her out into the gardens. They walked in comfortable silence for several minutes before they stopped at a point overlooking the marshes. The wind whipped at Emma's dress and bonnet as she held her face to the sun.

"It is beautiful," she said.

"I did not think so when I was growing up here, but I found myself longing for it after I left. I suppose knowing it would never be mine did not endear it to me."

"What is Newton Park like?"

"It is a charming property. Once the house is redecorated to your liking, I think you will find it pleasing. The house is situated in a meadow, surrounded by rolling hills."

"I am sure it will be lovely."

"Emma, I owe you some explanations," Colin said, looking her in the eye.

"You do not."

"I do. I owe you the truth, even though the dishonesty was for a good cause."

She remained silent.

"William and I have been working for years to catch Lofton. We long suspected his nefarious activities—but I get ahead of myself and shall start at the beginning.

"I believed myself in love with Lofton's sister, Cassie. I

was a young officer and was sent away to the Continent. In those days, Lofton was also a second son and a year younger than I. He was placed under my authority as a young lieutenant, much like your brother was. However, unlike your brother, Lofton was constantly in trouble, and I grew tired of his gambling debts and of bear-leading him. We were home on leave together one time, and I spoke with his father about transferring him to another unit. I felt it would do him good to be under someone he could not take advantage of. His father agreed. Melvyn was furious with me and, of course, blamed me for everything."

Emma remained quiet.

"The next morning, my dogs were found brutally killed—and there was evidence of Lofton having been at the scene. His handkerchief was there, covered in blood."

Emma gasped in shock and covered her mouth.

"I will spare you the details, but they had not merely been shot. Someone had deliberately mutilated them. My dogs were my companions in life, in war—my family," he said.

Emma could see he was trying to control his emotion.

"How could anyone hurt a harmless dog?" she asked in disbelief.

He shook his head and looked away. The memory was obviously still very painful for him, all these years later.

"He is a sick man. He knew how much they meant to me. William and I saw Lofton leaving his estate that night and followed him to the caves not far from the village. We suspected him of being the culprit and having plotted some manner of revenge. A few hours later, we saw him dragging something heavy near the grave, though we did not witness anything directly. We returned the next morning to investigate.

"Expecting illegal goods, we instead discovered a smuggler's body in a shallow grave near to where we had buried the dogs. When we went to confront Lofton, we found him with bandaged arms, claiming he had fallen into some thorns while a little top-heavy. I recklessly grabbed his arm, and blood oozed through the poultice. I ripped the bandages off and would have likely killed him, for he was covered in scratches and bite marks, but because he claimed to have been drunk, William held me back."

"So it led you and Falteroy to concoct the scheme to catch him? Did he admit to killing the smuggler?"

"Melvyn never admitted to any wrong-doing. He claimed he happened upon the man already dead and buried him near the dogs to allay any suspicions of revenue officers. Smuggling was—is—common in these parts near the coast, and most look the other way. However, the old Viscount Lofton and Melvyn's elder brother died in a mysterious accident not long after, and many suspected it was retaliation for the smuggler's death."

"Why would they think so? What happened to them?" she asked, full of questions about the man who had killed her brother.

"Nothing so strange it could not be counted an accident. Their small fishing vessel was found overturned, and their bodies were discovered in fishermen's nets two days later."

"How horrid!" Emma exclaimed.

"Indeed, it was a wretched business, and the sudden change in circumstances never felt right. William had begun to pay more attention to the operations of the estate since returning from university; he, of course, noticed Cassie. Melvyn had taken over as Viscount Lofton, and he thought to give Cassie to William to spite me. Our calf-love had dwindled, and William had not been aware of my feelings to begin with. He had been away at school during our brief courtship, but Melvyn knew of my intentions towards his sister."

"What of Cassie? Was she a mere pawn in this?" Emma asked, feeling defensive on behalf of her unknown sister-in-law.

"No. Cassie was nothing at all like her brother. She was a beautiful soul. However, it was a perfect situation to publicly work against Lofton. William had begun to suspect Lofton's activities with the French went beyond smuggling into treason when documents began to go missing in conjunction with Lofton's military duties. William worked with your uncle—who was his contact at Whitehall—spying for the Crown, and I began to plant information to try to trap Lofton through various orders and missives. He was suspicious and clever. I did not know the entirety until Lofton signed the confession."

"Why did my uncle allow Lofton to court Jane?"

"He did not believe it would come to anything, and he had no evidence to confirm my suspicions. It might have alerted Lofton had he refused."

"Poor Jane, but I do not think her heart was touched."

"It is a shame she must suffer the repercussions of it all. I wish I could have caught him sooner."

"Christopher did not play a part in it, did he?" Emma asked worriedly.

"No, nothing traitorous. He did do something careless, which is why he never made the delivery to my brother."

"What was it? Please tell me," she pleaded.

"Lofton wrote he had been . . ." He coughed. "Ah . . . making an *exchange* with a female French spy when Christopher happened upon them. Christopher mistook the *exchange* and decided to play the hero. I presume he believed the . . . the *exchange* was not by mutual consent. Ahem. Lofton says the Frenchwoman shot him so he could not identify them. Dead men tell no tales, I am afraid."

Emma felt her cheeks heat. She understood his meaning well enough. "And he chose to incriminate Christopher by placing a note on his body?" she asked.

"Yes. One intended to divert attention from himself."

She nodded sadly.

"Now what happens to dear Jane?"

"We have a plan for dear Jane, if she is agreeable." He leaned forward and pulled Emma to him. "But I do not wish to speak of Jane at this moment," he whispered huskily.

A warm, nervous sensation spread through her, and she could feel his chest rise and fall as his arms slid around her. He smelled faintly of sandalwood, earth, and horse, and she wanted more. Despite her nerves and the upheaval in her life during the past week, she realized she accepted what he was saying. She wondered how she came to be here—married to a stranger, rescuing her cousin from a traitor, finding her brother's killer, and in the arms of her husband—but her thoughts abandoned her as he brushed her lips with his.

He murmured her name against her neck, and the soft wisps of air sent shock waves to her very core. Unfamiliar feelings burned through her, and she suddenly felt beautiful, secure, loved. Emma blinked and looked at this man whom, she suddenly discovered, had already commandeered her heart.

Hesitantly, she raised her arms and pulled his lips to hers. He kissed her slowly and gently until her knees were weak and she was lost with desire for something more. Several more minutes passed before Shelton pulled away.

"We should perhaps take this upstairs, my beautiful wife," he whispered through ragged breaths.

Emma could not think. She could only nod. She could not explain the strange feelings but knew she wanted more, that this was right. Reaching down, he swept her into his arms and carried her upstairs.

Ten

Jane turned over, wondering where she was. She was in a strange bed and a strange room. She blinked to clear the sleep from her eyes, and that was when it all came back to her. She would like to go back to sleep and hope when she awoke next time it would have all been a bad dream. How much her life had changed in a single day!

She expected her mother would be here soon, having spread word around town she was ill or had gone to a house party. There was bound to be scandal—it was unavoidable with the way gossip spread in London—for no one left town at the height of the Season without good reason. She had meant what she had said to Lofton. She would rather be a spinster than be married to that monster. Nevertheless, it did not mean it would be easy.

Her mother would have a plan. Her mother always had a plan. It would likely include marrying her off quickly to someone in need of a fortune who would look the other way. Was that not what Lofton had been? She shuddered.

A light tap sounded on her door a few minutes later.

"Enter," she replied.

A maid looked in. "My lord has asked me to see if I can be of assistance, miss? Would you care to dress for dinner or would you prefer a tray in your room?"

Had she slept through the entire day?

"I suppose I will dress for dinner." There was little point in being alone, and she needed to thank Lord Falteroy for rescuing her earlier. She had been too overcome to do it properly.

"Mrs. Shelton brought some clothes for you."

"I had not even thought of it," Jane confessed.

After she was dressed in a simple blossom-pink muslin and her hair had been piled in loose curls upon her head, Jane went in search of her cousin. The maid had thought she might be in the nursery.

At first, Jane wondered what Emma would be doing in the nursery, but then she stopped mid-thought and reflected that perhaps Lord Falteroy was married and had children. She shook her head and chastised herself for being silly. She had no doubt imagined the look he had given her earlier. Besides, two days ago, she had thought she was to marry Lofton. Her narrow escape should be sufficient for now, she thought as she climbed the final flight of stairs to the nursery, without already thinking of another man.

"Papa, you hold the cup like this," she heard a sweet little voice say with a lisp.

"Yes, Lady Evangeline," she heard Falteroy say with amusement.

Jane peeked in through the doorway to see Lord Falteroy sitting at a small table with an angelic little girl whose head was covered in red curls.

Evangeline saw Jane and smiled.

"Want to join our tea-party?" she asked, surprisingly articulate.

"I did not mean to intrude. I was told my cousin was to be found here," Jane said.

"Lady Jane," Lord Falteroy said, rising to his feet. "May I introduce you to my daughter, Lady Evangeline?"

The little girl curtsied gracefully.

"Pleased to meet you, Lady Jane. Please have some tea and some blackberry biscuits."

Jane looked to Falteroy, who inclined his head with a smile.

Jane sat on a tiny chair, and Evangeline served her. "Blackberry biscuits are my favourite," she told the little girl, whose face lit up at the admission.

"Mine, too!" she exclaimed.

Jane's heart ached with pain, knowing she might not know the joy of motherhood because of the scandal. She wondered if Falteroy knew how fortunate he was. She studied him watching his daughter and could tell that he did by the pride in his eyes.

"Well, Lady Evangeline, I do think it is time for your bath."

The little girl sighed. "I know, but I wish it were not."

"I will be back to tuck you in later."

"Yes, Papa. I hope you will come back for tea soon, Lady Jane."

"It would be my pleasure, Lady Evangeline."

The maid directed the little girl to her bath, and Jane stood to leave. For some reason, she wanted to cry and hurried from the room. She thought to seek reprieve in the garden, hoping fresh air might calm her nerves.

"Lady Jane?" Falteroy called to her as she made her way through the house. "Are you all right? I was going to ask you to walk with me."

She turned and tried to control her emotions with a smile. She nodded and took his offered arm.

"She is a beautiful child," Jane said as he directed her down the stairs and out to the terrace.

"I am happy you were able to meet her. It has been hard for her, without a mother's love. Why the tears? Did Lofton harm you?" he asked gently.

She shook her head. "Not in the way you may think. I realized when I saw your daughter that I might never marry because in the eyes of Society I am ruined. I may also never have the chance to be a mother. Silly, is it not? I should be grateful to be alive."

He stood close enough to touch her and lifted her chin to meet his gaze.

"No. I do not think it silly at all." He was very close and looked deep into her eyes. For a moment, she forgot about her troubles.

He pulled back to an arm's length. "I am sorry I was unable to prevent Lofton from doing this to you."

"Surely you do not blame yourself for his reprehensible behaviour?"

"Not his behaviour, but I should have stopped him before he kidnapped you."

"I shall recover. It remains to be seen what repercussions there will be, but I am trying to remain hopeful. My mother is very resourceful."

Falteroy was quiet and appeared lost in thought as he looked skyward into the night. He finally spoke. "Let us hope the focus is now on Lofton and thus diverted from you. I am glad you are safe from him now."

"Lord Falteroy, thank you," she said softly, feeling the inadequacy of the words as she spoke them.

He inclined his head and returned to the house.

Lady Wetherby burst through the parlour door, not waiting to be announced. "Jane! Where is my dear Jane?"

"I am here, Mother," Jane said as she walked in from the garden, where her father and Lord Falteroy were talking.

"What has happened?" her ladyship cried as she hurried to embrace her daughter. "You are being forced into this marriage, then?" Lady Wetherby asked, as she was joined by her husband who had come into the room to greet her. "I was certain, my dear Lord Wetherby, you were arranging this match to save us from scandal."

"She is not being forced into anything, Tilda. Lofton is dead," Lord Wetherby explained.

He caught her before she swooned and helped her to a chair. Jane found her mother's smelling salts from her reticule and wafted them under her nose.

"You should allow me to be seated before shocking me, Lord Wetherby," Lady Wetherby said when she had recovered.

"I was unaware you were so easily shocked, my dear. How did you leave things in Town?"

"Oh!" She waved her kerchief. "I made Jane's excuses for the party, saying she had the headache. Then I put it about we were all to attend a house party here in celebration of Emma and Shelton's marriage, so the bride and groom could have time together before he sets out again for the Continent."

"I knew you would think of something, Mother. I am happy I will have a few days before going back to Town, but I know I must," Jane said bravely.

"Indeed, you must," her mother agreed. "We cannot

allow rumours to be fed. We must find you a new suitor quickly, before anyone remembers who Lofton was."

The door opened, admitting Emma and Colin. "Good evening, Aunt. I could not help but overhear you, and if Jane wishes, she may stay here with me until I leave for Dorsetshire."

"I do not know if that would be wise, Emma," her aunt said with a frown.

Lord Wetherby intervened. "We need not decide tonight."

He turned to William and Colin. "I hope the two of you will now feel free to retire from your duties to the Crown. I certainly would if I were in your shoes," he said with a smile.

"I feel my mission to be completed," William said.

Everyone's eyes turned to Colin. A look of surprise crossed his face. "I suppose I should ask my wife if she minds having a resident husband." Clearly noticing Emma's face flush, he continued, "But I believe that is a discussion for privacy. Would you care to join me for a walk in the garden, wife?"

Jane watched her cousin and new husband leave with a pang of wistfulness, though she was truly pleased for her. Emma seemed to have found happiness. How could she not, with a husband who so clearly adored her?

Lord Falteroy was playing a game of spillikins with his daughter on the other side of the parlour, while Jane's parents discussed her future in hushed tones. She would very much prefer to be absent from the conversation. She had no desire to be forced to wed whoever would have her, but her parents were speaking of leaving in haste to do just that.

"Lady Jane," she heard a little voice say to her. When she looked up, Lady Evangeline was standing before her.

"Yes, Lady Evangeline?"

"Papa says I must go back to the nursery now. Will you promise me you will not be gone tomorrow?"

Jane was unsure what to say. She did not know what her future held. But the little face was looking at her expectantly.

"I promise I will not leave without a proper good-bye," Jane answered with a smile.

"I do not wish for you to leave at all," the little girl said sweetly.

"Thank you, Lady Evangeline," Jane replied.

"Good night," the child said and made her curtsies to everyone in the room before leaving with her nurse.

"What an adorable child!" Lady Wetherby exclaimed.

"Thank you. I am very proud of her," Lord Falteroy said, taking a seat.

Jane felt acutely aware of the tension in the room. Her parents had been discussing her future and were now silent. Would it be unconscionably rude for her to excuse herself? It was not as if she would have much say in the matter at this stage. She would suffer for her poor judgement, possibly for the rest of her life. She wished Emma were still here to support her.

"Would you mind if I took some fresh air?" she asked, not feeling brave enough to be present for the discussion of her future—not in front of Lord Falteroy.

"Jane, you should be involved in these decisions," her mother insisted.

"May we not wait a few days? Will it make any difference?" she pleaded.

"I beg your pardon," Lord Falteroy said. "I will excuse myself. I did not realise you were discussing personal matters."

Lord Wetherby let out a sigh. "Not at all. I beg you will forgive our manners. We are naturally very distraught, and we are all exhausted. Perhaps everything will look clearer in the morning."

On his words, Lord and Lady Wetherby excused themselves for the night, but Jane felt too restless to go to bed.

"Would you still like some fresh air or was that merely a way to avoid the impending conversation?" Falteroy asked.

"Both," she said with a slight smile.

"The gardens are pleasant at night. I would not, however, recommend walking out to the marshes alone after dark."

"Thank you. I am sure the gardens will suit my purposes."

She stood to leave, feeling disappointed, wishing Falteroy would join her.

He stood up as well, and she felt a fool. She must have imagined the earlier attraction between them. Anyone who had been rescued in such a manner, and by a hero dreams were made of, would likely be as self-deluding as she.

"Jane," he said as she walked slowly to the terrace door.

"Yes?" she asked, reaching for the handle.

"May I accompany you? Or would you prefer solace?"

"I would prefer your company, sir," she replied, her heart beginning to pound.

He brushed his hand with hers as he held the door open for her to pass. They walked to the stone balustrade and stopped to look out over the garden.

"I was hoping to have a few days with you here," he said.

"My parents wish to return to London to arrange a match

as soon as we may," she explained, hoping her voice was not shaking as much as the rest of her was.

"I see. Is there a particular person in mind? One of your other suitors, perhaps?"

"I do not know," she said, beginning to feel absurd. She did not wish to speak of other men with him.

"I had hoped for more time," he whispered.

"More time?" she asked, confused.

"More time for you to recover from your ordeal. More time for you to get to know Evangeline and myself. More time for you to forget your feelings for Lofton."

"Please do not mention his name again! Any amiability which existed between us was dispelled some time ago."

"Then your heart is not injured?"

She shook her head. "Only my pride," she whispered.

"I would propose another option to you, then, and you need not answer me now."

She turned to look at him, and he was watching her with such intensity, her breath caught. Dare she hope?

"You could stay here and become Lady Falteroy. I hope, in time, you could feel happy here with us."

"You would marry me?" she asked. Tears began to fill her eyes.

"It would be my pleasure, Jane."

"I do not deserve such redemption. I do not know what to say."

"You need no redemption, Jane." He wiped away the tear which was falling down her cheek. "Rest on it and decide later."

"No. Yes."

He looked up in confusion.

"No, I do not want to decide later. Yes, I will marry you, William."

His eyes smiled first before his entire face lit up. He seemed genuinely pleased.

"I will make you happy, Jane," he said as he cradled her face.

"I do not doubt it for one moment," she replied earnestly, a moment before her mouth was covered with his. It was a promising start, to be sure.

Eleven

Colin led Emma through the house, down the terrace steps, and onto a pebbled walk that led away from the gardens. They walked over a mile into the fading sun, then she felt the breeze from the sea and heard the squawks of seagulls. Colin did not speak until they reached the edge of the marsh.

"This is where I always came to think when I lived here," he began.

"I can understand why," she replied as she looked around at the marsh, which faded into the sea.

"It has been rather a whirlwind for our first two days of marriage. I cannot promise such excitement everyday," he teased.

"I would not wish for it! But now Christopher's death is no longer a mystery," she replied sadly, "and a cold-blooded murderer can no longer kill."

"Yes, he would have eliminated anyone who stood in his way, including me."

"Must you return to those duties? Will you forever be in harm's way?" She turned and searched his eyes.

"Would you mind if I stayed? Do you regret marrying me, Emma?" he asked as he stared out over the sea.

"How shall I answer a question such as that?" she chided.

"Honestly." He turned back to her.

She could see by the look on his face he was in earnest.

"How could I? I feel I know you in part already from Christopher's letters, and I am forever in your debt for what you have done for my family. I only wish we had met in different circumstances . . . and you had not felt it necessary to marry me out of pity or mercy."

"Mercy? No." He looked down and kicked a stone from the path. "True, I never intended marriage, but I did feel responsible for Christopher's death and therefore wanted to provide some means for your family."

"What *did* you intend?" she asked, searching his face for answers.

"To draw enough attention to you for suitors to notice you and to provide you a dowry anonymously through your uncle."

"Then why did *you* marry me?"

He hesitated, then reached up and ran the back of his fingers down her cheek.

"I saw you, Emma."

For several seconds, she stared blankly at him. Her pulse quickened again. His eyes were dark, heated and intent. He touched her ever so gently, and as if being pulled by an unseen force, she moved closer to him.

"One look at you, one dance with you, and I wanted you. I wanted you to bear my name."

"'Tis a poor way to begin a marriage," she chided, although she now understood the unseen forces nature could exert, following their initial interlude as husband and wife.

"Is it, Emma? Many marriages have much less. In those first moments with you, I saw a beautiful woman who was willing to sacrifice herself to save her family." He stared at her

94

knowingly, and butterflies flitted about inside her in anticipation of what would follow. "I also saw a beautiful woman who made me feel alive inside. One whom I could admire and desire." He cradled her face in his hands before he lowered his head and brushed his lips over hers. "I do not feel poor, Emma," he whispered into her ear, sending shivers down her spine as he proceeded to place soft kisses on her neck.

"So you will stay?" she asked breathlessly as his hands slid around her and she melted into him.

"Just try to make me leave you," he said as he continued to show her how he felt, making her feel very rich, indeed.

About the Author

National bestselling author **Elizabeth Johns** was first an avid reader, though she was a reluctant convert. It was Jane Austen's clever wit and unique turn of phrase that hooked Johns when she was "forced" to read *Pride and Prejudice* for a school assignment. She began writing when she ran out of her favorite author's books and decided to try her hand at crafting a Regency romance novel. Her journey into publishing began with the release of *Surrender the Past*, book one of the Loring-Abbott Series. Johns makes no pretensions to Austen's wit but hopes readers will perhaps laugh and find some enjoyment in her writing. Johns attributes much of her inspiration to her mother, a retired English teacher. During their last summer together, Johns would sit on the porch swing and read her stories to her mother, who encouraged her to continue writing. Busy with multiple careers, including a professional job in the medical field, author and mother of small children, Johns squeezes in time for reading whenever possible.

Visit Elizabeth online: ElizabethJohnsAuthor.com

Edward & Emily

By Heather B. Moore

One

"You are nearly thirty years of age," Edward Blackwood's mother said in her sharp voice while she peered at him through a raised quizzing glass. "It's time you pull your head out of your books and take up your responsibilities. You are now the master of the estate and must attend to our guests who are here in your honor."

The conversations of the guests in the main hall filtered into the library and filled the tense silence between Edward and his mother. She'd invited their closest neighbors to a small dinner party—all to welcome him home. Any party at all, small or otherwise, hardly seemed appropriate in light of their recent family tragedy.

Edward would never forget the day that the morning post arrived at his hotel in Germany. The words scrawled across the pages had changed his life forever.

Peter was gone. Gregarious and generous Peter—who was always the life of any event, who had been engaged to be married, and who had been running the family estate these past ten years.

Since his older brother's death in a terrible carriage accident, Edward's mother had suddenly turned her eye to him. Edward was the scholarly one in the family. Eton and Oxford had opened his eyes to the world of literature, and he continued with his education, taking it as far as he could. Of course, he could not take on his ideal position—that of a university professor—but he had been invited to lecture and present his studies of the classics, in literature and art, equally.

And so it was when he was on a lecture tour in Germany that the blasted letter found him, bringing heartbreaking news. Peter was dead, and Edward was the heir. He'd returned home well after the funeral, unable to help the traveling delays that beset him. And now, he'd been home less than three days, and his mother was throwing a dinner party.

On the other side of the library walls were the neighbors chatting in the grand hall, and, according to his mother, waiting to greet Edward, offer their condolences, then proceed into the dining room.

"And don't forget, dear Edward, to pay special attention to Emily Foster," his mother said in a whisper. "Tonight is her first social event since her father's death. And as you know, Mrs. Foster is my dearest friend. She's sending Miss Foster with a cousin for the London Season in a few days, and tonight will be testing her fortitude, to be sure. You'll remember her aunt, Lady Gerrard, and her cousin, Miss Adele Gerrard. They've spent a few summers in the country with the Fosters."

Edward tugged at his cravat and met his mother's gaze full-on, which wasn't an easy task since she was a full two heads shorter than he. He couldn't give a fig about Emily Foster, a girl he could barely remember anyway, or her cousin Adele. He had a vague recollection of Emily as a dark, curly-haired girl who ran about the gardens like an imp with his brother. They'd played the silliest games, nothing that remotely interested Edward. As a boy, he'd always preferred an interesting book or a long horse ride over running around with the neighbor children. And now he was supposed to console Emily? Her father might be recently dead, but so was

Edward's brother. It seemed life never went as expected, and one had to simply learn to endure.

"Returning from Germany *is* fulfilling my duty, Mother," he said in a measured tone, despite the difficulty he had in keeping his temper in check—his temper and his grief, which had turned out to be a sorry combination. "Taking Peter's place is also fulfilling my duty." He released a breath. "It's not my duty to entertain the neighbors and comfort their daughters!"

The moment his voice rose above an acceptable pitch, he regretted it. His mother's eyes widened, and the guests had suddenly quieted. Had they overhead him? Even to his own ears, he'd sounded cruel. Cold and cruel. When in truth, he was never any of those things, but ever since his future turned upside down, he hadn't quite been himself.

Edward swallowed against his dry throat and rubbed his hand over his face. He closed his eyes for a moment, focusing on regulating his breathing. Then, he opened his eyes, looked his mother square in the face and extended his arm. "Shall we?"

She blinked a couple of times, then stepped toward him, and placed her hand on the inside of his elbow. She gave a regal nod, and together, the two exited the library, rounded the short hallway, and approached the gathering of guests.

It was going to be a very long night, and Edward was already looking forward to when he could return to the library after the last guest had departed and pour himself a healthy measure of brandy. Maybe two.

Two

Emily Foster wanted to flee the estate she now approached in a carriage. It seemed all of the candles in the entire house had been relocated to the main floor and lit. Or perhaps it was the contrast of the bright light to her dark mood that made the Blackwood estate seem afire. With the loss of her father and her mother's proclamation that she was to go and live with her aunt's family in London for the foreseeable future, Emily's mood felt very black indeed.

London was the last place she wanted to go right now. She wanted to stay home and help the steward with matters of the estate. Her father had always let her join him in his rounds of visiting tenants and speaking with the farmers about their crops and livestock. She'd rather be on horseback than sitting straight-back in a drawing room discussing the latest London scandal. Besides, the steward needed her help. Emily's brother Stephen had one more year left of Eton before he would take on his new estate responsibilities.

"Another pin is coming out." Her mother's voice interrupted Emily's gloomy thoughts.

Emily's gloved hand went to her coiffure, feeling for the errant pin. Her thick, black hair had a mind of its own. No matter how carefully or tightly the maid fixed Emily's hair, something was unraveling less than an hour later, and the jostling carriage wasn't helping any. In fact, the ruts in the private lane leading to the Blackwood estate had undergone a space of a few weeks where repairs weren't kept up on account of the disorganization that took place with Peter's death.

The next bounce nearly sent Emily and the other women off their seats.

"Oh dear," Emily's aunt said. "This road would be a disaster in the rain."

If Emily's aunt had noticed, then the condition of the road was poor indeed. Lady Gerrard only chose to see what she wanted to see. She usually avoided any and every unpleasant thing. She and her daughter, Adele, had come for Emily's father's funeral, but after the funeral, Lady Gerrard said it wasn't good to speak of the dead. Which only made their household more depressing as Adele's constant chatter was frequently one-sided.

"We should mention the state of the roads to the Black-woods," Adele said with what sounded like true distress.

"No," Emily said, compelled to speak up. "That would be exceptionally rude, and besides, they have undergone their own family grievances."

"You are so wise," Adele said immediately.

This didn't surprise Emily. Adele agreed with everyone and everything. She was two years older than Emily and had already had three seasons in London, none of them with a proposal worthy of a granddaughter of a duke, or so Lady Gerrard had said.

Emily's aunt wanted Emily to accompany Adele to all the social events in order to keep Adele company and cheer her up. The task seemed overwhelming at best since Emily could barely keep her own chin up. She also suspected that Lady

Gerrard was trying to cast Adele in better light, as Emily was clearly the plainer of the two. There might be some feelings of family duty in there as well, now that Emily's father had passed away.

"Here we are," Emily's mother said in her quiet voice. Compared to Lady Gerrard, Emily's mother was a timid mouse.

Lady Gerrard exited the carriage first, of course, followed by Adele, then Emily's mother, then Emily. Everything always had to be accomplished in order of precedence, it seemed. When the Gerrards were not staying with them, the Foster household stood on much less ceremony. It had become something of a joke between Emily and her father. When his sister was in town, all was prim and proper, and when she was away, everyone could, what her father called, "loosen their buttons."

Emily's eyes stung at the memory of her father, and she blinked quickly to discourage any real tears from forming. She stepped out of the carriage and looked up at the towering house with its brilliant glow.

"Oh my goodness." Lady Gerrard's voice sounded in Emily's ear. "What's that in your hair?" Another rebellious pin? Emily reached up to the side of her head just as Lady Gerrard plucked something out.

"Paint?"

"Oh," Emily started. "I was painting this afternoon."

"What? An entire wall?" Lady Gerrard shook her head. Then she grasped Emily's gloved hands. "At least gloves are fashionable."

Emily drew her hands away, her cheeks flushing with mortification. Her father had encouraged her painting, and her mother had allowed it so long as it didn't interfere with working on her other skills of piano and embroidery. But Lady

Gerrard had been vocal more than once about her shock that Emily could get so lost in painting, spend an entire day, in fact, producing portraits. Lady Gerrard had also made it clear that portrait painting wasn't ladylike when one spent so much time on it instead of other, more feminine pursuits. If Emily wanted to paint, it should be of flowery landscapes and delicate bowls of fruit, and only when she had no other obligations to attend to. Painting portraits of brooding ancestors relocated along a rocky seashore were simply a waste of time.

Emily hadn't confessed to her aunt that the two paintings she'd seen were only the start of the dozens more Emily had stored in the attic. Ever since her first governess taught Emily how to wield a brush, she'd been fascinated with the human form and the characteristics and moods that could be shown with a few strokes. Emily had started experimenting and grew more daring at the age of twelve by painting her great-grandmother, copied from another portrait, as a young woman, sitting on a grassy knoll as she looked out over the ocean, watching an incoming storm.

Her father had praised her, her mother had raised her brows, and Emily took it all as encouragement. So she continued.

"You'll be putting away your paints next week," Lady Gerrard said as they walked up the polished steps of the Blackwood home. "London is no place for that type of messy hobby. We can't have you greeting men with the smell of turpentine about you."

Emily almost smiled at the thought of riding in Hyde Park while she tried to discreetly pick paint splotches from her arm. She well knew that her perfume covered up any errant drops of turpentine that might not have been scrubbed away. At that moment, the front doors swung open, and the butler bowed low and greeted each of them in turn. He then announced to those beyond the names of the newest arrivals.

Lady Gerrard was announced first, of course.

Emily didn't mind the wait in the least. Her attention had been suddenly captured by the interesting appearance of the Blackwoods' new butler. He had a prominent nose, deep-set eyes, and hair as black as night. His appearance reminded Emily of a gypsy, and an idea for a portrait flashed through her mind. What if she painted the butler wearing gypsy clothes, a long dagger gripped in his hand, as he strode—

"Emily," her mother said. "Mrs. Blackwood will be wanting to speak with us. Stop dawdling."

Emily blinked, noticing for the first time that the drawing room off the hallway was filled with guests. Most of them stood with a glass of wine in hand. She followed her mother dutifully into the drawing room and picked out Mrs. Blackwood immediately by her deep auburn hair. Emily still couldn't believe that her childhood friend Peter was gone. She had hardly seen him since he'd gone off to Eton, followed soon by his younger brother, Edward.

The knowledge that he was permanently gone was hard to believe, especially with the gaiety that surrounded her now. But like her aunt had been saying for weeks, life went on, whether you were ready for it or not.

Her mother steered Emily through the crowd, greeting others as they went. They must be quite late for the host and hostess to no longer be welcoming guests in the grand hallway. Emily studied Mrs. Blackwood. Her faded auburn hair used to be more of a red. It seemed her advancing years had darkened her hair. And next to her . . . Emily found herself staring at Edward. It had been years since she'd last seen him. He had always been the serious brother in the family and couldn't let himself be bothered by playmates.

Anytime the families of the neighborhood got together for a child's birthday party, Edward would sit under a tree somewhere, his nose in a book. She could practically see in her mind his skinny shoulders hunched as he held an overly large book in his hands, intently reading page after page, hardly lifting his gaze for anything.

And that was possibly why Emily had never noticed how blue his eyes were. Not the dull gray-blue of Peter's, but the blue of the morning sea beneath an early golden sun.

Emily didn't know why she noticed this small detail, since Edward had rarely crossed her mind over the years at all, except now he was staring straight at her with a look of surprise mixed with curiosity. Emily's skill with painting portraits and altering them had trained her to read expressions, more specifically what lay behind a person's gaze. She almost turned around, to see whom Edward might be looking so intently at, but she knew she wasn't mistaken. For some reason, Edward Blackwood had just noticed her for perhaps the first time in his life.

Three

"Be gracious, Edward," his mother whispered to him. "The Fosters are making their way over here. You remember Emily, the dark-haired girl. And you just spoke to her cousin, Adele, the blonde woman."

Whatever Edward's mother was rambling on about, he knew for a fact that the Emily walking toward him right now was no longer a *girl*. She was certainly Emily Foster, but the thin, awkward girl he remembered as having brown eyes too large for her face had grown into a statuesque beauty. And the ironic thing of it was, he could tell she had no idea how much she was drawing the attention of every man in the room—married or unattached.

"Mr. Blackwood," Mrs. Foster said. The woman was just as diminutive and mousy as Edward remembered. Her daughter had gained her striking looks from Mr. Foster. "We offer our condolences to you and your family. Our only comfort is that you have returned home safely and can now find solace with your mother."

Another condolence, but this time, he could see into Mrs. Foster's eyes that she understood grief. She'd lost her own husband, and although he had lived a longer life than Peter, it was still painful.

Edward thanked Mrs. Foster and found his gaze again drawn to Emily. She remained quiet, nodded as her mother spoke, and now he was sure she might say something, but she did not. In fact, she was entirely opposite her talkative cousin, Adele. It was with guilt when he saw her blink those large brown eyes that now seemed to fit her face perfectly that he realized her mother's condolences should be returned. His mother was right. He was irresponsible. Clueless. Selfish.

"Mrs. Foster and Miss Foster," he began. "I, too, must offer my condolences to you. I hope you know that you are always welcome here if you are in need of an empathetic word."

"Thank you," Mrs. Foster said, but Edward's eyes were on Emily's. Her lips had lifted just slightly in acknowledgment, and she was looking straight at him.

Something unspoken passed between them, and Edward wasn't sure he could put a name to it, not if he searched all the literature in the world. It was like they shared a kinship—not over lost members of their families, but over being survivors in their families, facing each day in a changed existence.

And he suddenly felt an odd sense of protectiveness for her. He'd never had a sister, and wondered if this was how a brother felt toward one. But he didn't think a man with brotherly feelings toward a woman would find it so hard to look away from her.

Then Emily was turning away, her arm linked with her mother's, and he wanted to somehow detain her. But of course he didn't.

"Well done," his mother said. "We'll give everyone a few more minutes, then go in for dinner."

Edward could only nod. He watched Emily's departure, her mother pulling her into one conversation after another. Emily barely spoke a word. She looked as lost as he felt. She smiled politely at those she and her mother conversed with, but that smile never extended beyond her lips.

If there was anything Edward could understand, it was that polite smile.

"It's time," his mother said, nodding to Edward. "Escort Lady Gerrard and the rest will follow."

Edward hesitated, wishing he could escort Emily instead, if only to tell her that he commiserated with her. But formalities must be followed.

He sought out Lady Gerrard, and as he was escorting her to the dining room, the other guests followed behind. Like her daughter Adele, Lady Gerrard was not one to shirk on her conversational duty.

By the time he was seated, he knew most of her activities over the past month. But he listened carefully for any mention of Emily. So far, it had been all of Adele. He noted that Emily was seated halfway down the table from him, meaning there would be no chance of conversation between them.

"You must hear Adele play," Lady Gerrard said. "After dinner, she could play for us all, bring some cheer to this place." As the soup was brought in and served around the table, she added in a lowered tone, "I'm ready to return to London and escape all the melancholy at the Fosters."

Edward felt as if he'd been slapped. He glanced over at Emily. Certainly she'd heard. Lady Gerrard hadn't exactly been whispering.

Emily was looking down at her soup, her spoon in hand, as if she were seriously contemplating something.

"Will you be coming to London this Season?" Lady Gerrard pressed. "Now that you are heir, surely you are in want of a wife."

Edward had just spooned the first bite of soup in his mouth and nearly spat it out. Lady Gerrard was perhaps the most impudent woman he'd ever met. He looked to his mother for help; not even she would be so brash in mixed company.

Fortunately, her eyes flashed fire, echoing his exact feelings. But when his mother spoke, it was with all the decorum that befitted an excellent hostess. "Edward will be tending to the estate this autumn," she said. "There is much to do, and I'm afraid I cannot spare him to other frivolous activities."

Edward could have kissed his mother if the width of a dining table hadn't separated them.

"Well, the choosing of one's wife and partner and mother of one's children could hardly be considered frivolous," Lady Gerrard said in an imperious tone.

"Indeed not," his mother was quick to concede, although her tone was equally imperious. "When the time is right, Edward will choose a most excellent bride that the entire county will be pleased with."

Edward picked up his glass of wine and took a lengthy swallow. "A tall order," he said. "Any bride of mine might dread coming to our estate if word got out that she was to be measured against every lady in the county."

"Oh, Edward," his mother said with a conciliatory smile. "We'll keep that just amongst ourselves here at the table."

"All fourteen of us?" Lady Gerrard said.

His mother kept her smile on her face, and Lady Gerrard had no other choice but to pick another topic, which she promptly did.

"Now, my niece Emily is not a great musical talent like my daughter," Lady Gerrard said. "You might already know that since you are neighbors."

While she continued talking, Edward's gaze strayed again to Emily. She was eating her soup, not speaking to anyone, yet he caught the faint blush on her cheeks. Edward had no doubt her blush was due to her aunt's indelicate conversation.

"She paints," Lady Gerrard declared. "It's quite unusual, if you ask me."

Edward couldn't stop the words from tumbling out of his mouth. "Many ladies paint," he said. "It can be an impressive talent."

His eyes connected with Emily as she raised her head. Her blush deepened, and Edward wondered if he'd just made everything worse.

"Impressive, to be sure," Lady Gerrard said. "If the young lady in question is painting landscapes or perhaps a vase of flowers. But Emily's paintings are quite . . . unsettling."

Emily's face darkened two shades, and Edward snapped his gaze to Lady Gerrard.

"Explain yourself," he said, his voice cold. The other guests around the table had grown silent, absorbed in Lady Gerrard's newest conversation thread.

"She paints portraits," said Lady Gerrard, "of people long since passed and she . . . relocates the subjects."

Edward couldn't even choose which question he wanted to ask. He looked over at Emily. "That sounds quite interesting," he said, although he wasn't sure he quite understood.

She glanced at her aunt, and then at Edward. "Thank you." It was nearly a whisper.

"Can you tell us more about it, Miss Foster?" he asked, pointedly directing his question to her personally.

She cleared her throat and straightened her shoulders. Edward found himself admiring her resolve greatly. She might be quiet, and she might be embroiled in grief over her father, but she clearly had a passion for painting. Her brown eyes were brighter than he'd seen that night so far, and the embarrassed blush of her cheeks had faded to a healthy rose.

"I try to imagine people how they were when they were younger, when they were alive, and what sorts of things they liked to do." Her voice was soft at first, but grew in strength as she spoke. The entire group of guests was listening now. "For instance, my great-grandmother loved to take walks along the beach and was known for her daydreaming. So I used her portrait as a starting place, then painted her looking out over the ocean."

Edward found himself smiling. "That sounds quite wonderful and innovative." He slid his gaze to meet Lady Gerrard's gaze as he said *innovative.* "Not unsettling at all."

He thought of what his mother had told him earlier, that Emily would be going with her aunt to London to take part in the Season. Compassion surged through him. How would she cope?

"I'd love to come see your paintings," Edward's mother said, surprising him yet again. Although he didn't quite think she was doing it out of interest in Emily, but more to spite Lady Gerrard.

He was quite enjoying his mother's handling of Lady Gerrard.

"You are very kind," Emily told his mother.

"We're afraid Emily is quite busy since she is preparing to leave for London soon," Mrs. Foster cut in.

Everything inside Edward deflated as he thought of Emily going off with Lady Gerrard.

"We are hoping for double fortune this Season in the form of two proposals," Lady Gerrard said, one side of her mouth lifted in a knowing smile. "Perhaps the two cousins will be entertaining spring weddings." She cast a benevolent smile upon Emily and Adele.

Edward had never been more grateful to his obligations at the estate now. His brother had told him of the London scene a handful of times, but Edward hadn't believed much of what Peter had said about mothers parading their daughters before eligible gentlemen. Now he could fully believe it.

Emily was looking at her plate of food again. Braised chicken with an herb sauce had been brought out sometime during Lady Gerrard's diatribe on painting. While Lady Gerrard prattled on about eligible bachelors who might be spending the Season in London, Edward cast glances at Emily.

She seemed to be in her own world. Perhaps her aunt's comments didn't bother her? Or more likely, she'd heard them often enough that she was smart enough to ignore them. Edward didn't think he could do the same.

"How about we organize something for all of us to do tomorrow?" his mother suddenly said. "We could have a picnic while the weather is unusually fine."

Before Edward could protest, his mother was collecting excited agreements from around the table. He swallowed back his frustrated sigh. He'd hoped that after this evening's dinner party, his mother would give him some peace and quiet. Maybe before the appointed picnic time, he'd be able to come up with a good excuse not to attend. Even though he wouldn't mind trying for another chance to speak to Emily, he really couldn't lose his focus on the monumental task of putting the estate to rights. Besides, he didn't think he could endure much more of Lady Gerrard's conversation.

Four

It *was* rather silly, Emily admitted to herself. The portrait she'd started, and thought would be of her great-grandfather, actually looked nothing like the man at all. In fact, it was looking quite a bit like Edward Blackwood. She'd painted the man standing among castle ruins, but instead of examining the ancient structure, he was looking off into the distance, a book in one hand. His hair was brown, like Mr. Blackwood's, and his shoulders broad—again, like Mr. Blackwood's. She hadn't put in the finer details of his face, but as she started mixing paint, she knew the man's eyes would be blue.

Another glance at the portrait of her great-grandfather she'd sneaked off the gallery wall confirmed that her great-grandfather's nearly black hair and brown eyes and narrow shoulders were nothing like the man she had put onto the canvas in front of her.

"Miss?" A knock sounded at the door of the east attic, Emily's favorite place to paint in the mornings.

Her hand nearly jerked the brush across the canvas. "Yes?" she said, setting her brush down as Jenny entered the room. The woman was about ten years older than Emily, but she'd become a great confidante over the years—an unusual development Emily was grateful for.

"Your mother said the carriage is ready," Jenny said, her eyes darting to the canvas, then to Emily's hands that were splotched with paint. "Oh dear."

Emily looked down at her hands. She was sure she could be ready quickly, although the idea of going to a picnic with a great number of people didn't appeal to her.

"I'll need help," Emily said, putting her brush in a jar of spirits, then rising to her feet to take off her apron.

Jenny smiled and shook her head. "We must hurry. Lady Gerrard is in fine form this morning."

Emily hadn't even gone down to break her fast, so she hadn't been able to detect her aunt's moods, which usually ruled the entire household.

"Oh, your hair," Jenny said.

Emily lifted her hand to search for stray locks. "Is it that bad?"

"Don't touch it," Jenny said. "Your hands!"

But it was too late. Emily lowered her hands and said, "Can you fix it?"

Jenny narrowed her eyes. "Do you have anything that will take out paint?"

Emily glanced at the jar of spirits and raised her brows.

Pursing her lips, Jenny found a cloth that wasn't too badly used and dipped a corner into the spirits, then she tried to rub out the paint in Emily's hair.

"Good enough," Jenny said. "We haven't time for anything else."

Emily took the cloth from Jenny and scrubbed it against her hands, getting the worst of the paint off. She'd have to stop by her bedroom to fetch her gloves.

"Here you are, miss," Jenny said, pulling gloves out of her apron pocket.

"You're a dear," Emily said, taking the gloves and pulling them onto her paint-splotched hands. "I'm so glad you'll be coming to London with me."

Jenny nodded. "Me, too."

Emily blinked against the sudden burning in her eyes. Now was no time to get emotional about leaving her home for London. She'd only be gone for a few months. Her aunt had promised she could return home for the summer.

Emily navigated her way down the narrow stairs from the attic to the third floor. By the second floor, she could hear her aunt ordering a servant to do one thing or another. When she reached the staircase that descended to the main hallway on the ground floor, her aunt had already walked out the front door.

"There you are," Adele said, coming out of the drawing room. She wore yellow and looked as fresh as a flower.

Emily knew she could never compare with her dark blue dress, a half-mourning, which Lady Gerrard said she'd have to lighten up in London.

Adele was all smiles, and Emily had the feeling it had something to do with the fact they were going on a picnic and Edward Blackwood would be in attendance. On the carriage ride home the night before, Lady Gerrard had commented more than once how Edward had paid Adele special attention.

When Emily then pointed out that perhaps they didn't need to go to London after all if Adele had a love interest here, Lady Gerrard had immediately gone on the defensive. "We need to keep all of our options open. Mr. Blackwood is a fine man with a fine estate, but a title would also be nice."

Perhaps it was with those thoughts swirling in her head that Emily found herself painting the man in question this morning. Otherwise, it would mean that Emily had been paying Edward her own special attention, which would not do at all.

Emily was bustled into the carriage with her aunt and cousin. Apparently, her mother had pleaded a headache and would be missing this impromptu event. Sitting stiffly in the carriage, Emily watched the scenery go by as they drove to the picnic location, where they'd also explore the ruins of an old monastery.

"Edward Blackwood is quite wealthy," Emily heard her aunt telling Adele. "But we will see what London has to offer first."

Adele nodded and gave her mother another smile. Her eyes had that faraway look in them, almost dreamy. In fact, the more that Emily thought about it, Adele had been acting like this for several days now. Could her cousin be so smitten with Edward in such a short amount of time? But then Emily realized that Adele had only become reacquainted with Edward last night, and her distracted behavior had been going on previous to the dinner party.

When the carriage stopped, Lady Gerrard was handed down first. As Emily waited for her turn to climb out of the carriage, she determined to watch Adele's reactions to Edward very closely.

The day's weather proved to be ideal for a picnic. Soft white clouds meandered across the sky, pushed by a gentle breeze that stirred up the sweet fragrance of the meadow flowers. There were just over a dozen guests, as well as two servants who'd come along to carry the picnic baskets.

After all of the greetings were exchanged, Emily walked with Mrs. Blackwood, who seemed determined to cheer her up. Emily quickly noticed that Adele and Edward had paired off, although they were still part of the main group.

"Are you looking forward to the Season in London?" Mrs. Blackwood asked Emily.

She had always intimidated Emily as her stern personality gave little margin for error. But Emily preferred this to any conversation with her aunt. "I am sure it will be enjoyable, although I'll miss helping the steward about the estate, and I'll miss my freedom to paint."

"Yes," she said, peering over at Emily. Her quizzing glasses were nowhere in sight, so Emily assumed she'd left them behind for the picnic. "You have been very useful, your mother tells me. I'm sure you'll be relieved when your brother finishes up school."

"I love helping on the estate," she said, not sure why she was being so forthcoming. Perhaps it was because of Edward's questions about her painting the night before. "If I had been born a male heir to an estate, I would be forever content."

Mrs. Blackwood barked out a laugh. Emily wasn't sure if she'd ever heard the woman laugh in such a way. It made Emily smile back. "Don't we all wish for that at some time in our lives."

"*What* do you wish for, Mother?" a male voice said behind them.

Somehow, Edward must have disentangled himself from Adele and the other women. Emily felt her pulse speed up.

Edward looked fine this morning. He wasn't wearing the formal black of the night before, but his jacket was a pale gray that emphasized the blueness of his eyes. His cravat was tied simply, and the breeze had tousled his hair. Emily secretly wondered how his shoulders had grown so broad and his thighs so muscular and sturdy if he spent his days lecturing and researching.

"Good day, Miss Foster," Edward said when their eyes connected.

"Good day," she said, and then she noticed something she hadn't the night before. Perhaps it was because of the natural light, or the way a cloud had covered half the sun just then, but Edward's nose was slightly crooked. And Emily knew, could testify to it, that his nose hadn't been crooked before.

Edward arched a brow at her, and Emily realized she'd been openly staring at him. Her face heated immediately, and she looked forward again, feeling embarrassed, yet not able to stop the racing of her thoughts. Had Edward broken his nose? And if so, how? She thought through the different possibilities and was forced to suppress a smile.

"We were just discussing the newest colors in ribbons," Mrs. Blackwood was telling Edward, "and how we wished to add them to our purchase list."

"Mother, you really expect me to believe that?" Edward said.

This bantering between mother and son surprised Emily. It was a side of Mrs. Blackwood Emily hadn't seen before.

"If I know anything about you and Miss Foster here," Edward continued, "it is that you are the last two ladies to enter into a serious discussion about colored ribbons. You're far more likely to discuss something infinitely more significant."

Mrs. Blackwood looked at Emily with arched brows over twinkling eyes. "Do you agree with my son?"

"I think we've been found out," Emily said.

Edward laughed. "How about I show you our formidable ruins, Miss Foster?"

The question couldn't have startled her more. First of all, she'd been to the ruins dozens of times as a girl. It had been one of her favorite places to play hide and seek with Peter and her brother. In the second place, she was surprised that Edward had sought her out in this way.

A quick glance behind her showed the others in their party spreading out across the ruins while the servants set up the picnic.

"I'll have to leave you to it, Edward," his mother said. "I've got to discuss a few things with Mrs. Christensen."

Edward bowed his head at his mother's departure, and just like that, Emily was left with Edward.

Five

E dward couldn't help himself. When he'd seen his mother and Miss Foster walking arm in arm, apparently in cahoots, his curiosity got the better of him. Adele's conversation about all of the balls she was looking forward to in London had grown tiring very quickly, and Edward needed a break. He didn't have anything against Adele—plenty of young women thought one-sided conversations were somehow enjoyable for the other party—but Edward had spent half the night thinking about Emily and her painting. He determined that if he talked to her at the picnic, some of his curiosity would be sated, and he could sleep in peace tonight.

"Shall we?" Edward asked Miss Foster, extending his arm as an invitation. After all, the ground about the ruins was uneven at times. He didn't want her to twist an ankle.

He needn't have worried. Although, Miss Foster did take his arm, her touch was feather-light, and she was more than steady on her feet.

They walked for a moment in silence, and Edward felt surprisingly tongue-tied. He'd never had trouble speaking his mind to anyone else. He was more than curious about Miss Foster—in a way he couldn't ever remember being before. "How is your brother doing?"

"He is well, thank you," Miss Foster said, peering up at him with those large brown eyes.

Edward almost missed a step. "Will he return for the holidays?"

"I'm not rightly sure," she said. "I'll still be in London, and I'm sure that Stephen will take every advantage of holding on to his freedom for as long as possible. He's rather young to take on the responsibility of an entire estate."

Edward understood more than he probably ought, although he was nearly thirty years of age. "I've much to learn myself," he said in a solemn tone.

"Yes," Miss Foster said. "I suppose, as the second son, you were always free to follow other aspirations."

"That's one way to look at it," he said. "I don't necessarily view it as freedom. I didn't have a choice, really."

Miss Foster nodded. "I'm really sorry about Peter," she said softly. "You've probably tired of condolences by now."

"And I'm very sorry about your father," Edward said. "I know you were close to him." He realized that they'd stopped walking and were merely standing and looking at each other.

"Thank you," Miss Foster said, glancing down. "I'm actually quite angry at him."

"Oh?" Edward said, finding this amusing, although he didn't think she meant it that way.

Her gaze met his. "Now I have to go to London and prance around at all the balls in order to secure a husband while my father's steward gets to do the more enjoyable tasks at home."

Edward stared at her. "Your father's steward?"

"Yes, Mr. Billings," she continued. "He's the overseer, you know, and I used to help him and my father with the maintenance schedules and visiting the tenants to write down their needs." She looked away from him, and Edward noticed how thick her eyelashes were. "How can one trade the beauty of the country for the dampness and smog of London?"

"A woman's lot can be trying," Edward said.

"Are you teasing me?" she said, arching one of her dark brows.

Edward smiled. "I'm not sure. It was just an observation."

"I'm certainly fortunate in many things," she said. "But the limitations placed upon my sex can be vexing."

"Is that what you were speaking to my mother about?" He started walking again, guiding her toward a crumbled wall.

"You are very observant," Miss Foster pronounced. "But you'll find that I'm quite observant, too."

"Oh?" Edward asked. This conversation was infinitely more appealing than what he'd had with Miss Adele earlier.

"What happened to your nose?" she said, casting a sideways glance at him. "I knew you looked different when I first saw you last night, but it wasn't until I saw you again today that I realized you'd broken your nose."

Edward laughed. And when a nearby couple turned to look at them, he steered Miss Foster around the wall.

"I'll give you that, Miss Foster," Edward said. "You are observant."

She smiled at him, then released his arm and put her hand on her hip. "Well? What happened?"

"If I tell you, I must swear you to secrecy," he said.

"Was it something horribly embarrassing, then?"

"Not in the way you might think," he said, scanning the mischievousness on her face. "I wasn't reading while walking and happened to trip." She opened her mouth to protest, but he rushed on. "I know what Peter and you were always saying about me."

"Well . . . you did read quite a bit," she said.

Edward chuckled at that. "Here's the thing," he said,

leaning closer and noticing Miss Foster's rather pleasant rose scent. Then he noticed something else—bits of white in her hair just near the nape of her neck. "What's in your hair?"

"Oh." She drew away as her hand fluttered to her hair. "I suspect I didn't get all of the paint out."

Edward watched her with amusement as she fussed with her hair. "It's hardly noticeable." He stepped forward. "Wait." He reached up and picked out a fleck of paint, then tucked a stray bit of hair behind her ear.

Miss Foster froze, and Edward did, too. Then he quickly lowered his hand and stepped back, but not before he again caught her sweet scent of roses.

"I apologize," he began, but she raised her hand to halt his speech.

"It's all right," she said. "My aunt doesn't like reminders about my hobby. So the less paint specks visible on my person, the better."

Edward wanted to laugh out loud, but he'd already noticed Lady Gerrard look in their direction more than once.

"Let's keep moving," Edward said, holding out his arm again. "I'm supposed to be regaling you with the historical details of the ruins."

"I probably know more than you, Mr. Blackwood."

"You probably do," he said. "If I remember right, you spent more time at the ruins playing games than I ever did."

"And you're avoiding my question about what happened to your nose," she pressed.

Edward looked around to make sure that they were out of hearing distance from the other picnic guests. "Will you swear never to tell another soul, as long as you live, especially my mother?"

"I am intrigued." Miss Foster's eyes rounded with interest. "And I swear upon my life."

"Have you ever been abroad?" Edward asked.

"No, and that cannot be the answer to my question." She folded her arms with a slight pout.

"It's the beginning of the answer," he said. "I'm finding you quite the impatient young lady."

Miss Foster pursed her lips together and tapped her foot.

All right, then. "Other countries are not quite so steeped in social customs as our dear England is," Edward said. "And I've found that I've enjoyed activities outside the academic ones."

"Such activities where you might find yourself with a broken nose?"

"Precisely."

Miss Foster lifted a single brow, waiting.

"I've been known to fight in a few fisticuffs matches," Edward said. "And I'll have you know I'm a fair fighter and have won more than half of my matches."

As expected, Miss Foster gaped at him. "You . . . Edward Blackwood . . . a *pugilist?*"

"I wouldn't define my life pursuits as a pugilist competitor," Edward clarified. "I've enjoyed it as a pastime, though. Although when I brought it up to my mother as a lad, she promptly forbade me to participate in any sort of fisticuffs—was worried I'd break my nose."

Miss Foster looked like she wanted to laugh, but instead her expression gave way to a deep blush.

"Are you all right?" he asked her. Was she about to cry? He didn't understand what had upset her so much. He was well aware that it might come as a shock, especially to his mother.

"I . . . I am fine," she said, exhaling. "I had wondered something about your physique, and you just answered my question."

It was Edward's turn to redden. He couldn't quite believe what she'd admitted. Yet, it pleased him nonetheless. "You are right, Miss Foster. You are quite observant." He tapped his nose. "I believe you're the first person, family or otherwise, to notice the slight change."

"I am a portrait artist, you know," she said, her complexion returning to its original pale creaminess.

"I would like to see your work sometime," he said.

Her eyes focused on him, clear surprise in them. "You were in earnest last night?"

"I was." The small smile that curved her lips sent a jolt through his heart.

"I am no great master, mind you."

"May I be the judge of that?"

She gazed at him for a moment longer, and Edward found himself noticing everything about her face—from the slight smile of her rose-colored lips to her dark brown eyes with endless depths.

"You may," she said softly. "I hope you will not be disappointed. I don't purport to be a great talent, but painting is something I find I am quite enamored to."

"I understand the feeling," Edward said, moving back slightly. Standing so close to Miss Foster was making him feel quite warm. Besides, Lady Gerrard was moving in their direction. "Shall I regale you with the history of these ruins?"

Miss Foster glanced over her shoulder, seeing the approaching woman, and turned back to face him. "I'd love to." She stepped forward and slid her hand around the crook of his arm.

Six

"**W**e are about to have company," Edward Black-wood said in a half whisper.

Emily nodded and continued to walk with him between the crumbled walls of the ruins. "Why am I not surprised?" she said, then closed her mouth firmly. Had she said too much? Surely her aunt wasn't pleased with Emily dominating Mr. Blackwood's time. But she had enjoyed their private conversation immensely. He had surprised her at nearly every turn. And now she looked up at him, seeing him with different eyes now that she knew the slight crook in his nose was from a fisticuffs match.

"I've enjoyed conversing with you, Miss Foster," Mr. Blackwood continued, echoing her own sentiments. "When you are in London . . . would you consider writing to me?"

Emily was startled at the bold request. "Would you want your mother to read my letters?" she asked.

"I receive the post first every day," Edward said, his eyes gleaming.

It would be a bit of a trick to avoid her whole household wanting to read Edward's letters. They would think an engagement was on the horizon. But as she held his very blue gaze that matched the sky beyond, she found herself saying yes.

"Very good," Edward said. "I have many more questions about your painting, but it looks as if our time here is no longer ours." He glanced over at the approaching matron.

"I would love to," Emily said, hoping she didn't sound like the breathlessly stunned woman she was. Mr. Blackwood had asked her to *write* to him. He'd spoken more to her in the past twenty minutes than in all of their youth. She didn't know what to make of it. Perhaps he'd asked Adele to write to him, too, and Emily shouldn't be letting her heart gallop to conclusions.

"You two have been on your own for quite some time," her aunt said, her voice raised as if she were calling to them from another hillside.

Mr. Blackwood turned to face Lady Gerrard, steering Emily with him.

"We are finished with our exploring, and we were about to rejoin the others," he said sincerely. "How fortunate you've arrived just now. I'll have the privilege of escorting two lovely women to the picnic."

Lady Gerrard's thin lips curved into a smile, and Emily was startled to see a faint blush tinge her aunt's cheeks.

Lady Gerrard tucked her hand into Mr. Blackwood's arm, and the three of them began walking to where the servants had set up a rather extravagant picnic. Mr. Blackwood commented on the weather, and then Lady Gerrard regaled on about something Adele had said.

Emily wasn't entirely following their conversation. She was still thinking about Mr. Blackwood's request to write to him while she was in London. Several opening salutations ran through her mind. How would she address him? How would she bid him farewell?

After everyone was settled for the picnic and the conversation buzzed about her, Emily looked over at Adele. She didn't seem perturbed that Emily had spent so much time with Mr. Blackwood. In fact, Adele's rosy glow made her look perfectly content speaking with each neighbor in turn.

And then Emily noticed something unusual. Adele was holding a letter in her hand, partially hidden by her skirts, mostly out of sight. But every so often, Adele would look down at the letter and read a few lines.

Emily watched with interest throughout the picnic as Adele stole away half moments to read the letter in her hand. Why had she brought it along? Why hadn't she just read the letter in its entirety and left it at the house?

By the pink on Adele's cheeks, Emily guessed it was a flattering letter. Was it a beau, then, and if so, did Lady Gerrard know anything about it? They could all save themselves the cost of a Season if Adele were to become engaged. And Emily could stay home and watch over her mother and help run the estate until Stephen returned.

All too soon, the picnic was over, and the servants were packing up the food and drink. Emily found herself climbing into the carriage with only a brief farewell to Mr. Blackwood and his mother. He didn't renew his sentiment of writing, but he had certainly held her gaze long enough to let her know that his wishes hadn't changed.

Her heart felt as if it might float all the way to heaven if she allowed her imagination to run away with her.

In the carriage, Emily scanned for the letter on Adele's person, but it was nowhere in sight. Adele looked perfectly pleased, as if she'd had an exceptional day. Lady Gerrard was also smiling to herself. The day had been a success for all of them, albeit in different ways.

Once home, Emily made her exit as gracefully as possible and hurried up to the attic to check on the painting she was working on. She stood in the slanting afternoon light and surveyed her work. It was definitely Mr. Edward Blackwood. She'd gotten his nose just right. Fisticuffs, huh? The thought made her giggle. Then her imagination leaped to a scene of Edward standing on the edge of a fight ring, preparing to join in a fight.

Before Emily could find a reason for her behavior, she'd set up a new canvas and twisted the cap off her oils. She dipped her brush in and started to paint.

When Jenny appeared to announce it was time to dress for dinner, Emily already had the background painted and was starting on the male figure.

"Can you please give my excuses?" Emily said. "I've started something new, and I want to get it right before it flees my mind."

Jenny came to stand next to Emily and stared at the painting for a long time. Normally, Emily wouldn't allow anyone to view her work before it was completed, but Jenny was the keeper of many confidences, so Emily made an exception.

"Oh, that's . . ."

"Yes," Emily said. "Don't tell anyone. It's one I'll never show anyway."

"Not even Mr. Blackwood?" Jenny asked.

"He would be the last person to see it." Emily gave a nervous laugh. "Regardless, I want to keep working on it."

"I'll tell your mother you want a tray brought up," Jenny said, turning to leave the room. She paused by the attic door. "You look different tonight."

Emily put down the paintbrush she'd just picked up. "How so?"

Jenny lifted a shoulder. "It's hard to explain. But the light is coming back into your eyes."

Emily knew exactly what she meant, but she didn't want to confess to Jenny about Mr. Blackwood's request for correspondence.

The door clicked shut quietly, and soon Emily was lost again in her painting. Beneath her brush, the scene came to life as only Emily could imagine it. She'd never seen a fisticuffs match in person, had only read about them a few times, but she hoped to do it justice.

Emily continued to paint, and when the shadows deepened in the room, she lit all of the lamps. She hoped that her mother wouldn't venture up here, or Emily would be sure to receive a lecture. But all stayed quiet until, at one point, Jenny brought in a hot cup of tea.

"It's quite late, miss," she said.

Emily took the interruption as an opportunity to stretch and survey her work. "I'm nearly finished," she said, marveling at all she'd accomplished in one afternoon and evening. "I'll let it dry tomorrow, and then I'll be able to store it before leaving for London."

Jenny set the tea down, and Emily tried to see the painting through her abigail's eyes. There was no hiding the fact that the man in the painting was Mr. Blackwood, although Emily had obviously never seen him with his shirt off. But she did know at least that pugilists fought without their shirts, which meant it was not a gentleman's sport at all.

"Well," Jenny said. "That's certainly a deviation from your portraits."

Emily only nodded. This was another reason why the painting would never be for public viewing. It was completely and inarguably a creative piece.

Jenny left again, and Emily continued to paint. Tomorrow, final preparations would be made for leaving to London, and the following day they'd set out on their journey. Tonight was Emily's only chance to finish this painting. She wasn't sure why she felt so driven, but the lateness of the hour didn't deter her.

As Mr. Blackwood's form took shape and gained definition over the next thirty minutes, Emily found herself smiling. Here she was, cloistered in the attic in the middle of the night, painting her neighbor in a fisticuffs match. It was as if they shared a great secret between them. If her father were still alive, Emily knew he'd be amused, and perhaps a bit impressed, too.

And yet, she'd never be able to show this painting. To show it would reveal Mr. Blackwood's secret hobby and bring embarrassment and scandal to her. The painting would just have to remain her secret.

Seven

Edward reined in his horse before the ground became too uneven around the ruins. The morning mist had yet to lift from the surrounding meadow, and it gave the illusion that Edward was the sole person in the entire county. He dismounted his horse and let her graze while he trudged to one of the crumbling walls—the exact place he and Miss Foster had sat during the picnic.

She'd been gone a fortnight now, and Edward had almost given up on her ever writing him. Surely, she was beset with balls and musicales and trying to please Lady Gerrard and Miss Gerrard. Edward had been incredibly busy with learning all that went into running an estate and the surrounding properties. It was an exhausting prospect. When one problem was solved or a repair made, another one came up. Thankfully, his brother had kept immaculate accounts, and the finances were in order. It was just a matter of keeping it all in top shape and running smoothly.

Edward had been at his desk early this morning, as usual, when the post arrived. The butler had brought it in, and Miss Foster wasn't even on Edward's mind when he shuffled through the envelopes. His hand paused at the thick folded paper of snowy white, sealed with dark wax. The handwriting was decidedly feminine, but certainly not one he recognized.

"That will be all, Johnson," Edward had quickly told the butler, dismissing him so the man wouldn't see Edward's interest in the envelope. The return address bore no name, but he knew the London street was where Lady Gerrard owned a house. As understanding dawned on him that the letter must be from Miss Emily Foster, he realized how much he had been hoping she'd write.

And now, Edward had come to the ruins in order to read the letter with absolutely no distractions. It seemed fitting to be in the place he'd last seen Miss Foster and to read her words here. If he'd taken time to step back from the situation, he might have thought it was a bit strange to go through all of this trouble just to read what was probably a simple and mundane correspondence. Miss Foster had been his neighbor his whole life, and he'd had many opportunities to speak with her at various gatherings and dinners held during the holidays over the years. Yet the arrival of this letter felt vastly different.

Edward settled onto a level part of the wall and broke the seal. Exhaling, he slid the folded paper from the envelope. There were two pages, and judging by the shadowed script on them, she'd filled them both. Edward was tempted to read quickly and get to the end, then start over. But instead, he read slowly, line by line. And when he finished, he was smiling, and his heart was pounding.

Miss Foster was certainly more observant and wittier than anyone had ever given her credit for, he decided. She described a couple of the balls she'd attended with her cousin and aunt and detailed humorous descriptions of the who's who—specifically, the men her aunt was hoping would court Miss Adele Gerrard.

I believe my cousin Adele has a secret, perhaps a secret love? She goes about with one of those Madonna smiles on her face and agrees with everything her mother says. More than once, I've caught her reading a well-creased letter, only to have her hastily put it away. What do you make of that, Mr. Blackwood?

What did he make of that? Edward hadn't written Miss Gerrard, so whatever letter she so treasured wasn't from him.

Edward continued to reread.

I suppose you know the names of all the great pugilists and perhaps follow their competitions. I must admit I've never taken much interest in the sport until I discovered that my lifelong neighbor has a great secret. Now I find myself looking forward to the morning papers each day so that I might read any news. I've had to become quite secretive about my new interest and have hidden away the fisticuffs report when I'm unexpectedly called upon.

Edward chuckled at this. It seemed Lady Gerrard's home had become a house of clandestine reading and hidden letters and papers. Miss Foster's letter was begging for a reply, and Edward knew that before the day was out, his note back to her would already be posted.

After reading the letter for perhaps the third, or maybe fourth time, Edward tucked it into the safe confines of his pocket and mounted his horse, then rode back to his home.

The scents of warm scones reached him as he entered the hall, and he made his way to the morning break room. His mother turned from where she stood at the sideboard, filling her plate with food.

"You've been out?" she said, not needing her quizzing glasses to make such a deduction.

"I went for a short ride," Edward replied. "I've been working on accounts since early this morning and needed a break."

His mother studied his face for a moment. "Johnson said he already delivered the post to you. Any invitations?"

Edward didn't answer for a moment, wondering if Johnson had told his mother about the letter from London.

"I haven't opened everything," Edward said. "But nothing looked like an invitation."

"That is surprising." His mother turned away then, and he wasn't sure if he understood her right. The social events were at a minimum with the London Season and many of their neighbors in attendance.

When Edward had filled his plate and sat down at the table, his mother said, "You are looking peaked."

"Peaked?" Edward said, taking a bite of warm potato.

"Flushed," his mother amended. "Was your ride so long?"

"Only to the ruins and back," Edward said. He took a sip of juice and wished his mother would for once focus on something other than him. "What are your plans today, Mother?"

"Well . . ." she started.

Edward snapped his gaze up to meet hers. His palms were suddenly moist as if he dreaded his mother's next pronouncement as if she were about to inform him they would be hosting a dinner tonight.

"I'll be having tea with Mrs. Foster," she finished.

"Oh." That was all. Tea. Nothing he had to be involved with. But if it was at the Fosters' home, perhaps if he went along, he'd be afforded a view of Miss Foster's portrait work. "Do you mind if I accompany you?"

His mother couldn't have looked more surprised and

142

pleased. "Why, that would be wonderful, Edward. But whatever can you have interest in at a ladies' tea?"

"I thought if Mrs. Foster gave us permission, we could view her daughter's paintings," he said as nonchalantly as possible. "I remember hearing about them at our dinner the other week."

"Ah, yes," his mother said. "Frankly, I was intrigued as well." She gave him a conciliatory smile. "Come with me, and I am sure Mrs. Foster will not turn down our request."

It was all Edward could do not to smile and show his immense pleasure. He merely nodded and returned to his food as his mother spoke of some matters pertaining to the gardens. Then she switched the topic to something far less pleasing. "Miss Marybeth Sorenson has written to me," she said.

The name was familiar, in fact—

"Peter's betrothed asked specifically after *you*," his mother continued.

That's right. Marybeth Sorenson had been engaged to his brother. Edward hardly remembered her. It had been years since he'd first met her, and that was long before Peter was interested in marrying her.

Edward forced a polite expression on his face as his mother said, "I wonder if it wouldn't be too forward to invite her here, with her younger sister, of course, so that it's all proper."

"So that *what* is all proper, Mother?"

"Marybeth's visit, of course."

Edward blew out a breath, trying to curb his frustration. "If you're going to be entertaining and hosting her, I don't think there will be a question of propriety."

"Oh, you are very right," his mother said. "But there is an unmarried man in our household."

Of course there was. Edward shook his head. "I have many responsibilities, Mother. I can't be caught up in whatever entertainments you might plan."

"That's rather blunt, son."

Edward picked up the napkin next to him and wiped his mouth. He had other things to deal with. And arguing about houseguests with his mother wasn't one of them. He excused himself and returned to his study where he took out a couple of fresh sheets of paper. He wanted to write Miss Foster right away, but would it be too fast and presumptuous? Perhaps he should wait until after the ladies' tea and he could give her his good opinion of her paintings? No, he decided. He'd rather not sound like he'd been spying on her home and her artistry. Better to respond only to her recent letter.

Edward smoothed the pages of the letter from Miss Foster and reread the words, finding himself smiling all over again as he imagined her secreting herself away to read the reports of fisticuffs matches. His gaze went to Miss Foster's closing salutation. She'd written "Your Friend, E.F."

She was his friend, he realized. They hadn't interacted much during their childhood, but they were certainly familiar with each other. And now that familiarity had transitioned into friendship—one in which they could confess their secrets to each other.

Edward picked up his pen and began to write.

Dear Miss Foster,

It was with surprise that I received your letter this morning. I'd nearly given up hope that you'd write and regale me with the intricacies of the London Season. I'm pleased that you are enjoying yourself and in good spirits. I'm also pleased to see that you've increased your interest and knowledge of my favorite sport, which I won't mention here unless this letter falls into ominous hands.

Edward chuckled at his own quips and imagined that Miss Foster would surely be smiling at this point in his letter. He continued to write of the rather monotonous activities he was engaged in about the estate and how he hadn't quite given up on his "pugilism" just yet. He just hadn't found an opportunity in the country.

When Edward closed his letter, he added:

Someday in the future, I hope you will show me your paintings. I've been looking forward to seeing them ever since your aunt brought your talent to my attention. And perhaps someday, I'll take you on a tour of my personal library, which is not the family library, mind you. Each book in my personal library has been read more than once and is dear to me for one reason or another.

Your friend, E.R.

He studied "your friend" for a few moments, wondering if he should have closed differently than she. But if anything, it was honest. And it felt good to share parts of his life with someone. He was certain she'd tease him about having a personal library. Only his family was aware of the collection that he kept separate from the main library of the home. He kept all of his favorite books there, ones he wasn't willing to let guests browse through or neighbors borrow.

But Miss Foster might just prove to be the exception.

Eight

Emily smiled up at Mr. Gifford as he complimented her on her dark green dress. It was not quite the fashionable pastels most of the other women were wearing, but since she was in half-mourning, it would do. Besides, she was not a debutante.

Mr. Gifford was nearing forty, and a widower in need of a wife for his two young boys, according to Emily's aunt. Mr. Gifford also happened to be a second cousin to her aunt. Emily decided that Mr. Gifford was a decent man, if a bit hairy about the ears and eyebrows. And he had the habit of leaning quite close when she was speaking, which told her he was hard of hearing. It would be rude to comment upon a man's hearing loss; her aunt had admonished her after she overheard Emily complaining to Adele.

"Shall we?" Mr. Gifford said, offering his arm to escort her into the musicale that was to start in a few moments.

Emily had arrived at the Jensen's home with her aunt and Adele. The musicale was another in a long string of events they'd been attending since their arrival in London. Tonight, her aunt had urged Adele to pay particular attention to the Jensens' eldest son, Bartholomew. Adele had simply smiled and agreed with her mother.

Emily had yet to discover with whom Adele was in secret correspondence. And of course, Emily made certain that no one in the household knew about her letters written to and received from Edward Blackwood. Jenny delivered her letters to the post office and then retrieved anything that came from Mr. Blackwood. Emily was collecting quite a few, and now had nearly a dozen locked away in the bottom drawer of her jewelry box. In fact, a letter from Edward had arrived with the evening post, but Emily had decided to save it until she returned home that night.

Mr. Gifford led her to a chair, and they sat next to each other. Emily's aunt passed by them, offered an approving nod, and then sat one row up to the right.

Adele was sitting next to Bartholomew Jensen, enjoying herself, if her smiles at his comments were any indication. But Emily knew better. Adele was hiding something.

When another man sat on the other side of Adele, greeting both her and Mr. Jensen, Emily watched in fascination as Adele's face and neck flushed pink. What was the new man saying to Adele to cause her to blush? Emily didn't recognize him, but admitted to herself that he was young and handsome. Perhaps too young to be looking for a wife.

"Who is the man sitting on the opposite side of Mr. Jensen?" Emily asked Mr. Gifford.

He looked over to where Adele was sitting. "Oh, that's the young Mr. Downs. I thought you'd know him. He's to be the new vicar of your parish."

"Oh," Emily said. "Yes, I guess I do remember him." She hadn't seen Jonathan Downs for years, she realized. His father was to pass on his ministry to his son, who was now sitting by Adele and apparently causing her to blush.

It was with trepidation that Emily looked at her aunt, who had surely noticed the man sitting next to her daughter.

Sure enough, Lady Gerrard was staring openly at Mr. Downs, not that he or Adele noticed her.

Was this . . . could it be? Emily wondered if Jonathan Downs was the man Adele had been corresponding with. It wasn't a farfetched idea that they'd crossed paths before. Although, Emily couldn't think of when it might have been— perhaps during one of Adele's visits to her home.

The soloist began her musical number, and all conversation hushed. Emily couldn't help but steal glances in Adele's direction, both fascinated and mortified. She could very well imagine her aunt's objection to Adele's apparent love interest. Emily decided that it had to be Jonathan Downs who was writing her letters.

The next hour was a strain as Emily's thoughts jumped around, both in defense of her cousin and in disbelief at what she was seeing unfold right before her eyes. More than once, Mr. Downs whispered something in Adele's ear, and each time, she blushed.

And it was with very little imagination that Emily read her aunt's thoughts and predicted the conversation that would take place during the carriage ride home. At the end of the musicale, Emily had let herself become so distracted that she barely managed to thank Mr. Gifford. Jonathan Downs disappeared almost immediately, after kissing the top of Adele's hand and giving her a confident smile.

Lady Gerrard bustled her way over, slowed by the crush of people leaving their seats and moving to the refreshment tables, so that when she reached her daughter's side, Mr. Downs was nowhere to be found.

"Excuse me," Emily said, moving through the crowd, greeting a handful of people, but making her urgency apparent.

Lady Gerrard had a tight grip on Adele's arm, although

she was smiling so that anyone looking over wouldn't suspect there was anything amiss.

"We need to offer our regrets to the Jensens and leave now," Lady Gerrard was whispering as Emily joined them. She saw Emily and said, "Oh, thank goodness you're here. We need to leave immediately." Her voice might have been calm, but Emily heard the furious tension coming through.

"Of course," Emily said. The least she could do was keep Adele company while her mother ranted in the carriage.

Moments later, they were outside as the carriage was brought around, and soon after they were loaded inside, Lady Gerrard started in. "I thought I told you that Mr. Jonathan Downs was beneath your consideration."

"I—I couldn't very well ask him to leave, Mother," Adele said. "He sat by me before I knew what was happening."

Ah, Emily was beginning to understand. Mother and daughter had already covered the ground of Mr. Downs's ineligibility for a woman such as Adele, esteemed granddaughter of a duke.

Adele might have sounded humble in front of her mother, but Emily plainly saw the gleam of defiance in her cousin's eyes.

"Earlier tonight, Mr. Jensen approached me and said he'd like a private audience with me later this week." Her gaze bore into Adele as the lanterns outside of the carriage created a half glow inside.

At this statement, Adele went very still, and her face drained of color. Emily found herself holding her breath as well.

"He plans to offer for you, Adele," Lady Gerrard said. "And I advise you to inform Mr. Downs that all further communication will cease right away. I will not allow any gossip to spread about your disloyalty."

"I have been disloyal to no one," Adele said, the fire in her eyes growing.

Lady Gerrard leaned forward, lowering her voice although there was no one to hear them in the confined carriage. "You *flirted* with Mr. Downs. He's nearly a vicar, for heaven's sakes. Can you go any lower?" She shook her head. "What sort of life can you expect to have with him? Twice-mended gowns? Days spent putting together charity baskets? Sending your children to the village school for their education?"

Adele looked down at her clasped hands, and a tear dripped onto her cheek. "I've . . . I've done nothing wrong. There is nothing to gossip about."

Lady Gerrard sat back, her lips pressed together. "You will accept the hand of Mr. Jensen, and all of this foolishness will come to an end."

Emily's heart hurt to see Adele's shoulders sag and her sunny demeanor cloud over. She turned her head toward the window, saying nothing more, as her mother sat primly on the bench the rest of the ride home.

No one spoke as they entered the house and silently went up to their rooms.

Emily closed her bedroom door behind her to find Jenny sitting in the corner, working on mending. "You're early, miss," she said, rising to her feet.

"It will be nice to turn in early," Emily commented and said nothing further.

Jenny knew her mistress well enough not to continue questioning. She helped Emily out of her gown and was gone, leaving her alone in her room to wonder how Adele was doing.

Was there truly a *tendre* between Adele and Mr. Downs? Emily wondered. She could not believe that Adele would defy her mother, but if she was exchanging secret letters with him, then that was already in defiance.

Emily glanced over at the side table where she'd hidden Mr. Blackwood's latest letter. She wasn't exactly immune from keeping her own secrets, but Mr. Blackwood was only a friend, and besides, he wasn't beneath her station.

She moved to the door that connected to the hallway and listened for a moment. The house was silent. She ventured out of her room, opening the door carefully so as to not make a sound. Adele's room was on the other side of her mother's. Emily walked quietly past, halting at every creak. Finally, she reached Adele's door, surprised to see a faint light coming from within. At least it told Emily that her cousin was awake.

Emily turned the handle of the door and found it open.

As she swung it wide, she spotted Adele at her writing desk, her eyes wide and luminous in the lamplight as she stared at Emily.

"Oh, you startled me," Adele whispered.

Emily stepped fully into the room and closed the door behind her. "I've come to see how you are doing."

Adele wiped at her cheeks, then looked down at the letter she held in her hands, saying nothing.

"Is that from Mr. Downs?" Emily asked.

For a moment, she didn't respond, and then she gave a slow nod. "Emily," she said in a rasp. "I don't know what to do. Jonathan and I are engaged, and I don't know how to tell Mother."

A gasp escaped before Emily could stop it. She covered her mouth, staring, then said, "You're engaged? Truly?"

"Yes." A fresh round of tears started down Adele's face.

Emily took a handkerchief from the pocket of her robe and handed it to her cousin. "When did this all come about?" That was the first question in a long line of many.

"Last Christmas season when we visited you for the week," Adele said. "Vicar Downs came to your Christmas party and mentioned that his son would be arriving in the next day or two. I didn't think much of it, but then your mother had me deliver sweet breads to the parish, and I met Jonathan." She wiped at her face and took a deep breath. "When I first met him, I knew he was different than any man I'd met in the social circles of London."

"Well, he's training to be a vicar in a small county," Emily said.

Adele gave a small laugh. "I thought it was quite provincial at first, just like my good mother taught me to view those below our station. But I was curious about Jonathan, and over the next couple of days, I volunteered to deliver goods to the parish. I'm sure your mother thought it was odd, but there was so much going on with your father's poor health, no one seemed to pay me much mind."

Emily nodded. Her father was indeed very ill last Christmas season, starting his slow decline.

"We started corresponding," Adele continued, "and that's when I fell in love with him."

Emily let this information settle over her. "What are you going to do?"

"I don't know," Adele said in a soft voice. "Mother will never give her permission, and if we elope, then Jonathan will never be a respected vicar."

Everything that Adele said was right. Emily took a deep breath. "Then, dear cousin, we must convince your mother to say yes."

When Emily left Adele's room, she was already regretting the promise she'd made to her cousin. How could Emily help Adele convince her mother of a marriage to a vicar?

Emily crept down the hallway and quietly entered her

room. The fire was burning low against the chill of the night, and she withdrew the latest letter from Mr. Blackwood from its hiding place in the side table. She curled up on the settee and opened the seal. Unfolding the pieces of paper, her pulse drummed in anticipation.

She already had a smile on her face before she started reading. She'd been giving Mr. Blackwood advice about running his estate—well, not exacting advice, but she'd dropped hints about what her father had been doing, whom he'd hired for specific projects, and the like. It was good to see that Mr. Blackwood took her seriously.

You were right about taking my mother when visiting the tenants. The women shared more things with her than they ever do with me. We were able to stave off several problems just by listening to their concerns.

Now, I have a confession. A couple of weeks ago, I visited your home with my mother on the express purpose of convincing your mother to show me your paintings.

Emily gasped and read faster.

She took us into the library where three of your altered portraits hang on the wall.

Emily exhaled with relief. Were those three the only ones he saw, then? She wasn't worried about the painting of him— it was tucked away in her attic workroom—but there were painted canvases in the utility room that weren't quite ready for public viewing. Some were simply experiments in color and form.

I must say, Miss Foster, that you are a talented artist. And

I am not speaking from the viewpoint of a friend, but from the viewpoint of a man who has visited endless museums throughout Europe.

A warm shiver traveled through Emily. This was a compliment, indeed.

Your paintings are perfect for family homes where families want to remember their loved ones engaged in their favorite activities. It's my opinion that every family home needs such a rendition.

She already knew her paintings would never be museum quality. She continued to read through Mr. Blackwood's letter, smiling and nodding several times. He reported on his secret workouts to stay in shape in case he ever had the opportunity to fight again, and Emily tried to stop her imaginations from picturing him shirtless. Her painting had already captured that image for all time.

Then she paused on his closing salutation.

Fondly Yours, E.R.

This was much different than the previous "Your Friend." Mr. Edward Blackwood had just signed his name as an endearment.

Suddenly, Emily couldn't gather her stationery and pen fast enough. She knew just whom she'd confide in about Adele and how to ask him for help.

Nine

I am in urgent need of your assistance, the letter began. Edward folded it in half and tucked it into his waistcoat as he heard footsteps outside of his private library. Because of the infernal rain that had been falling for two days straight, he'd come to his library to read Miss Foster's latest correspondence instead of riding out to the ruins.

"There you are, Edward," his mother said. "I've just received a note from Mrs. Foster inviting me to travel to London with her and stay for a couple of weeks at the Gerrards. Apparently, Lady Gerrard claims to be in need of some sort of familial support." A small frown marred her face. "Mrs. Foster wasn't sure of any other particulars, but she asked if I might accompany her. It sounds quite dire."

Edward was listening to his mother speak, but all he could think of was that she'd be seeing Miss Foster. And, Edward realized, he'd like nothing better himself.

"What do you think? Will you go with us?" his mother asked.

Edward stared at his mother. "The invitation included me?"

"Of course not," his mother said. "But you don't need an invitation. We can send word and have the London residence made ready."

The only reason he would go to London was to see Miss Foster, he admitted to himself, but the matters of the estate were just coming together, and he could think of nothing less productive than attending balls and soirees.

"Besides," his mother continued, "Peter's betrothed, Marybeth Sorenson, will be there. She's such a dear girl. You'll be reminded of that as soon as you see her again."

Edward tilted his head. "Why are you so adamant that I be reunited with Miss Sorenson? What have you told her about me?"

"Nothing personal, of course," his mother said, looking down at the note in her hand. "It's just that she has great empathy for you, and she is still unattached." His mother looked up again, feigned innocence in her eyes.

"I'm not going to court the woman who was in love with Peter," Edward snapped, and then immediately regretted his sharp tone.

"Ah, I thought you'd say something to that effect," his mother said simply, appearing completely unruffled. "I'll begin packing. We leave tomorrow." She turned as if to leave.

Edward took several strides and blocked her exit at the door. "I have duties here, Mother. You should be glad I'm taking on my responsibilities. I'm sorry to say that I won't be accompanying you to London."

His mother looked up at him, her brows raised. "You'll need a wife soon, Edward. Marybeth is a dear, and you shouldn't put your nose up at her."

"I don't even know her," Edward ground out. "And she doesn't know me either, so how could she have any expectations?"

"Well," his mother said, looking away.

"Don't tell me you've given her anything to go on," Edward said.

His mother gave a slight shake of her head, but didn't reply. Instead, she moved past Edward and left the library, presumably to start packing.

He stared after her, disbelief coursing through him. Even if he didn't go to London, if his mother wanted him to become acquainted with Marybeth, she'd find a way. He turned around and walked back to the plush chair in the corner of the library and sank down on it. He'd met Marybeth at a dinner party a few years ago, before she and Peter were even interested in each other. Edward knew that Peter had fallen in love with her before he knew it himself.

His letters had been filled with all things Marybeth, and so it was an easy deduction to make, and Edward wasn't surprised in the least when Peter had written of his engagement. Edward had thought he'd next return home for a wedding, not a funeral.

As tempted as he was to go to London in order to see Miss Foster, he wouldn't let himself be drawn into his mother's plans. Edward leaned back in his chair, pulled out the hidden letter from his waistcoat pocket, and continued to read.

I am in urgent need of your assistance, the letter began. *Is there any way possible for you to come to London?*

Edward stared at the writing, then reread the words a second and third time. With a pounding pulse, he continued to read, learning that Adele Gerrard had a secret beau in the form of the vicar's son, Jonathan Downs, who was to take over from his father after Christmas. Just as Miss Foster surmised, there was no way Lady Gerrard would give her blessing or consent to such a match unless . . .

Edward's eyes narrowed as he read through Miss Foster's plan.

If you could influence Lady Gerrard with your good recommendation of a certain gentleman caller and discourage others who might seek Adele's hand in marriage, my aunt will eventually see that Mr. Downs is an excellent choice for her daughter and her daughter's happiness. I know my aunt thinks well of you, Mr. Blackwood, or else I would not ask this. And I hope that I'm not taking advantage of our friendship. If it is too much to ask, I understand, and I will continue to read the fisticuffs reports and think of you.

Affectionately, E.F.

Edward stared at the "affectionately" and then reread the entire letter again. There was no doubt that Miss Foster's plan was probably going to fail. But how could he tell her no?

Edward rose and crossed to the writing desk in the library. It didn't take him long to pen his reply, and then he went to find Johnson to tell him to post the letter immediately.

He found his mother in her bedroom with her lady's maid, directing the selection of gowns that were to be packed for London.

"Edward," his mother said, turning upon his entrance.

"I've changed my mind," he said, bracing himself for her reaction. "I'm going to London."

"Oh, wonderful." She clapped her hands. "I am certain you will enjoy yourself more than you can imagine."

For once, Edward agreed with his mother. He bid her farewell, and then arranged to meet with the estate steward. In his absence, he didn't want any of the scheduled repairs to be put off, and he needed that harvest accounting double-checked and recorded. But mostly, he had to contemplate how in the world he was going to fulfill Miss Foster's wish.

As it was, Edward slept very little that night, anticipating the journey as well as the woman he'd see at the end of it. They took two carriages since Edward knew he'd most likely be returning sooner than his mother, and she could ride back with Mrs. Foster.

Word had been sent ahead to prepare their London house, a townhouse that Edward had only stayed in briefly in the past. They arrived just before nightfall, and separated from Mrs. Foster, promising to return for the dinner that Lady Gerrard had invited them to.

Edward's valet brushed out his clothing and shaved him for the second time that day. In the glow of the lamplight in the townhouse bedroom, Edward checked his reflection. The circles beneath his eyes were barely noticeable, at least he hoped, since he didn't want any comments from someone asking after his health.

And then it was time to journey to the Gerrards with his mother. Edward met her in the foyer.

"You look nice, Edward," his mother said, lifting her quizzing glasses as if he'd never made that sort of effort before.

"And you look lovely," Edward said. "Are you ready?"

"Yes," she said, looking entirely too pleased with herself.

With dread, Edward wondered if somehow his mother had worked Marybeth into the attending guests tonight. He wouldn't be surprised if his mother had.

The carriage ride was short, and Edward realized that the Gerrards' London house was within walking distance on a fine day. As he helped his mother out of the carriage, he glanced up at the house and the warm glow coming from the large windows. The thought of Miss Foster behind those window-panes somewhere made his heart rate quicken.

They walked up the handful of steps and were greeted by a butler, then led inside.

Edward saw her first, but it wasn't long before Miss

Foster raised her gaze to meet his. She wore a dress of deep violet, which set off the dark curls that had been arranged about her face as a cascade.

Lady Gerrard came forward to greet him and his mother, but Edward hardly heard a word she said. Miss Foster's hint of a smile seemed to wend its way around his heart. He watched as she greeted her mother first, then his mother, and finally she was standing before him. There was so much that he wanted to say, but it would all refer to their private correspondence. So he merely grasped her gloved hand and bowed over it.

"I'm glad you had a safe journey," Miss Foster said. "I assume it was uneventful."

Edward let his own smile escape and was rewarded by one of Miss Foster's in return. "Yes, quite uneventful."

"Adele and I have been looking forward to your arrival."

Edward glanced over to where Adele was speaking to another young woman, whose back was to him. But then the other woman turned. It was Marybeth Sorenson. The blood left his face as Miss Gerrard and Miss Sorenson walked over to where he stood with Miss Foster. He wished he could draw his mother into a separate room and give her a stern talking to, but instead he stood there, keeping a pleasant look on his face while he greeted both women.

Marybeth Sorenson was much as he remembered, a petite blonde woman who didn't have any trouble keeping up her end of the conversation, similar to Miss Gerrard. The two seemed fast friends, and Edward wondered how well they all knew each other. Edward supposed that Miss Sorenson was a pretty woman, and the fact that they both had Peter's loss in common was endearing, but he was also bothered by his mother's obvious scheming. He cast his mother a glance, and she was positively beaming.

This trip to London was certainly favorable to her.

Edward tried not to scowl, because he was then introduced to a Mr. Todd, a second cousin of Lady Gerrard's who looked to be in his fifties, and his two sons, both young men under twenty. It appeared that Lady Gerrard had managed to assure even numbers at the dinner. When dinner was announced, Edward led Lady Gerrard into the dining room, and then was required to sit next to her. On his other side, he was surprised to have Miss Foster seated next to him. Perhaps they'd have time for conversation after all. As the soup course was brought in, Lady Gerrard dominated the table conversation with accounts of the social events they'd attended.

"Which gentleman am I to discuss this evening?" Edward said in near whisper to Miss Foster.

She took another bite of her soup before replying. "Mr. Bartholomew Jensen," she whispered back, and then turned to look at her mother with a smile as she commented on something.

A moment later, Edward asked, "What is his grievance?"

"My abigail has discovered that his father has an affinity for gambling and is in great debt."

Edward gave a brief nod. It was enough. Many gentlemen gambled quite harmlessly, but there were those who became entrenched in the underground world and lost fortunes upon the gaming tables.

Several more moments passed, and when Lady Gerrard brought up a recent musicale event they'd attended, Edward saw his opportunity.

"How is Bartholomew Jensen doing?" he asked. "I haven't seen the fellow in ages and hoped to look him up on this trip."

"Oh, you know him?" Lady Gerrard asked, her hand

fluttering to her chest. "How wonderful. He's paid particular attention to Adele. In fact," she said, leaning closer as if she didn't want any of the others to hear, although she made no effort to lower her voice, "I'm expecting an official visit from him soon."

"Well," Edward began, "That sounds quite serious indeed. I'm assuming if he's in a position to court a young lady that his financial woes have reversed."

Lady Gerrard straightened. "Financial woes?"

"Surely you've heard?" he said, glancing about the table, making sure he had everyone's attention. "His father is quite the gambler. A couple of years ago, he brought his family to the brink of ruin. But if Bartholomew is back in the social circles, apparently they've made a miraculous recovery."

Every person at the table was silent. Edward could only pray that his ruse would be accepted. If the elder Mr. Jensen was a gambler, then the details wouldn't matter. Edward just needed to get across the fact that Bartholomew might be a fortune hunter.

"Hmm." Lady Gerrard pursed her lips and picked up her wine glass, then set it back down without taking a sip. She cast a glance over at her daughter, who was staring at Edward with wide eyes, and possibly a grateful expression.

Edward could practically feel Miss Foster smiling, although her face was expressionless.

"Who performed at this musicale?" Edward asked. "Was it someone famous?"

Lady Gerrard picked up her wine glass and this time she took a long swallow, then she turned her eyes upon Edward. "No one too famous, although she was a talented singer."

Edward continued to listen politely as his hostess spoke of the singer's talents and which songs she sang. The main course of roasted chicken and steamed and buttered vegetables was brought in.

When the topic turned from the Jensen's musicale to an upcoming ball at the Garrett family's newly refurbished house, Edward cast a glance at Miss Foster.

"Do you think that will make a difference?" he whispered.

"Thank you," she said in a breathless voice. "You don't know what this means to me, and to my cousin." She moved the hand in her lap and patted his forearm, all concealed from the others by the table in front of them. She quickly placed her hand back in her lap as if she hadn't moved at all.

Edward was momentarily speechless. "My pleasure," he said at last.

And then he realized with horror that his mother was inviting the women over to their townhouse the next afternoon for tea. Edward had hoped to take Miss Foster out riding so that they might have some privacy at last.

It seemed that would have to wait.

Ten

Adele came to Emily's room long after she'd thought everyone had retired for the night. She almost didn't hear the soft knock at the door since her subconscious was hovering on the edge of dreaming.

Emily rose from her bed, pulled on her robe and opened her door a crack. When she saw Adele's tearful face illuminated by the oil lamp she carried, Emily pulled her into her bedroom.

"Come in," she said. "Whatever is the matter?"

Adele set the oil lamp on a side table, then wiped the tears from her cheeks.

"I don't know what's wrong," Adele said, moving to stand near the fireplace that only contained glowing embers now.

Emily set a small log on top of the embers and stoked the fire to life.

"I mean," Adele started again in a trembling voice. "What Edward Blackwood did tonight was marvelous. I still cannot quite comprehend it."

Emily couldn't agree more. Not only had Mr. Blackwood cast doubt into Lady Gerrard's mind about the eligibility and intentions of Mr. Jensen, but he'd also regaled Mr. Jonathan

Downs at a later time in the evening. Mr. Blackwood had asked in a discreet voice if anyone had caught sighting of his friend and good man Mr. Downs.

"Everyone in the county is looking forward to his ascension to the ministry," Mr. Blackwood had said. "He and whoever his future wife will be will be esteemed members of the community their whole lives. Doing the Lord's work is the highest honor a man can aspire to in this earthly life."

Emily had never heard Mr. Blackwood speak a thing about religion. By the absolute silence in the room, she had surmised it was the same with everyone else. But by some small miracle, his mother rallied first and said, "You are quite correct, Edward. Did I ever tell you your father was interested in the ministry as a lad?"

When Mr. Blackwood shook his head, Mrs. Blackwood continued, "If he hadn't been the oldest son and set to inherit, I think he might have taken it on." And then she said something that had nearly brought tears to Emily's eyes. "Being a vicar's wife would have been an honor had my life taken that direction."

And now, Emily could understand Adele's emotional state.Emily crossed to her cousin and grasped her hand. "It's my sincere hope that your mother's heart will be softened, and she'll turn her mind toward Mr. Downs."

Adele sniffled and nodded. "I have worn my carpet out with pacing tonight, and I knew I couldn't sleep until I was able to talk this through with someone."

"Come," Emily told her, and drew her to the settee where they sat together.

"It's my regret that I haven't been a kinder cousin to you, dear Emily," Adele began. "But sometimes my mother hasn't been the best influence on me. What you have done for me, and what you have asked Mr. Blackwood to do, is something that has touched me deeply and profoundly." Another tear leaked down her face.

"Oh, Adele," Emily said. "You've been a wonderful cousin. You can't help who your mother is."

Adele giggled, and Emily laughed with her.

"Let us just hope that your mother won't concoct any more plans, at least until after Edward has left," Emily said. "Or else we'll have to beg him to stay the entire Season." The thought wasn't hard to digest, although she knew it would be impossible. Edward had an estate to manage now.

"Marybeth asked me all sorts of questions about Mr. Blackwood," Adele said. "If I didn't know better, I would have thought she's interested in getting to know him better."

Emily felt her face heat up, making her grateful that the only light in the room was the firelight. "But she was betrothed to his brother."

"Yes," Adele said, leaning closer. "Isn't that quite perfect, though? She lost her intended, and it was a great tragedy, but perhaps she could have a perfect ending after all. Her dreams of becoming the mistress of the Blackwood estate could still happen if she married the younger brother."

Emily's stomach twisted into a hard knot. "Dreams? Was she aspiring to be mistress, or was she in love with Mr. Peter Blackwood?"

"Both." Adele settled back and gazed at the fire, a faraway look in her eyes. "She's lost one of her desires, but by marrying Edward Blackwood, she'd have at least one thing. Besides, Marybeth could bring some life to the place. Mr. Blackwood is so serious and studious and only cares about his books, and Marybeth is cheerful and perhaps a bit frivolous like me." She gave a faint laugh. "But that would be perfect for the Blackwoods—bring them out of their gloom."

Emily opened her mouth to reply, then closed it again.

The man who Adele had described was not exactly the man Emily had come to know. She knew about his worries over running the estate, his trepidation of taking over what was supposed to be his brother's duties, his sorrow over his brother's death, and his secret passion for fisticuffs. The letters exchanged with him had shown Emily that Mr. Edward Blackwood was anything but a gloomy man. He was highly intelligent, very caring, witty, and when he looked at her with those intense blue eyes, she quite lost her breath.

"I thought your mother had designs on him for yourself at one time," Emily ventured, if only to see what her cousin's reaction would be.

"Ah, yes," Adele said. "That is my only worry about Mr. Blackwood being here and taking down the reputation of every man my mother wants to present me to. What if her ideals turn toward Mr. Blackwood himself?" She grasped Emily's hand. "Which brings me to a new plan we must implement. We need to encourage Marybeth's affections toward Mr. Blackwood. Once my mother sees that in action, she'll not concern herself with matching me to him."

Emily couldn't speak for a moment. This was not what she intended when she'd questioned Adele about Mr. Blackwood. But now Adele was speaking faster than Emily could keep up with about how they'd direct Marybeth into Mr. Blackwood's affections.

"I'm so blessed to have you for a friend and a cousin," Adele gushed at the end of her diatribe. She leaned forward and embraced Emily, and it was all that Emily could do to usher her cousin out of the room before her own tears fell.

She shut the door behind Adele and leaned against it. Staring at the dimming fire, she replayed the conversation in her mind. It wasn't hard to admit to herself that she felt possessive of Mr. Blackwood. She'd grown to know him as she had never thought possible, and if Marybeth had been marrying Peter Blackwood for his estate, then marrying his brother would only be another loveless marriage. And Emily wanted more for her friend. She wanted him to have a wife who would appreciate all of his qualities, a wife he could share his secrets with, a wife who would be grateful for the sacrifices he was making in the wake of his brother's passing.

A woman like herself, Emily thought. But writing a few letters to Mr. Blackwood hardly presented herself as wife material. Besides, she was sorely needed at her own home in the coming years as her brother would take over the estate affairs and would need a lot of guidance. And even when he married and had a family of his own, her mother would need a companion. If only her father hadn't died and left a too-young heir and a grieving widow, then Emily might have been able to consider her own future as a wife of so-and-so. But as it was, she wouldn't allow her heart to take a risk such as pining for what she'd never have.

No, she was much too practical for that.

It was with these thoughts that Emily climbed into bed and finally drifted off.

When she awoke to the morning sun brightening her room, she was at first surprised that she'd slept so well and deeply. Then she remembered the conversation with Adele from the night before, and dread coursed through her, chilling her body so that she burrowed deeper into her covers.

This morning, they were to attend tea at the Blackwoods' townhouse, and Marybeth had been included in the invitation. Mr. Blackwood would certainly greet them if not spend part of the tea social with the ladies. Emily finally rose from her bed and rang for Jenny. After she'd dressed, and Jenny had arranged her hair, Emily excused Jenny and pulled out her sketchbook.

She hadn't been able to bring her paints to London, so the sketchbook had served as a place to express her overflowing thoughts. She flipped through her pages, stopping on more than one of Mr. Blackwood. She'd sketched him walking through the ruins, mist clinging to his long coat. She'd sketched him in his library, reading a book. She'd sketched him standing by the fireplace in the drawing room, looking out one of the long windows.

And now, Emily picked up her sharpened pencil and started to draw. She drew Marybeth first, sitting prettily on a settee in the downstairs drawing room. Then she sketched Mr. Blackwood standing behind the settee, as if he were about to come around and sit next to Marybeth. But Emily's pencil seemed to have direction of its own, and Mr. Blackwood's head was turned toward the hearth, watching a different woman. And before Emily could put a definition to her logic, she'd drawn a woman in her own image sitting near the hearth, holding a book in her hand.

It was clear from the sketch that Mr. Blackwood was looking at *her*, but it was only her artist's imagination that had put him in such a position. In real life, they were friends. And Emily valued that above all else.

A tap on her door brought Emily out of her thoughts. She hastily snapped the sketchbook closed, and said, "Come in."

Jenny entered and crossed the room to hand over a sealed note. "This came in the morning's post."

"Thank you," Emily said, taking the note.

Jenny curtsied, then moved out of the room.

Once Emily was alone, she cracked the seal. She already recognized Mr. Blackwood's handwriting and couldn't imagine why he was sending her a note this morning. When she read, the heat crept up in her neck.

Dear Miss Foster,

It was a pleasure to see you again last night. I only wish we could have been afforded more privacy than a large dinner group provided. Would you like to accompany me on a ride through Hyde Park tomorrow morning? We can continue in our plans.

Yours, E.F.

If Emily hadn't known that Mr. Blackwood was merely fulfilling his agreement to help, and Marybeth was angling for Mr. Blackwood, Emily might have let her thoughts get carried away. But that wouldn't do. Yet, her gaze went to the closing salutation: *Yours.* It was so simple, yet felt so intimate.

Another knock sounded at the door, and Emily hurried to tuck away the letter just before Adele poked her head in. "You're ready? Oh good. Mother is already in a state this morning."

Emily grimaced. "Whatever is the matter?"

"She's received an invitation to tea at the Jensens, and she wants to decline."

"That's good news, right?" Emily asked. "She's taken Mr. Jensen off of the list of potential husbands."

"Yes," Adele said, flashing a smile, but it didn't spread to the rest of her face. "But Mother is worried that declining the invitation would set of a round of questions. And so she's now saying that we've wasted too much of the Season on one man."

Emily released a breath. Something had to be done, but she wasn't exactly sure what. If only she and Mr. Blackwood were riding through Hyde Park today, they could discuss this. "When does Mr. Downs leave London?"

"In a few days, I believe," Adele said.

"Then we must do something to turn your mother's head in favor of Mr. Downs," Emily said. "But, what, I don't know."

Before they could come up with a solution, Jenny was at the door, announcing that Lady Gerrard was ready to leave.

Soon, they were all in the carriage heading to the Blackwoods. Emily hadn't realized she was both dreading and anticipating the tea. When Marybeth arrived at the same time, Emily's stomach plummeted. Marybeth looked radiant in a pale peach gown, while Emily was still in her half-mourning dark blue.

They stepped out of the carriage and as the butler swung the door open, Emily saw Mr. Blackwood coming out of what must be a study or library on the left side of the hallway. He greeted Marybeth first, but instead of seeing a glowing appreciation in his eyes for Marybeth, he barely looked at her. Instead, his blue gaze locked with Emily's. It was then she knew she'd gotten the sketch of him from that morning all wrong. She hadn't drawn his expression nearly intense enough or his features handsome enough.

Emily's face warmed, and she hoped that she wasn't blushing. She suddenly realized she hadn't replied to his note. The group moved into the drawing room where a cheerful fire was burning, and Mr. Blackwood made his apologies, saying he had a prior engagement with Mr. Jonathan Downs. And he said all of this while casting glances at Emily. Her face flamed again, and she hoped no one else in the room noticed the silent attention he was paying her.

"Perhaps we can invite him over one evening, Mother," Mr. Blackwood said. "He'd love to meet familiar neighbors amid all the London Season whirl."

"I am in agreement," his mother replied.

For a moment, Emily wondered if Mr. Blackwood had informed his mother of their plan. She was playing into it so well.

"What do you think?" his mother said, turning to the rest

of them in the drawing room. "Shall we put together an evening that includes our future vicar?"

It was everything that Emily could do to not meet Adele's gaze.

"That would be wonderful," Marybeth spoke first, and for once Emily was grateful for the woman's presence.

Mr. Blackwood gave her a half bow. "I'll inform Mr. Downs then today, and I'm sure he'd be delighted to accept any manner of invitation. But I'll leave the specific details to the ladies."

His mother murmured something, and then bid him farewell.

Mr. Blackwood was out of the room and leaving the townhouse before Emily could quite comprehend what had just happened. If it had been up to her, she couldn't have planned this better herself.

Eleven

"No, hand me the navy vest," Edward told his valet. He wasn't usually so particular in his appearance, but he'd awakened early this morning with thoughts of what the day might bring. First, this morning he'd be taking Miss Foster for a ride in Hyde Park. Since it wouldn't be the fashionable hour quite yet, he hoped that they'd have plenty of time for undisturbed conversation.

She'd written to him last night accepting his invitation. And then, Edward had promptly stayed awake most of the night, thinking about Miss Foster and her dark curls and the way they'd shared a secret smile and how he wouldn't mind kissing her.

When he pulled up to the Gerrard's home, the weather had played havoc already. The sun had settled behind a bank of clouds, and a stiff wind had started. As he strode up the stairs, he found that his heart was pounding. Partially because he was looking forward to this time with Miss Foster, and partially because he was becoming more and more convinced that despite what his mother said, he wasn't willing to enter into any marriage of convenience.

He wanted to marry someone he could love as well as be friends with. Someone who would be a good companion and a good mother and someone with whom he could share his interests.

The butler opened the door after Edward knocked on the door, and moments later, Miss Foster appeared. She wore a dark lavender pelisse over her dress, trimmed in off-white. Not that Edward made a habit of noticing details of a woman's clothing, but he noticed quite a few details about Miss Foster.

"Are you ready?" he asked. Thankfully, no one else came to the hall to greet him. No Lady Gerrard to deal with.

"I am," Miss Foster said, giving him a smile that brought warmth to the depth of her brown eyes.

He extended his arm, and she wrapped her hand around it, and then he walked her down the steps toward the carriage.

As Edward settled next to her, he said, "The weather is a bit brisk, so we might have the park to ourselves. Unless you want to bow out and do this another time."

She turned her face up to meet his gaze. "I rather like the idea of being the only ones in Hyde Park."

He smiled, then flicked the reins of his two horses. "Then here we go."

They spoke little on the journey to the park, and Edward regretted not bringing a heavy blanket to place over Miss Foster. She didn't act particularly cold, but the wind wasn't all that enjoyable. Thankfully, once they started to circle the park, the wind was cut down by the surrounding trees.

A handful of other carriages were moving about; most of them had hoods up. It seemed their occupants had paid much more attention to the blustery weather.

"I wanted to thank you for coming to Adele's rescue," Miss Foster said. "What you have done for her cannot be repaid."

"Before you thank me entirely, let's see it through first," he said. "By the way, your aunt and mother will be receiving an invitation this morning to a soiree that my mother is hosting that will include one Mr. Jonathan Downs."

"Oh," Miss Foster said, grasping his arm. "Truly? You've arranged it already?"

Edward chuckled. "Apparently my mother appreciated my suggestion." He looked down at Miss Foster's hand still on his arm and was quite pleased to see it there.

"Does your mother know of our concoctions?" she asked.

"I might have dropped a hint or two," he said, glancing at her.

Her eyes widened. "You told her? What did she think?"

Edward paused a moment. "She thought I shouldn't meddle, and then she questioned why I had involved myself so much."

Miss Foster removed her hand and folded them in her lap. "And what did you say?"

Edward slowed the horses and brought the carriage to a stop near a grove of trees that offered more protection from the wind. He looped the reins on the foot post, then shrugged out of his overcoat.

He turned toward Miss Foster and draped his coat over her shoulders. The article of clothing practically drowned her, but made her look much warmer. Edward was plenty warm himself. He'd probably stay warm even if it started to snow.

"My mother is a smart woman," Edward said. "If I hadn't told her, she would have figured something was going on anyway. I have turned down invitations to London all of my life . . . until now."

Miss Foster was staring at him, her expression quite unreadable.

But that didn't slow Edward down. He intended to find out exactly what this woman was made of and if he was in the right to put his heart on the line. "After the soiree tonight, there's a fight near Bond Street."

Her eyebrows shot up. "Really? Can I go with you?'

Edward stared at her. "Go with me?"

"Don't women ever go to the matches?"

"Uh, not proper ladies," Edward said. This was unexpected. "A fisticuffs match isn't a place you'd enjoy."

Miss Foster bit her lip and looked away. If it wasn't for the sound of an approaching carriage, Edward might have bent toward her and kissed those lips.

"What if I was able to escape the house unnoticed and meet you somewhere on the street?" she said at last.

Edward stilled. She meant to sneak out and attend the fisticuffs match? He scrubbed a hand over his face. It would be an adventure to take her along, but he feared for her reputation if she were caught. "Are you willing to take that risk?" he asked, hardly believing she'd go through with it.

"My Abigail can help me," she said. "Jenny is as loyal as they come. I'll disguise myself, and no one will know."

Edward wasn't sure if he should laugh or try to dissuade her.

"What do you think?" she asked, peering up at him.

Apparently she was completely serious. The other carriage had long since passed, and the only thing that accompanied them was the wind blowing her curls against her neck. Edward couldn't help himself, not if his good sense told him that Miss Foster might not be romantically interested in him. He leaned closer and she didn't move; in fact, she turned more fully toward him and closed her eyes. This brought a smile to Edward, since it appeared that she was waiting for him.

He pressed his mouth against hers, gently. Her lips were cool from the wind, but when she placed her hand on his chest and curled her fingers around his lapel, everything seemed to warm between them. Edward deepened the kiss, testing, and she responded by moving closer and softening against him. He wrapped his arms around her and pulled her even closer, kissing her until they were both breathless.

When they finally broke apart, Edward's heart was pounding, and he felt as if he were weightless. "Miss Foster . . ." he started, not entirely sure what he was about to say.

"You might need to call me Emily now," she said, the edges of her kissed lips turning up.

Edward laughed. "My mother would be the first to notice the change."

"All right, then how about only in private then?"

"Only if you call me Edward."

Her smile bloomed.

Edward touched her cheek, running his fingers along her smooth skin. "You have been in my thoughts night and day, dear Emily," he said. "How will I ever sleep now?"

Her brows lifted as she stared at him, and he wanted to kiss her again, but was afraid he'd already taken too much liberty.

"Perhaps you can ask a physician for a sleeping draught," she said, her face flushing.

"Perhaps," he murmured and kissed her again, this time briefly because the unmistakable sound of a carriage could be heard. He drew away reluctantly, but also gratefully. His thoughts had scattered in multiple directions. But most of all, he was wondering what Emily Foster would say if he proposed to her right here, right now. The realization should have shocked him, but it didn't. In fact, it had probably been a long time in coming. It had just taken a moment of privacy to solidify his thoughts.

"Good morning," a male voice called out.

Edward turned to see a gentleman who looked vaguely familiar. The man was riding in a carriage with an elderly woman, who Edward surmised was the man's mother.

"Hello, Mr. Gifford," Emily said.

Ah, Gifford. Edward had crossed paths with him at Oxford years ago.

"And Mr. Blackwood," Gifford said. "What a surprise. I didn't expect to see you here with Miss Foster." He nodded to the woman next to him. "This is my mother."

Both Edward and Emily murmured their greetings.

Gifford slapped his hand against his thigh. "Oh, that's right. You two live in the same county. Practically neighbors."

Edward decided not to correct him. He stole a glance at Emily. Her cheeks were still flushed and her lips swollen from their shared kisses. He wondered exactly how observant Gifford was. Apparently, not very.

"Are you free tomorrow, Miss Foster?" Gifford asked her. "If the weather is fair, I'd love to take you for a ride."

Edward almost smirked. Why would another man invite a woman on an outing when she was clearly on an outing with another gentleman?

Emily gave him a pleasant smile. "My mother just arrived in London, so I will need to speak with her first in case she has already made plans."

"Excellent," Gifford said, completely nonplussed. "I'll send around a note."

After they made their farewells, Edward was relieved to see Gifford go. Edward was very interested in questioning Emily about her acquaintance with the man. "Have you formed a bond with Mr. Gifford?" he asked when the carriage was well away.

"Heavens no," Emily said. She slid her hand around his arm, nestling against him. "Why ever would I do that?"

Edward swallowed. "Well, then. That is pleasing to hear. We best get back before your mother or aunt send out a search party."

Emily just nodded, keeping her gaze forward, but he didn't miss the smile curving her lips.

He flicked the reins, and the horses started to move again, heading through the park and back to the residential streets.

Edward had to admit to himself that this had been a successful venture into the park. He hadn't intended to kiss Emily, but now that he had, it was easier to approach his mother on a serious topic since his decision had solidified. A decision that didn't involve Marybeth or any other woman of his mother's choosing. Marriage was really the only solution now for him and Emily, because he fully intended in securing many more kisses in the future.

As he pulled the carriage in front of the Gerrard's house, Emily said, "Tonight at the corner, then?"

She'd remembered.

"I'll be waiting," he said, fully expecting for her to cancel beforehand.

Twelve

"**I** love you," Adele gushed to Emily. "Tonight was a dream, and if Mother doesn't give her blessing to a union between me and Mr. Downs, then there's nothing else to be done."

Emily hugged her cousin, her heart swelling. She was truly happy for Adele. Mr. Blackwood's—Edward's—brilliance had played beautifully tonight at the soiree his mother had hosted at their townhouse. The party was only an intimate number of guests, including Mr. Jonathan Downs.

From the moment of the vicar's arrival to well after his departure, both Edward and his mother had paid him compliments and presented him in the greatest light. *There is nothing more important in this life than caring for another's needs,* had been repeated more than once by Mrs. Blackwood. *The entire parish will welcome the new vicar,* was another phrase repeated.

And Mr. Downs had been the perfect gentleman, elegant in both dress and manners. He'd paid the sincerest compliments to Lady Gerrard that she couldn't help but be pleased with. Emily had caught Edward's gaze upon her more than once, and it was all that she could do to refrain from blushing every few minutes throughout the evening.

The thought of his stolen kisses in the park had made her feel over-warm. And by the noticeable absence of Marybeth, it was clear that Edward had said something to his mother. This realization had only sent her heart racing. First, there was Mrs. Blackwood's favorable behavior to Mr. Downs, and then there was her extra kindness toward Emily. Another person might not have noticed it, but she had.

"Well, good night," Adele said with a broad smile. "I, for one, will be dreaming of a future I thought I might never have." Her words came out tremulous.

"You deserve every happiness," Emily said, grasping her cousin's hand and kissing her cheek.

When Adele had finally left her room, Emily rang her bell for Jenny. Once her abigail had arrived, Emily told Jenny of her plan to attend the fisticuffs match. Jenny listened in astonishment, her eyes wide as Emily unfurled her plan to meet Edward at the corner of their street.

"And, you're calling him Edward now?" Jenny said, folding her arms and narrowing her eyes. For an abigail, she was certainly cheeky.

"Well, he asked me to," Emily said, not mentioning the fact that she'd asked him to call her Emily first, and that was after a rather thorough kiss.

Jenny was quiet for a moment. "Miss Foster, I've gone along with your desires to date. I've even delivered and picked up letters for you. This new venture is quite the extreme, and I know it's not my place to say so, but I can't keep quiet on this."

"I've already made the decision," Emily said, crossing to the wardrobe and scanning the contents. "None of these cloaks will do. I need to borrow clothing from you so that I'm not seen as upper class."

Jenny didn't move for a moment, then she lowered her

head and left the room. When she returned, she had several items of clothing draped over her arm. Emily changed quickly, and then they only had to wait until the house had settled for the night and all was clear.

The next hour felt like ten hours, but finally, Jenny declared that all was quiet and everyone in the household was sleeping. Jenny led the way as they crept through the hall, down the back set of stairs and out the servant's door that led to the small herb garden on the side of the house. From there, they made their way around the house and out the front gate.

Once on the street, the night air was colder than Emily expected, and she was grateful for the heavy cloak she wore and one of Jenny's warm wool dresses.

They hurried along the sidewalk and turned the corner. There, not a dozen paces away, awaited Edward's carriage.

Emily had never been so relieved in her life. If they'd had to wait on the street, there was no telling who might come by and see them.

Jenny opened the carriage door, and Edward reached a hand out, helping Emily inside, and then Jenny.

"There you are," Edward said, a brow raised as if he couldn't quite believe she'd followed through.

Emily climbed inside and settled onto the bench opposite Edward. The velvety blackness surrounded them inside, and Edward explained, "I thought it would be better not to light the lanterns and attract any undue attention."

"Thank you," Emily said, feeling breathless with the excursion and all the intrigue surrounding it.

"Are you sure about this?" Edward said in a quiet voice as Jenny joined them inside the carriage.

"I am," Emily confirmed.

They rode in silence, but there was nothing silent in her

heart about sitting across from Edward, riding through the streets of London in the middle of the night.

Finally, the carriage slowed, and Edward opened the door and climbed out first, handing both women down.

Emily looked around them, gaining her bearings. She didn't recognize this part of London, but she knew they were close to the river, since she could smell the wet foulness upon the air. And from the building in front of them came a great deal of noise, like a mob of people shouting.

Edward turned to her. "Are you ready?"

She swallowed against the sudden thickness of her throat and nodded.

"Come on then, and stay with me at all costs," Edward said. He linked one arm with Emily and the other arm with Jenny. Then he led them toward the door that had just shut after another patron had entered.

After a sharp rap on the door, it was opened and Edward handed over a few bills of money. And then suddenly they were inside, surrounded by noise and chaos.

Edward steered them around the perimeter of the crowd. The cheers from the primarily male audience rose and fell, obviously timed with the events inside the ring, although Emily couldn't see a thing over everyone's heads. Edward led them up a narrow staircase where they came out onto a row of balconies. He picked the least crowded one and they muscled their way next to those standing at the rail and watching.

"Hold your ground," Edward said into her ear above the noise. "And don't let go of my arm."

Emily could only nod. There was no way her voice would outmatch the noise around them. Her gaze swept over the hundreds of men circling the ring, then her gaze landed on the two men who were fighting. A deep blush flamed her face at the way they were dressed, or *undressed.* Their shirts were off, and perspiration dripped down their faces, making their muscled chests and shoulders gleam.

One of the pugilists, a blond man, took a violent swing at the other man in the ring. Emily watched as every muscle in his torso and arms and neck bunched. And then the second man crumpled to the ground. The crowd went wild, and even Edward was cheering—yelling something that Emily couldn't decipher.

The crowd started chanting a countdown as the man on the ground struggled to open his eyes, and finally climb to his feet. His nose was bleeding, and Emily almost had to look away as lightheadedness took over. Thankfully, holding onto Edward and the crowding spectators behind her, helped her stay on her feet.

The fight continued with the blond man swinging again, but this time the second man ducked and threw a punch into the blond's stomach. Emily felt her own breath leave her as the crowd moaned. It was clear that the blond man was everyone's favorite. When he gained the upper hand again, Emily found she was cheering along with Edward and everyone else in the room.

Each punch and blow made her wince and her stomach knot, but exhilaration coursed through her as the fight progressed. The sport was so raw, but Emily could see the skill that was being used by the blond man against his opponent.

The crowds on the balcony thickened as more and more people came up to get a better view, and Emily pressed herself against Edward. He held her close, and on his other side, Jenny remained as well, transfixed by all the action. Emily spotted a few other women in the crowds below, but they were women she'd never normally cross paths with if she were to judge by their low cut bodices and bawdy ways. It made Emily all the more grateful for Edward's presence and protection. And then the blond man delivered a final blow that was deafening even if there was no way possible that Emily could have heard the fist-to-skin contact.

The crowd cheered and undulated below. Emily yelled, too, caught up in the moment and those around her as people slapped each other's backs in congratulations and shillings and pound notes exchanged hands.

"What are they doing?" Emily called out to Edward.

He looked down at her with a grin. She noticed he was perspiring, too, and realized that the heat of the room and so many people would outmatch a gentleman's outer cloak. "They're paying off their bets."

Emily's mouth rounded, and the crowd started chanting something she couldn't quite grasp.

Edward looked back toward the ring, then shouted over the noise, "Come on, we need to get out of here."

She wanted to ask why, but Edward was already ushering her and Jenny down the narrow stairs, through the crowd on the main floor, and then out the door where the sharp, cold air felt like a slap.

As the door shut between them and the crowd, the quiet outside rang in her ears.

"What's going on?" Emily asked Edward as he started down the street, keeping his arms linked with each of theirs.

"The German pugilist is calling our man a cheat," Edward said.

"How can a man cheat at fisticuffs?" she asked.

"New rules are always being made." He slowed as they came to the carriage and the waiting driver. Edward opened the door and helped both women inside.

The inside of the carriage was warm compared to the outside, but Edward still draped carriage blankets over their laps.

"Thank you," Jenny murmured. The expression on her face echoed the awakening Emily had just felt as well.

This area in London was unlike any she'd ever visited, and that crowd . . . so much shouting and cheering and emotion.

"What did you think?" Edward asked her, his gaze on her face.

"It was wonderful," she said. And it was true.

Edward's brows shot up, and then he laughed. "You are truly a remarkable woman, dear Emily."

Emily felt her face heat in a way that even the warm competition room hadn't brought on. "It was fascinating, really," she said. "Not that I enjoyed watching the men hurt each other, but they were so intense and so determined. I felt like I was watching two men fight for what was dearer to them. Even though fisticuffs is just a game."

"It is a game," Edward conceded. "But you might be onto something. Some of these pugilists make their living out of this sport. To lose is to lose money, and perhaps their livelihood, if their injuries are severe enough."

Emily leaned forward, catching the expression on Edward's face in increments as they passed by glowing street lamps. "What does it feel like? To be hit like that and to keep fighting even after the pain."

Edward's eyes bore into hers, and it was too dark for Emily to properly read into his gaze.

"It's a shock, I'd say," Edward said. "Then once you realize you've been struck, the pain roars through your body, almost crippling it. But then, miraculously, it fades into a strange numbness, and you just keep moving. The pain becomes a motivator, and you want to fight harder, faster, and avenge yourself."

Emily nodded, captured by what he was saying, and even

more captured by the way he was looking at her and speaking to her. It was like he was sharing an intimate part of his soul. And Emily knew she'd cherish this entire night for the rest of her life.

As they turned a corner that was more familiar to Emily, she noticed Jenny had fallen asleep, leaning her head back, her eyes closed.

Edward seemed to notice the same thing for he moved forward on his bench so that his knees brushed against hers. Warmth shot through Emily at the touch, spinning her thoughts into a dozen directions.

"Emily," he said in a soft voice, taking both of her hands in his. "I'd like to visit with your mother tomorrow and request your hand in marriage."

She stared at him, and knew that even though they sat in fractured darkness, his eyes were a deep blue. For a moment, she couldn't breathe. "Truly?"

"Truly, dear Emily," he said. "Think of it. You could help me run my estate, *our* estate. I wouldn't have to wait days to get an answer to one of my questions. You would be nearby to help your brother as well. And . . . you'd be able to paint day and night without interruption. Well, with minimal interruption."

"It sounds like I'd be of great use to you," she said.

"More than that," Edward said, leaning closer until she could feel the warmth of his breath. "I don't want you to marry anyone else. *I* need you." He brushed his lips against hers ever so gently. "I love you, Emily."

She blinked and drew away. "You love me?"

He nodded and kissed her again. This time the kiss lingered and was just as gentle, but Edward made no move to draw away, even though the carriage started to slow, which meant that Jenny would be waking up.

When he did draw away, it was only a short distance, which felt like no distance at all. "Do you love me?" he whispered.

She didn't have to think in order to answer. She did love him, but hadn't dared to hope that she'd be united with a man both in love and friendship, and now she wouldn't move far for marriage.

"Yes, Edward Blackwood, I do love you," Emily said. "And my mother would be more than happy to receive you tomorrow and consider your request."

Edward's laughter was light, and Jenny stirred, mumbling sleepily.

He released Emily's hands and sat back in his seat. "Now that it's settled," he said in a quiet voice, "let's see what we can do to advance the cause of Jonathan Downs and your cousin."

"Did I tell you that I love you?" Emily asked.

Edward grinned. "You did."

Epilogue

A double wedding might have been a groom's night-mare, but for Edward, he couldn't be happier. In fact, if Peter were still alive, Edward knew his brother would be impressed.

This morning, Edward would meet Emily at the altar, right after Jonathan Downs and Adele Gerrard were married by Jonathan's father. Then Jonathan, in his first act as a new vicar, would pronounce Edward and Emily man and wife. And Edward couldn't be more pleased, or more impatient.

His mother had taken on the wedding plans with the force of a gale wind, and from the moment he had announced his engagement, his mother had determined to invite anyone within traveling distance to come to the wedding feast. A handful of relatives had arrived a full two weeks in advance of the wedding, filling the spare rooms, and areas of the house that hadn't been breathed upon in years had been cleaned and prepped.

And not one thing bothered Edward. No, his mother could throw a ball fit for the royal family if she cared to. In fact, she could throw an entire week full of balls. Edward's thoughts were only filled with Emily. Since their engagement, she'd allowed a few more kisses, which Edward had enjoyed with increasing intensity, but it was more than the attraction he had for his future wife that kept his thoughts consumed. He was retrofitting a set of rooms in the east wing of the house into an artist's studio. It had been completed two days ago, and Edward couldn't wait to show it to Emily.

She'd promised to meet him at the ruins early this morning, and he'd escort her back to the house before any of the guests awakened from their late nights. Edward couldn't wait to see her expression. Emily had been curious about what his wedding gift might be, but then she told him she had a wedding gift of her own, and that she'd be bringing it to the ruins. Which meant it was small enough to carry.

As Edward finished dressing on his own, since it was much too early to be bothered with the help of his valet, he thought of the one thing that would have made this day more perfect. Peter. And he knew that Emily wished her father could have lived to see her married.

Edward gave up on knotting his cravat and left it in a simple loop. He would spend all of his time and energy making sure Emily was happy. They'd both been through enough sorrow, and hand in hand, they'd greet the future.

As ready as he was going to be this early, Edward strode out of his bedchamber and down the stairs through the main house, then out the door. The groom was already waiting out front with his horse, and within moments Edward had mounted and was riding through the mist toward the ruins.

When he reached the first signs of the outcroppings of crumbling stone, Emily was nowhere in sight. Edward dismounted and let his horse graze. He hoped Emily would still come. If he didn't show her the artist studio early, he might not get a chance to until after their honeymoon. Their day and evening was packed with events, and they'd be traveling by carriage tonight to the next village where they'd spend two nights at a small house Edward had rented out. He wanted his bride all to himself before they set out on their honeymoon.

The sound of approaching horse hooves cut through his thoughts, and he turned to see a form coming through the mists. Within moments, Emily's shape was defined, and as her face came into view, Edward found that his heart was pounding. A familiar feeling now. He scanned her luminous features, her brown eyes, and the dark curls that framed her face. She wore a deep green riding habit.

Edward approached her horse as it slowed and handed her down. Her hand fit perfectly into his, and he drew her close, leaning down and saying, "Good morning," before brushing his lips against hers.

"Good morning," she answered with a smile, and Edward felt as if he were falling into the depths of her eyes.

He leaned in for another kiss, pulling her closer, but she placed a hand on his chest, and said, "I've brought you something. I want to show it to you before I change my mind."

He drew away, and before he could say anything, she turned back toward her horse and unbuckled a satchel she had attached to the saddle.

Edward was surprised to see her face pink as she handed over the satchel for him to see inside. He grasped the satchel and put his hand inside and touched something square and thick, yet too lightweight to be a book. Taking it out, he realized it was an unframed canvas. When he turned it over, he could only stare for a moment at the man standing in a fisticuffs ring. Edward knew immediately that the shirtless fighter was him, and that the opponent, mostly in shadow, was Mr. Gifford.

He examined the detail and lines and shapes, marveling how the scene seemed to be moving although it was only paint on a canvas.

"You painted this for me?" he asked Emily at last, still overcome with amazement.

"Not exactly," she said, moving to stand next to him so they could both gaze at the work of art. "I didn't intend to draw you at all, but I actually started this before leaving to London. And when we returned, I had to finish it. I'd seen an actual fisticuffs match in person and so I had to make a few changes from my original creation. But you . . . you were mostly the same."

Edward met her gaze, and in the brown depths of her eyes, he saw her insecurity and her desire to know what he thought. It wasn't hard, and he didn't need to gloss over any truth. "This is remarkable, Emily. And not because I'm your subject, but because you captured the emotion perfectly." Surrounding the image of Edward were spectators in all stages of watching the impending match. Edward recognized several of the characteristics of the people they'd seen that night. Emily had brought them all together in a riot of color and action.

And then there was his image. Strong, muscled, determined, yet there was a hooded look in his eyes that spoke of the knowledge that what he was doing had many risks.

"I'm going to hang it up," he said.

"Oh no," Emily protested. "I couldn't possibly let my mother or your mother know that I've painted your bare torso."

"Well," Edward said, smiling and sliding an arm around her shoulders. "That would be quite the scandal, wouldn't it?"

"My aunt will probably faint if she sees it." She smiled back at him, her face flushing pink again.

Edward moved his head close to Emily's and breathed her in. "Would that be such a terrible thing? I mean, we're about to be married. And I have the perfect place to hang it."

When she shook her head, he continued, "Don't say no until I've shown you the wedding present I've prepared for you."

Emily turned up her face, her brows raised with curiosity. "Is this the present that no one else can know about yet?"

"Correct," he said. She was so close to him that he had to take the opportunity to kiss her again. He loved the way her body softened against his, chasing away all the space wherever they connected.

"We should go, then," Emily said, sounding breathless. "The sun is rising."

The mist was quickly dissipating as well, and after Edward helped his almost-wife onto her horse, he mounted his own. They rode through the summer meadows and down the sloping lawn leading to the house. They took the horses to the stable, and then Edward led Emily around to the back of the house where they entered through the garden parlor.

The house was silent save for the murmur of voices coming from the kitchens where the cook and maids were beginning to prepare yet another feast. Edward kept Emily's hand in his as he led her up the back stairs the servants used, then up another flight of steps until they were on the third floor of the house. Guests were staying in one wing, but Edward led Emily to the east side.

He'd had double doors installed when he had the carpenters combine two rooms into one.

"Ready?" he asked as they came to a stop in front of the doors. "Close your eyes and walk with me."

She dutifully closed her eyes, and Edward opened both doors then led her inside. Once he had her in the middle of the studio, he stopped and let go of her hand.

"You can open your eyes now," he said.

When she opened her eyes, Edward watched Emily's expression shift from amused patience to astonishment. He looked around at the room, seeing it anew through her eyes. The tall windows had been scrubbed inside and out and the draperies removed so that the morning light spilled in pink and orange. The floors had been cleared of the rugs, and the wood had been sanded and refinished. Canvases of all sizes were stacked up along one wall, and a large wood table sat against another wall. Upon the table basic paint colors were arranged, and next to the paints sat new brushes in all sizes.

Several easels stood proudly in front of the windows, and in addition to an artist's stool, sat several other chairs in different sizes that would accommodate whatever Emily needed to sit on. Most importantly were the portraits hanging along the back wall—portraits Edward had helped Jenny take from the attic where they had been practically hidden. Now, displayed on a wall in the light of the morning, they virtually shimmered with color and movement and life.

"Edward," Emily whispered in a reverent voice, turning in a full circle to take in the entire view of the room. "How did you do this . . . Is it all for me?" She looked up at him, her eyes moist with tears.

"Of course it's for you, dear Emily," Edward said, unable to stop the grin on his face. "I don't ever want you to hide your art again."

She took the satchel that he'd slung over his shoulder, then removed the painting of the fisticuffs ring. Carefully, she set it on the center easel where the light of the rising sun enveloped it into an ethereal glow. Emily stood in front of it for a moment, just gazing at the canvas and the views through the tall windows that looked over the estate.

"It's finally home," she said, then turned to Edward.

He was only a step away, watching her.

Emily brushed at a tear that had fallen on her cheek, then she took the two steps that separated them and threw her arms around his neck. "I can't believe you did this." Her voice hitched. "If you hadn't already proposed to me, I would have to propose to you."

Edward chuckled and tightened his hold on her. As he held her close, he breathed in her scent, and never wanted to let her go. If they hadn't their own wedding to attend, he might never release her.

"Let's go make our vows." He took her hand, and they walked out of the room together, back down the stairs through the silent house. When they stepped outside, the warm wind rushed about their feet. They hurried to the stables where Edward helped her mount her horse.

"I'll see you at the church?" she asked, reaching down for his hand at the same time he reached up to take hers.

"Nothing could make me miss it," Edward promised. He reluctantly released her hand and stepped away from the horse.

He leaned against the stable doorframe and watched as Emily rode toward her home, toward the rising sun that guaranteed the most brilliant of days. When she'd disappeared from sight, he finally turned back to his house, the one he'd soon be sharing with his new wife. A smile spread across his face as he strode across the lawn. It was a smile that would be there for a very long time.

About the Author

Heather B. Moore writes historical thrillers under the pen name H.B. Moore; her latest thrillers include *Slave Queen* and *The Killing Curse*. Under the name Heather B. Moore, she writes romance and women's fiction, her newest releases are the *USA Today* bestseller *Heart of the Ocean* and the historical romance *Love is Come*. She's also one of the coauthors of the *USA Today* bestselling series: A Timeless Romance Anthology.

For book updates, sign up for Heather's email list: hbmoore.com/contact
Website: HBMoore.com
Facebook: Fans of H. B. Moore
Blog: MyWritersLair.blogspot.com
Instagram: @authorhbmoore
Twitter: @HeatherBMoore

A Sporting Season

By Rebecca Connolly

One

A Season in London. What could be more exciting or perfect than that? It had absolutely everything one could want. Balls and parties with the most eligible men looking for equally eligible candidates for matrimony; fine fashions and the latest styles in absolutely everything; evenings at the theater where one's personal performance might be more important than the one on the stage; the overall feeling that at this time, in this place, one's life might just begin to change.

Provided, of course, that one cared about such things.

Daphne Hutchins did not.

She did not think any of this sounded remotely perfect or exciting, and she had absolutely no interest in anything the London Season could offer. She would much rather stay in her quiet home in Berkshire, where her only excitement lay in traipsing up to Reading for the limited entertainment a day there could bring.

London held absolutely no interest for her.

None whatsoever.

Especially not a Season there. Nothing could have prevailed upon her in any possible way for her to consider subjecting herself to the embarrassment and inanity of joining in the march of the misses.

Nothing, that is, except for a determined mother with unequaled skills in the arts and sciences of guilt.

One would have hoped that eighteen years of experience with these skills and their effects would have made Daphne equally as skilled in the defense against them, but one would be quite wrong.

As Daphne's awareness and combative skills increased, so too did her mother's cunning and tenacity. There was no adequate resistance to her attacks, and none of the Hutchins siblings could pretend otherwise.

The elder two chose complete avoidance as a manner of coping, which seemed to work well enough. But Ned was a man, despite their mother's denial of his adulthood, and with that came the freedom to do as he pleased. And Phoebe . . . Well, Phoebe was a different story altogether, and Daphne did not care to consider anything about her.

The point of the matter was that, despite the rather extensive arguments and apparently uncharacteristic behavior on Daphne's part against the matter, her things were packed, the carriage loaded, and she, her domineering mother, and absentminded father were on their way to London. All for the express purpose of marrying Daphne off after a triumphant first Season, delayed though it was, and regaining the pleasant reputation the family had enjoyed prior to the Incident.

Daphne wasn't aware they'd had any sort of reputation in London for good or ill, but her mother assured her it was so.

Apparently, Phoebe had ruined that, as well as everything else.

The Incident had all but destroyed her family, though the full scope of the matter never became public knowledge. Only the barest facts had escaped, though rumors were plentiful enough. Two years and still her mother had never mentioned Phoebe by name within Daphne's hearing. No doubt her parents spoke of her in private, as Phoebe had always been her mother's favorite, but she had never come back to Fairview Park, and that was a significant matter to note.

Everybody still seemed to recall that, while the family had indeed suffered from the indignity, it was Daphne who had suffered the most. It was Daphne who had been broken beyond repair. It was Daphne who deserved the pity and the apology and the indulgence.

They had all been very good about it—surprisingly so.

Had being the important word.

She had wondered how long the effects of the Incident would linger amongst her family. It had been a full year before her mother had proposed the idea of going out on social visits. Then she had gently encouraged Daphne to update some of her dresses, as well as reading a bit less, in favor of other accomplishments. Then had come the not-so-gentle suggestions of potential suitors, reminders of her prospects, and demands that Daphne had flatly refused.

She was never intentionally difficult . . . Well, all right, by the end she was blatantly difficult, which was a remarkable amount of fun, despite her mother's distress. Or perhaps because of it.

Whichever it was, Daphne had obviously worn out whatever sympathies she had engendered from the Incident and could no longer expect her mother's patience to endure, provided she had any patience at all. She was no longer "poor Daphne" or "sweet Daphne" or "unfortunate Daphne." Now she was "ungrateful," "willful," and "unfeeling."

Which, obviously, made her a perfect candidate for marriage and meant it was time to marry her off.

Daphne was no simpleton; she knew full well she was not

an heiress and could not expect to be fully independent at any point in her life. Should the worst happen and her parents died untimely deaths, Ned would only be able to support her for so long. Until he married, and married well, there was no real hope for either of them. The only way for Daphne to have her true freedom was through marriage, as backward as that was.

But eighteen hardly seemed the time to panic about such things. Daphne was perfectly capable of making a match in ten years to an elderly gentleman in need of comfort and companionship in his waning life. Comfortable and companionable and easy. Nothing to do with love or hearts or any such silliness. Perhaps she would have children, perhaps not, but it was the picture of a perfect life and marriage in her eyes.

If her mother ever actually listened to a single word Daphne said, she would know precisely what her daughter wanted instead of quite literally forcing her into the exact opposite course.

Then again, Daphne had grown quite spiteful in the weeks following the unpleasant announcement of the London Season, so perhaps her mother was not interested in listening to her in any case. And perhaps she had good reason.

Daphne mostly likely would not have listened to herself had the situations been reversed.

But she might have done.

Well, one thing was for certain. There was absolutely no possible way that Daphne was going through all of this without a proper fight. And there was no chance of her making a match this Season, she would see to that.

While all the other girls worried over making a single mistake that could destroy their hopes, Daphne was going to flaunt those mistakes. All of them. Every single thing she could accomplish without compromising herself or completely ruining herself, she would do. Short of ruining her brother's own matrimonial prospects by association, she would push every boundary possible. She would not become a household name, but she did intend to make a rather unfortunate name for herself. Men would flee her presence.

And if she could embarrass her mother on a regular basis throughout the whole of it, so much the better.

One gloriously failed Season should do the trick.

Despite her aversion to the reason for their departure to London, Daphne found herself smiling at the thought of her task.

Which was her first mistake.

"I knew it!" her mother insisted, pointing a bony finger at her. "I knew your resistance was all for show! Francis!" She elbowed her dozing husband, whose slim frame did nothing to muffle the jab, and he jerked away, spectacles askew. "Did I not say as much?"

"Yes, m'dear," he mumbled, rubbing absently at his ribs. He cleared his throat and adjusted his spectacles. "What did you say?"

Daphne's mother rolled her eyes dramatically, scoffing. "Never mind," she told him dismissively, then began muttering incoherently.

Her husband looked at her in confusion, then turned to face Daphne, expression inquiring.

Daphne raised a brow, smirking. "Apparently I smiled, and Mama thinks it means I am somehow secretly thrilled with our venture."

He raised both brows, gave his wife a look, then returned to Daphne once more. "Well, that seems rather unlikely, doesn't it?"

"Francis!" his wife scolded.

Daphne hid a smile, lest her mother think she was still pleased.

"Daphne has never been duplicitous, Mary," Mr. Hutchins reminded her, patting her limp hand weakly. "She truly does not desire to go."

It was odd, Daphne thought, but her father's words, though firm in statement, sounded pitiful in his placating tone of voice. He was a bland sort of man, his hair only a few shades lighter than his skin, and his eyes bore the sort of blankness that spoke of ignorance. She loved him dearly, but he had grown more obtuse with the years, and the endearing qualities he had once possessed were now something of an annoyance.

Still, he was attempting to aid her, and she was grateful for it, though it would fail in moments.

"No one simply 'does not desire' a Season in London," her mother insisted, shaking her head quickly.

Daphne raised her hand. "I do."

The glare she received was worth the brief insolence. "No one," her mother repeated in a tone that could have rewritten the commandments if she'd wished it.

It was no use, really. Daphne was stubborn, she always had been, but she had inherited that particular trait from her mother, and they were very well matched in this battle. She would never succeed in direct confrontation against the woman. It would take strategy and scheming to get anywhere, and as they were going into London a full two weeks before the Season began, there would be plenty of time for it.

But for now, she would have to continue at defiant reluctance, moody silence, and anything else she could think of to ruffle her mother's feathers.

She groaned and turned to look out of the window. "I'm not going to enjoy this," she grumped.

"You'll enjoy it or I will make you enjoy it," her mother barked sharply.

"I'd love to see you try," Daphne muttered, a laugh escaping.

"No. You wouldn't."

She smiled. "I have no intention of enjoying a single aspect of anything remotely connected to this idiotic festival. I would rather drink cold tea without sugar and walk barefoot over broken glass for the rest of my life than hunt for a match in this fashion."

Her mother screeched in distress while her father moaned. "Daphne, please. Think of your mother."

Daphne gave her father a withering look. "Are you suggesting this Season is for her benefit and not mine? I find that hard to believe, as it is my future that will be affected, not hers."

"I never had a Season!" Mrs. Hutchins lamented, wringing her hands. "Imagine what could have been if I had!"

It was probably not the best time to give her father a pointed look, but it seemed the natural thing to do. "Yes, you've suffered so much," Daphne replied in a dry tone.

Her father seemed to develop a twitch and looked down.

"And I've never put a daughter through a Season, either!" her mother rambled on. "Phoebe would have made such a splash, so beautiful and engaging and bright . . ."

There was complete silence in the carriage as she realized she had gone too far. Daphne stared at her coldly while her husband shook his head from side to side.

"Are you telling me," Daphne ground out slowly, "that I am suffering through this because you never got the chance with Phoebe? That you wish she were in this carriage instead of me?"

Her mother's widened eyes revealed her panic, and she reached for her daughter's hand. "Darling Daphne, I would never . . ."

Daphne wrenched her hands out of reach and turned away. "Leave me be. And remind yourself what I endured at the hands of your favorite daughter."

No one was foolish enough to speak after that, and Daphne felt ridiculous for still becoming so distressed about the whole situation. She ought to have been far enough removed from the Incident to remove the worst of the feelings, but the bitterness had taken root, and she had grown accustomed to it.

She closed her eyes as the carriage rocked to and fro, suddenly awash in memories.

Sixteen was too young for marriage. She had always known that, even before anyone had said anything. Her mother hadn't thought so, which had been all the encouragement she'd needed. And there had been no formal engagement, but it had been forthcoming.

He had promised.

They had promised.

Everyone knew about it. People outside their town and even outside the county had known. Daphne Hutchins was a most fortunate girl, and the envy of quite a few.

Their understanding had been the worst kept secret in Reading and all its inhabitants.

Sixteen or not, everybody agreed it would be perfection.

It was not until after the Incident that the gossip came to light. She was too young, he had a reputation, and it would never have worked. A poor match indeed and a most inappropriate familiarity.

And her sister . . .

Poor Daphne Hutchins.

What a silly, sorry creature.

There was no one to blame but herself.

Astonishing how they all turned when circumstances

changed. Friends, neighbors, complete strangers looking for any tempting bit of tittle-tattle all sang a different tune after that. The pity was overbearing, the avoidance telling, and the truth, such as it was, hidden beneath the elaboration the rumors had concocted.

Most people had forgotten about the whole thing by now. Daphne could not.

She didn't love him any longer, that had died along with her hopes and dreams. The hurt had lasted much longer, and the shame beyond that.

Somewhere along the way, she had vowed to never be so stupid or silly again. Never so weak or vulnerable or exposed. Never so trusting.

Never again would her life be so tied up in that of another that she lost herself.

Daphne Hutchins then was not Daphne Hutchins now.

And Daphne Hutchins now was not going to leave her happiness in the hands of others, not even for a London Season.

She had her own plans to see to, her own happiness and satisfaction to attain. She had her own mark to make, and make it she would.

She dipped her chin briefly in a nod to herself.

The games were about to begin.

Two

James Woodbridge could have done without the fuss of the Season altogether. It really was not worth all the effort that went into it—not that he'd ever put in any effort for it. Quite honestly, he did not care all that much. The quiet of a country life was all he'd ever imagined, though London certainly had amusements enough. He'd enjoyed a few turns at the festivities, but without any serious intentions, and only because it was the thing that a gentleman in England was expected to do.

He might not be very many things when one considered him, but he was a gentleman, at least. And he was also exceptionally bored, which seemed to be a common trend among gentlemen.

But Jamie had to be far more bored than most. His estate was now fully restored and sustainable, so he no longer had that to engage his time. He had no marriage prospects, which continually worried his mother, and his ambivalent attitude toward that particular facet brought him much grief from all his female relations.

But as those same females had been giving him grief every day of his life for various things, he was quite used to their plaguing.

217

Which was another reason for coming down to London, despite his aversion to the Season itself.

Unfortunately, this Season was doomed to be more trying than others had been. Now that Jamie had something to offer the material world, the relative anonymity he'd always enjoyed was disappearing. Too many people knew his name, despite no formal introductions. He had met so many fathers and brothers of apparently eligible women, it worried him. The look in the eyes of passing females was too keen, too excitable, and too calculating for his liking.

Oh, he wanted a wife, sure enough, but there was no need for haste, and he certainly did not have the prospects of his cousin Jonathan to elicit such responses.

But Jonathan was Jonathan, and it was well known by now that he was not going to marry without affection, and procuring that affection was rather impossible when the man did nothing to encourage it. The issue with Jonathan, as the entire family saw it, was his very particular tastes. He could judge a woman with one look and determine if they would suit, and, aside from doing his duty to wallflowers, he only danced with those he considered potentials. After one dance, he could determine if the female in question were appropriate for his needs. Not a single female in the world measured up to his standards, whatever they were.

Jonathan was like a brother to Jamie, but he had no idea what his cousin was looking for.

Jamie could say the same for himself, having been bored beyond belief with the field of young ladies he had seen.

He sighed and resisted the urge to tug at his cravat as he ambled toward Bond Street. Were the eligible females of London really so desperate for a marriage that they would consider a man with three thousand a year and a barely sustainable estate in Norfolk to be so appealing a prospect? It was a pretty estate, now that it was habitable once more after the neglect of fifteen years, but hardly tempting.

Jamie was fond of it, but only because it had been his father's, and now it was his. It wanted a new name for all the changes it had undergone, but as yet it was still Brimley—or Grimley, as he and his family called it. That rather seemed the nature of Jamie's life. Renovated, in need of a new name, waiting for a life of sorts to begin.

"Good morning, Mr. Woodbridge," greeted an attractive woman of some years in the company of two girls, obviously daughters.

Jamie inclined his head and tipped his hat, knowing he should know them, but not recalling their names. "Ma'am."

She inclined her head with a smile, and the girls blushed, averting their eyes quickly, smiling themselves.

He nearly rolled his eyes after he passed them. He was not one of the Mr. Woodbridges to be pursued, not when there were four others with far better prospects. But he would take the compliment, such as it was, and proceed as he was doing. Once the Season began in earnest, he would be long forgotten in the wake of other more engaging suitors.

He could not wait for such bliss.

His mother would string him up if she knew.

And so would his aunt.

The Mothers, as they were known to all the Woodbridge children. When Jamie's father, the younger of the original Woodbridge brothers, passed away early in Jamie's childhood, his uncle had insisted that his brother's widow and son should make their home with his family, as the property designated to his brother's care had not become prosperous enough to support them.

So they had done so, and Jamie had grown up as a sibling to his cousins, with the intriguing consequence of having two mothers, both of whom could instill fear and obedience into any of the children, whether hers or not.

His uncle had passed only last year, but the Mothers showed no inclination to change their living situation, and he could not imagine it any other way.

A sudden jostling of people broke his reverie. Bond Street was unusually crowded today, but the first events of the Season would start within a week, so he ought not to be surprised by the odd frenzy circulating around him. It was rather fascinating to watch as he continued on, examining faces and behaviors as he did so.

The determined mothers marching along, sometimes dragging their easily distracted daughters behind them, followed by servants heavily laden with boxes and parcels. Or young misses giggling with their friends, eying the gentlemen as they passed. Carriages rolling to a stop and emptying out with the finer females, sometimes quite overdressed, who bore the same energy as the rest. Even the men seemed more eager than their usual temperament, puffing their chests out and straightening cravats, or riding their stallions more proudly.

It was the oddest sort of promenade he had ever seen, and the bustling nature of it all was nearly as entertaining.

A movement across the street caught his eye, and he saw a young woman moving down the street, which was not at all unusual, as there were dozens of others just like her, dressed just as finely. She even had the older woman at her side and the servant trailing dutifully behind her, just as the others did.

What exactly had made him look, he couldn't have said, but now that he was, he was not particularly inclined to look away.

All of the other females he had seen had been excitable and flirty, alight with hope and fervor, but this one was different. He could only see part of her expression due to her bonnet and her slightly lowered head, but there was no lighthearted fancy here. She walked with determination, not noticing anything around her, a slight furrow on her even brow. If he did not know any better, he would think she was plotting something.

Come to think of it, he did *not* know better. He had no idea who she was, so he supposed it was entirely possible she was plotting something. She looked behind her at the maid and said something that caused her to laugh, and the older woman waved her up to join them, all three turning down another street.

Jamie stared after them, smiling in amusement. He had two female cousins. He knew full well women were capable of great strategy, and many of them used such in the grandeur of the Season, though Emma and Grace had yet to embark upon one for themselves. But something told him this particular stratagem had nothing to do with the usual games girls played for the Season.

And she was a pretty little thing; he could see that well enough from his vantage point. Unremarkable in dress and coloring, blending in easily with everything and everyone else, and no doubt unobserved by many. But wide-set, fair eyes and natural complexion appealed to his tastes, and he found himself wondering if her hair were fair or dark, curly or otherwise. Did she smile easily? Or was that something one had to work for?

He was intrigued enough to pursue. When he wanted to know something, he sought it out. He usually pursued what he wanted, no matter the obstacles, and it had landed him in a spot of trouble a time or twelve in his life. But in this case, he would resist the temptation. Imagine following a young woman purely for curiosity! That was something his cousin Ross might have taken on, and certainly Ethan would have.

Jamie was far more gentlemanly than either of them, even if Jonathan could outstrip him there.

No, his curiosity only extended as far as wondering, and an amused sound that escaped him as he turned from the spot and entered the boot maker's shop for a new pair of Hessians.

Perhaps an hour later, the order for the aforementioned boots in his possession, he continued down Bond Street toward a dressmaker's shop his cousins had insisted he visit on their behalf, something about an order they had placed by mail that he absolutely *must* see to. With the girls being restricted to half-mourning, he couldn't imagine what they would need, but he had agreed to assist them, against his better judgment.

There really were some severe trials that came with being too close with one's relatives, but he'd never been able to refuse Emma or Grace anything, and they knew it well.

Also, Jonathan had refused, point-blank, to do his sisters' bidding, leaving the task to Jamie.

It made no difference, as he had nothing else to fill his day with but errands about Town, all in preparation for the interminable length of the Season and its demands. As he approached the shop, he wondered about the curious looks he might receive from those who saw him enter. Perhaps it would cause some rumors to swirl about him, which he was sure could only do him good. Perhaps then he would not be confused with the other Woodbridge men and might have a chance of entertaining some females he might truly wish to know.

With that thought to lighten his step, he approached the shop with far less reticence and held the door for some suddenly giggling females, dipping his head in acknowledgment of each of them.

He glanced into the shop and saw the older woman behind the counter, looking rather pale and drawn for one who'd just had her shop patronized by several seemingly well-paying women. She had another customer before her, and it took him only a moment to realize that it was the same girl from before, her faded, green-striped muslin looking too old and flimsy to be worn out in public, and a yellow spencer that was too new for the outfit entirely, particularly with the frayed orange ribbons from her bonnet.

Her maid stood nearby, looking completely nonplussed about the entire situation.

Her chaperone, though similar to her in coloring, looked absolutely bored.

Jamie could not make out what the young lady was saying, but the shopkeeper swallowed with difficulty and nodded.

"Aye, I shall add it to the bill," the woman said in a stiff voice. She bit her lip for a moment, eyeing the parcel he could now see between them. She hesitantly pushed it toward the young woman.

There came a bob of the bonnet that he could only presume was an expression of thanks.

Still the dressmaker looked uneasy. "Please, Miss Hutchins," she suddenly said in a rush. "I beg of you."

The bonnet tilted slightly.

"Should anyone inquire as to where you purchased this dress," the woman went on, additional lines appearing on her face, "please do not reveal the truth."

Jamie nearly laughed in disbelief, but stifled it quickly. Why in the world would the woman sell a dress that she would not wish to own? It seemed rather counterproductive, but he had never presumed to understand women or their fashions, or the purchasing of said fashions.

The maid of the young woman seemed to be fighting a smile, which told Jamie that the young woman herself was smiling.

"I can assure you, Mrs. Farrows," the girl said in a low, throaty voice that positively rang with amusement. "Your wonderful reputation will remain intact. I will not betray your kindness to me."

Relief lit Mrs. Farrows's features, and she managed a smile. "Thank you, Miss Hutchins. You are too kind."

Miss Hutchins took the parcel in hand, then handed it to the maid, who had two other parcels in her grasp. "Not at all, Mrs. Farrows. Good day."

She turned away from the counter toward Jamie and the door, and he finally had a proper view of her.

It was difficult to say what struck him first: the natural grace of her features or the enticing glimpse of a secretive smile that played at her perfectly formed lips. She was fair-haired, but not brilliantly so. More of an aged gold that had been kissed by the sun, and he was surprised at the faint spattering of freckles across her cheeks and the bridge of her nose, which he found rather charming.

Refreshing. That was the word that escaped him. She was absolutely refreshing in looks and intriguing by nature.

He stepped back to let her, the older woman, and the maid pass, sweeping his hat off, dutifully not speaking, as good manners dictated. He might be witty and a little unconventional, but he was really quite a well-behaved man—outside of his family.

Miss Hutchins surprised him by looking directly up at him, her smile spreading and creasing the corners of her eyes. "I can't imagine what a gentleman such as yourself would have to do in here, but I applaud your unorthodox choice in shops.

There's some lovely tartan in the back, if you're feeling a bit Scottish."

Jamie did not even have time to get over his shock, or pretend to be taken aback, before she swept past him with a little laugh to herself. That laugh drew one out from himself, which she did not hear as she moved out of earshot. He shook his head, smiling his disbelief, and turned to the counter, where Mrs. Farrows looked ready to begin shaking all over.

He approached with great care. "Mrs. Farrows, I take it?"

She jerked a little, as if she had not truly been aware of him. "Yes. Yes, sir, how may I assist you?"

"I believe there is an order from my cousins, the Miss Woodbridges?"

She nodded briskly, color returning to her features, almost all trace of her discomfort gone. "Yes, of course. I only just completed it this morning. I shall fetch it, if you will wait here, please." She bustled away, her steps quick.

Jamie turned to glance back out of the windows, wondering who Miss Hutchins truly was and just what she was about.

Impossibly, and improbably, he continued to see Miss Hutchins as he went about his business, even when he had finished with his solicitor. She appeared to finally be leaving the area, though strangely enough without a coach to see her home in. He had no notion of where she lived, but to walk all this way with her companions was certainly cause for concern.

He pulled out his father's pocket watch and frowned. It had been nearly three hours since he had first seen her march with determination along the shops. Three hours? What could she possibly have had to do in Bond Street for three hours? Her maid was not heavily laden with parcels, and she did not look the sort to have an extensive fortune that would allow her to simply bill many things.

She still wore the expression he had seen on her initially, an almost speculative smirk and an air of indifference to her surroundings.

It was odd, but he found himself more drawn to her than to any person of his acquaintance, which was astonishing, as he was not even of her acquaintance. She had made a breach of etiquette in her address of him, which any young woman in the beginning of her Season would take great care to never do. Not that Jamie was offended by her actions or her words, he rather enjoyed it, but it did speak of a rare originality that could either be a spark of genius indicating a success in the making or the beginning of a downfall that could be the talk of the Season.

Ironically, Jamie found an eager interest in either outcome.

Before he knew what he was about, he was following her, crossing over to her side of the street and lengthening his stride to keep up with her brisk pace.

Even now as he closed the distance, he could not have honestly said why he was doing this. Would he be a gentleman and offer to escort them home, despite their not being introduced? Would he defy all convention and have a true conversation with the girl in spite of that? Would he embarrass her by his approach? Or find that she was not at all what he expected?

"Excuse me," he heard himself say to the maid. "Pardon me, but are you and your mistress without a carriage this afternoon?"

The maid, a long-faced, plain girl with a pointed chin, peered up at him. "Aye, sir, and what business be that of yours?"

Jamie smiled as kindly as he could. "Nothing but a polite interest, I assure you. The streets are busy, and I would not care to see harm come to any of you."

She seemed surprised by that, but her features softened noticeably as she fought a smile. "Aye, sir, I see that you're a gentleman in more'n name. I beg your pardon."

"Not at all." He glanced up ahead at Miss Hutchins and her companion, neither of whom seemed aware of their conversation. "Would your mistress take offense if I offered to escort you all?"

She frowned in thought, looking at Miss Hutchins herself. "I should 'ope not. 'Tis the mark of a gent, is it not?"

"Personally, I should say so," Jamie allowed, nodding. "But I am biased on the topic, belonging to that class of men myself. And we are strangers, so it is not quite the same."

The maid looked back to him with the same sort of scheming look Miss Hutchins had worn earlier. "A stranger's distance only lasts 'til introduction. I can arrange that, sir, if you'll allow it."

What a clever creature to have in one's company. Jamie grinned swiftly at his new conspirator and inclined his head. "James Woodbridge, at your service."

The maid bobbed quickly, then rushed forward. "A Mister James Woodbridge would like a word, miss."

Miss Hutchins stopped, as did her companion. "Mr. James Woodbridge? Do I know him, Aunt Josephine?"

"No," her chaperone said, shrugging.

"Perfect." She turned on her heel and faced him, her eyes sparkling.

Completely unprepared for that, and for the sudden loss of breath he felt at the sight of her, Jamie fell back a step.

Miss Hutchins looked him up and down, then scowled. "Oh, it's you."

That was not the response that Jamie had been hoping for, nor one he was accustomed to. "I beg your pardon?" he managed, offense quickly rising within him.

"Consider it begged," she muttered, shaking her head. "What's the point of speaking to someone to whom I haven't been introduced if I've already done it?" She glanced at the maid suspiciously. "Did you not recognize him?"

The maid's face was carefully innocent. "No, miss, I didn't."

"I could introduce myself," Jamie suggested, finding this whole situation utterly bizarre.

Miss Hutchins lifted a brow. "I already know who you are, Mr. Woodbridge, so what would be the point?"

"I could speak to you without defying protocol."

"We are speaking, and I don't hear any society matrons shrieking in horror." She glanced at the older woman. "Even my aunt isn't."

Jamie grinned outright. "Give them time," he told her. "They are out of practice in the months before the Season. They will shriek plenty when the time is right."

Miss Hutchins's lips quirked, but she did not smile. "Until then, I am quite safe without the formality."

He pursed his lips. "It would allow me the pleasure of your name."

Now she did smile, but it was slight. "But anonymity is my protection, is it not?"

Jamie sighed, sensing this was a battle he was not going to win, but enjoying the struggle all the same. "It saves me from being improper when I offer to escort you and your companions home."

Miss Hutchins tilted her head, still smiling. "So does my refusing your hypothetical offer, gracious though it would have been."

They stared at each other for a long moment, and Jamie could almost feel the pocket watch ticking in his waistcoat. "This is not going to work out for me, is it?"

She slowly shook her head. "I am afraid not, Mr. Woodbridge. But that is not your fault, so you may blame me freely."

"Oh, I would," he assured her, "if I but knew whom to blame."

Miss Hutchins shrugged and bobbed a curtsy, then turned away and continued on away from him.

Jamie stared after her, his smile fixed in place.

Refreshing, he had thought her. Yes, that was a perfect description. Whatever Miss Hutchins had planned for this Season, and he very much suspected her to have a plan, it was going to be anything but dull.

He turned and headed back toward the shops, meeting his cousin on the way to Dennison's stables, as they had planned.

"What kept you?" Jonathan asked in his low tone, gripping his hand firmly. "You're not the sort to be tardy."

Jamie told him an abbreviated version of the story, knowing how it would amuse his cousin. Despite his comparative reserve, Jonathan was a Woodbridge through and through, which meant a healthy dose of sarcasm and more humor than was good for a person.

As he suspected, Jonathan chuckled easily, shaking his head. "Well, I suppose you can cross her off the list of potential candidates, can't you?"

Jamie found himself smiling again, just to himself, and shook his head. "No, I don't think so. Not quite."

Three

The whispers began the moment Daphne removed her cloak, just as she hoped they would. As this was the first event of the Season, she would have to make a grand entrance shortly for the whole room, but the titters of the servants would suffice for the moment.

Her parents had already entered, not feeling the need to be announced, as they were not the ones in need of attention. They'd smiled at her and squeezed her hands, wished her luck, and bestowed all of their hopes and dreams upon her in one desperate look.

She had intentionally been quieter in the last few days to avoid drawing any attention to herself from her parents, which, if they had paid any attention, ought to have raised all of their alarms at the same time. With all of the protesting they'd heard from her since this stupid decision had been made, and how vocal that protesting had been, did they actually believe her silence to be some sort of acquiescence?

They had no idea what was coming.

She approached the entrance to the ballroom and handed the majordomo her card, though he seemed to have trouble moving his eyes down enough to read it.

Daphne barely noticed, now the thing was before her.

Could she really go through with this? She was a stubborn girl, always had been, but she had never been blatantly defiant. She was about to embarrass herself on purpose, and she had never been one to tolerate anything of the kind. She had always simply wanted to do as she wished and leave the attention for the others.

If this plan worked, there would be no attention left for anyone else.

It would be worth it.

It had to be.

No one would want to be seen with her after this.

She released a slow breath, steeling herself. There was only one chance to make this first impression, and she needed to make the most of it. Her mother had bristled at not having the privilege of dressing her, or seeing the final product of the family's well-spent funds, but Daphne had managed to divert her from interference, just as she had throughout most of the purchasing process. No one knew how she looked at the present, save for the horrified maids behind her and the scandalized majordomo before her.

She didn't understand the fuss. She was perfectly covered and modest. She had even added additional lace to ensure that.

Just because the gown was an unusual shade of brown with black velvet trim with black lace *engageantes* off the sleeves at her elbow that were at least thirty years out of fashion and a neckline that showed absolutely nothing of interest unless one enjoyed an expanse of lace patterns did not mean it ought to be shocking to see.

It was a downright ugly gown, but surely people had finer manners than to be so obviously distressed by it.

Her name was announced, somehow without any hesitation, and she proceeded forward proudly, her head held high. The murmuring gasps prodded a small smile on her face. She heard more utterances of "mourning," "horrible," and "heinous" than anything else. Her mother, who had been standing with several other ladies nearby, appeared somewhere between livid and appalled, though she had little enough coloring in her complexion to be considered truly ill.

She glared at Daphne more furiously than she had at Phoebe after the Incident, which was very telling, but Daphne only raised a daring brow at her. There was no way her mother would stoop so low as to publicly scold Daphne or make any scene at all, but she would certainly begin working on a row of epic proportions for when they were alone.

The entire room seemed unable to look anywhere but at her, and Daphne could only smirk at it and continue moving through the crowd. She had no particular location, as she did not know anyone present. While Daphne may have convinced her mother that Aunt Josephine was helping her prepare for the Season, the truth of the matter was that her aunt was clueless and knew absolutely no one—which made her a perfect excuse for day-to-day activities and a convenient chaperone, but alas, she had given Daphne no introductions.

Though if she had, they would hardly be approaching her after this.

Once she had crossed the room, she turned on her heel, reached for a glass from a footman passing at the perfect time, and downed the entire glass in one gulp.

This was not a particularly wise course of action, as she had been expecting a muted punch and not champagne, so the sudden burn and fizz of the beverage started raging against her throat and lungs at once. Her eyes burned, and her chest heaved with the need to cough. She swallowed a painful cough that racked her lungs and felt her body begin to seize in response.

Well, it would certainly do the job right if she died in the middle of the ballroom at the first event of the Season. She wouldn't have the privilege of enjoying the results from such a grand spectacle, but it would be enough.

Thankfully, the musicians started up, and the attention of the room returned to their own interests, and Daphne was free to hack several coughs at her leisure into her too short gloves.

Really, she was doing the thing as right as rain, as there were several people staring at her again with the noise she was making, their expressions a mixture of horror and concern. She would wager, when she could both see and breathe once more, that their concern was more for the scandal of somebody dying before their eyes than anything personally directed at her.

"You really ought, perhaps, to think about breathing one of these days."

Through her bleary eyes, Daphne looked up to see Mr. Woodbridge standing nearby, observing her mildly.

"You could be a gentleman and fetch me a glass of water," she managed, coughing at almost every word.

Mr. Woodbridge released a disbelieving laugh. "And have you choke on that as well? I think not. I am not that desperate to be a hero."

Daphne rolled her eyes as her coughing subsided at last. "Or a gentleman, it seems."

"I am always a gentleman."

"You are speaking to me without introduction," she pointed out as she straightened, wiping her eyes and tossing her hair before fixing a smirk to her lips. "Consider yourself contradicted."

Mr. Woodbridge narrowed his eyes, then bowed, holding up a finger.

She stared at his back in derision. He wanted her to wait? For what? Where exactly did he think she was going to go? There was twenty feet of empty floor around her in every direction, and that was not about to change, if the looks in her direction were any indication.

He was gone only long enough for her to consider tapping her toe in irritation, and then he was back with the reluctant hostess, whose name Daphne had quite forgotten, and who undoubtedly thought this was madness. She currently looked as though she smelled something foul.

"Miss Hutchins," she said in a weak tone of voice that perfectly matched her expression. "May I present Mr. James Woodbridge, who wishes to make your acquaintance?"

Daphne raised a brow at her and flatly said, "Charmed, I'm sure."

"I should hope so," the hostess huffed, fanning herself quickly, then swept away grandly.

"Well, that would make two of us," Mr. Woodbridge commented in a much friendlier tone.

Daphne turned to look at him speculatively. "Aren't you supposed to be a gentleman? Wasn't that the point of the ridiculous charade of bringing her over here?"

He bowed to her again, very properly. "It was indeed, Miss Hutchins, and a very great pleasure it is to have made your acquaintance. Tell me, have you been in London long? I cannot recall having the pleasure of seeing you in London before this."

"Steady on, Mr. Woodbridge," Daphne told him, restraining a snort. "Your politeness is overwhelming me, and I may be obliged to curtsy, and nobody needs to see that."

"A gentleman would not argue with a lady of such quality," Mr. Woodbridge continued with a mischievous light in his eyes, "but nor could he allow her to abuse herself so abominably. Tell me how to proceed, Miss Hutchins, so that I might be a true gentleman in your eyes."

Daphne stared at him, wondering what was wrong with him and if he was fully aware of it. For how attractive Mr. Woodbridge was, she would expect him to be more a man of flattery and less of contradiction. He had a sharp wit, she had seen, and now he was the epitome of proper behavior, though she suspected it was an act for her benefit. He was the only person in the room not appalled by her, which surely indicated some error in his way of thinking or dysfunction in his being.

She wondered about the wisdom of standing so near a person who was obviously afflicted.

Her silence prompted a curious quirk of his brows, his hazel eyes dancing more than before. "Miss Hutchins, are you quite well? Shall I fetch something for you? Or someone? Your mother, perhaps?"

Daphne coughed again, torn between a laugh and a snort. "Lord, no. Anything but that." She heaved a sigh, thinking she knew what he was after. "Fine, Mr. Woodbridge, I concede that you are a gentleman."

His smirk of a smile confirmed her suspicions. He hid it, though, as he inclined his head. "And will Miss Hutchins allow my acquaintance while she is in London?"

She rolled her eyes at his excessive politeness. "Oh, why not? Miss Daphne Hutchins, Mr. Woodbridge, a pleasure to officially make your acquaintance at last." She started to curtsy out of habit, then stopped herself, narrowed her eyes, and stuck out her hand as a man might have done for a handshake.

There were a few gasps around her, but nothing to truly mark, considering she'd had a much larger reaction for her dress only moments before.

Mr. Woodbridge did not seem shocked in the least, but

amused as he took in the sight of her outstretched hand. He grasped it lightly, then bowed over it politely as he would have done had she held out her hand in the usual way, effectively diffusing the situation for those watching.

"Very gentlemanly, I must admit," Daphne reluctantly praised, retrieving her hand easily.

"I know." He shook his head, heaving a mournful sigh. "And thus ends my impropriety and short-lived shocking behavior."

Daphne frowned, scanning his chiseled features for any clue as to what he was referring. "Impropriety? You could have given lessons on proper behavior just then."

He waved his hand dismissively, which dislodged a small sliver of his dark hair across his brow. It was really quite an attractive sight, truth be told, but she found herself more irritated by it than anything else. Insufferable people ought not to be attractive.

"That?" he was saying while she was fighting the internal battle between irritation and attraction. "That was rather true to my usual behavior. I meant everything that happened before that. And the other day."

Daphne took a moment to consider this handsome man, who apparently had the adventurous spirit of a tortoise. "That was the most improper thing you've ever done?"

"Of course not," he snorted, shaking his head. "I'm a Woodbridge. We wrote the book on impropriety as children, but I'm a perfectly behaved gentleman now, and being officially introduced to you, though polite, means that I must behave with that decorum henceforth."

"That's your own fault," Daphne reminded him as she took a glass from another footman—lemonade this time. "I was content with impropriety; it was you who brought the buffoon over to prove what a gentleman you are."

"Yes, true, true," he mused thoughtfully. "Don't choke on that," he added just as she sipped.

She caught herself on a laugh before his words could become true and glared at him in spite of her laughter and his smile. "Rude, Mr. Woodbridge. Not gentlemanly."

"Not sporting, you mean. A gentleman would certainly have reminded you to be careful of drinking beverages considering your history with them."

Against all reason, Daphne found herself grinning at this man, who might just become the sort of ally she needed in this scheme of hers. She'd not confide anything to him as yet. It was far too early in the Season to form any alliances at all, and, as a general rule, men were not to be trusted—especially not ones she found attractive. One could usually trust the plain men, but only with great trepidation.

Still, it had been nearly two years since the Incident, and she'd vowed never to look upon an attractive man with anything but venom for the remainder of her days, yet venom was shockingly lacking at this moment. This tall and particularly attractive man, with his impressive build and dark features, not to mention his wickedly dancing eyes, was a playful sort who did not take anything too seriously, and in the stuffy behavior of the day, that was a rare thing, indeed.

"Are you going to answer my question?" Mr. Woodbridge asked suddenly, breaking Daphne's study of him.

She frowned in confusion as she sipped her drink with a distinct care that made him smile. "Did you ask me a question? I wasn't actually listening. I rarely do."

He smothered a laugh with his glove, then clasped his hands behind his back. "Have you been in London long, Miss Hutchins?"

"Not long," she replied absently, scanning the dancing

with a brief pang of longing. "And never before. First Season, you know, and my mother is so pleased."

"Your tone says otherwise," he commented.

Daphne shook her head. "Oh, no, she is very pleased. Or she was, rather, before I came in like that. She has *expectations*," she confided.

Mr. Woodbridge smiled again. "What, that you'll catch a husband in a dress like that?"

She narrowed her eyes at him, but couldn't help smiling at the jab. "That my proper behavior and decorum, combined with my natural airs and graces, will render me irresistible to the wealthier gentlemen. She never said anything about my manner of dress."

"Then this gown was not her selection?" he asked, gesturing faintly.

Again, Daphne shook her head, sipping her drink once more. "She did not see it until I entered. And I highly doubt I'll be dressing myself for the rest of the Season. It was worth it, though, for the spectacle."

"It certainly captured the room's attention," he agreed. "Where is she now?"

"Scheming in the corner by the fern, just there," she told him, pointing boldly.

Her mother was watching her and blanched horribly, her eyes widening. The fan she held shook in her hand, and the ladies around her turned to look at what was startling her.

"Oh, blast," Daphne said without any remorse. "Ladies do not point. What a pity to be so uncultured."

"Apparently, I am being shocking as well, if my cousin's expression is to be believed," Mr. Woodbridge replied, gesturing faintly toward a man who looked extraordinarily like him, though a little fairer and with blue eyes. He certainly looked shocked and confused, though not in a way that would attract attention.

"I can hear him now," Mr. Woodbridge continued, "'Jamie, what the devil are you about?'" He snorted, shaking his head. "He won't be serious about it, unless he calls me James, and then we will really be in for it."

"Is this the sort of look that renders calling you James?" she asked, truly curious.

His lips curved. "You never know with Jonathan. It might be."

Daphne smiled at the deeper impression of his cousin. "Am I so shocking a sight that you are tainted by our very brief acquaintance? We can remedy that, if you wish to take it back."

Mr. Woodbridge turned to look at her directly, his mischievous glint surprisingly absent. "I don't wish to take it back. I don't believe I've enjoyed a London event more than I am right now, and that is entirely because of you, Miss Hutchins. I rather enjoy having made your acquaintance, and now that I have officially done so, I will not be shocking by asking if you will stand up with me for the next two dances."

She really shouldn't have, but Daphne reared back in shock, not bothering to moderate her expression. "What? James Woodbridge, have you lost your senses?"

"If you're going to be informal, call me Jamie. James means I am in trouble, remember?"

"This is definitely a James moment, Mr. Woodbridge," she insisted, shaking her head repeatedly. She scoffed at his stupidity and took a measured step away. "Do you think I came dressed like this to dance with anyone?"

"I saw you watching the dancing. You would love to dance."

Blast him, he was too observant for his own good, and thus was now the enemy to all her plans. She scowled at him. "Not with you, thank you very much. You don't have the sense to flee from the terrifying prospect I present, as everyone else in this room does."

Jamie, as he would forever be in her mind now, unfortunately, shrugged easily. "Apparently not, but I've never been easily terrified, and it would give me great pleasure to dance with you, as it would give you great pleasure."

This was only getting worse. She forced a smile through gritted teeth. "As it happens, I loathe dancing and was only wondering how to properly break it up. You would make a poor partner, and I must excuse myself before your addlepated nonsense becomes contagious."

She turned on her heel and marched defiantly away, directly into a group of people, none of whom looked pleased to see her. "Has anyone found a successful way to trap a rich man into matrimony? No less than five thousand pounds a year, mind. I have no wish to be a pauper's wife."

Hours later, when packed up and headed for home, after no dancing at all and at least seven ridiculous conversations on topics no woman should converse on, Daphne leaned her head back against the carriage seat, shutting her eyes and wanting nothing more than to sleep for days.

But she would be in for the scolding of a lifetime, and nothing would prevent her mother from exploding at her.

At least she had avoided Jamie for the rest of the night, except for two times when he had been near enough to make comments in the conversations she provoked. And he always seemed to look at her with a bemused smile, as if he already knew her game.

He was dangerous, and she considered writing to her friend Alice in Bath to see if she knew anything about him or his family.

She was not curious at all. She only needed to prepare herself where he was concerned.

The carriage rolled on toward home, and Daphne frowned. The scolding should have started already, and yet it was silent. She opened her eyes to look across at her parents, both of whom were watching her speculatively, their expressions eerily unreadable.

"Yes?" she prompted, feeling more uncomfortable with this than anything else that night.

Her mother sniffed softly. Her father swallowed visibly. Neither said anything.

Daphne looked between them, wondering if there was, perhaps, a heretofore unheard of torture that was about to be rained down upon her head for her betrayal of the family.

She gave a pointed look at her mother, who only exhaled slowly.

"Daphne," her father said in a tone that dripped with disapproval. "Your behavior was appalling. You owe your mother an apology."

That was to be expected. But it would not work.

She shook her head. "I do not. It is my Season, as you say, and I may act as I see fit."

"You will find, my dear," her mother replied coolly, "that your freedom to act at all is at an end." She eyed Daphne with distaste, though her gown was hidden by her cloak. "Your dresses will now be selected by me, and I will oversee your complete dressing to ensure every piece is in place. You will dance at least three times with a variety of suitable gentlemen at every ball, or you will find your room stripped of books."

Daphne gasped at the threat. "Mama—"

"Your mother is speaking," her father chided with more firmness in his tone than Daphne had heard in her entire life.

She clamped down on her lip, her face burning.

242

"I will be arranging all of your social engagements," her mother went on, barely blinking at her interruption. "Down to invitations to tea. Only your aunt or myself may chaperone you, and you will always be chaperoned. You will behave, Daphne, and garner a minimum of one invitation to call after every major engagement on your social agenda."

"Or else?" she whispered, trying for defiance.

Her mother's lips curved into a vicious smile. "Or else we will stay in London all winter, too."

Even her father was taken aback by that, and they both stared at her in gaping shock. The horror in that statement was enough to flirt with the idea of perfect behavior in every way.

"Try me and see, Daphne," her mother said with a firm nod. "Just try." She settled herself back, sighing. "And despite your attempts, the evening was not a complete waste after all."

Daphne had to swallow three times before answering, "No?"

There was an answering shake of her head. "You have secured a fine man for a courtship, Lord knows why. But your father gave his approval."

That could not be possible. There was absolutely no way, no conceivable chance, that any man would have wanted to court her after the evening she had just passed. There had to be a misunderstanding somewhere, unless her parents had secured a slow-witted man with limited sense and intelligence, but the notion that such a man would have a fortune they were interested in was slim.

"I beg your pardon?"

Her father nodded slowly. "Pleasant chap. Spoke highly of you and requested, most properly, to court you, though it is early in the Season. I asked around about him, and received all good reports, even from your aunt, so I gave my consent.

He will be by the house after luncheon to call upon you. Behave, please, as he was most kind about you, all things considered."

That was not likely, and she felt the need to snarl as she asked, "Who?"

Her tone did not go unnoticed, and her father looked bewildered by it. "Why the noise, Daphne? You spoke with him at length yourself. It's Mr. James Woodbridge."

Four

If Jamie's arm had had any feeling left in it, he would have wriggled his fingers a little, but the clenching grip on it at the moment left him rather immobile in that limb, and he desperately wanted to laugh about it.

Daphne Hutchins was furious with him and probably rightly so.

How dare he court her after the dismal spectacle at the ball last week. What cheek. What nerve. What a shocking lack of sense and taste and refinement.

That was what the gossips were saying, at any rate. And Jonathan had given him his own speech on the idiocy and folly of such a course of action, but Jamie kept coming back to only one thought: what fun.

And truly, it was only getting better.

He had called on her every other day, and she had always received him, only because she was in the company of her mother. Their conversations were stiff and painfully polite, but Jamie enjoyed them as much as anything else because he could see the torment it gave Daphne to do so. Tonight was their first chance to be alone in any fashion, but it was the theater. There were people everywhere, and her parents were not too far behind, but her hold on his arm, though polite by appearances, was going to leave bruises.

He needed her to speak without the restraint that their recent meetings had held.

That was not Daphne.

This was.

"You could smile, you know," he murmured, leaning over a little as they walked to the box he had reserved for them.

"If I had anything to smile about, perhaps I would," she ground out.

Jamie fought a smile at the palpable resentment. He had to prod her further, just to see what would happen. And he had an idea how. "Come, come, Daphne, what have I done to render you so irate?"

She slid her green eyes to him with the sort of look that told him he was an idiot for asking. "You know very well what."

"Because I asked to court you?" he asked, not keeping his voice down.

Daphne's eyes widened, and he could see that she almost laughed, but her will was too strong for that. "That, yes," she hissed. "And don't call me Daphne."

He gave her a mock frown. "You know, for a lady bent on flaunting impropriety, you have been surprisingly proper of late. Have I had that much of an influence on you?"

She gave him another potent look and replied, "No." Then she turned to face forward again, her expression devoid of anything remotely resembling enjoyment or pleasure. He might have been walking her to the gallows rather than a theater box.

"It's the theater, Daphne," he reminded her, using her given name again. "Everybody loves the theater."

"I don't," she replied tightly. "I have a dreadful fear of heights."

He stumbled a step and turned to her in embarrassment.

"Have you really?" he asked, panic rising. He hadn't thought of that. He hadn't a clue how to court anyone, and the theater seemed a logical place to go. He was going to have a time of it, as it was, courting her, what with her determination to resent everything and make scenes. But if he had been so careless as to thrust her into a truly fearful situation for her, there would be no recovering for him.

And as he realized how very important courting Daphne Hutchins was to him, he desperately needed to recover.

Daphne seemed amused by his concern and tilted her head at him, her eyes brilliantly green against the shimmering emerald silk she wore, her entire ensemble perfect and pristine and painfully breathtaking. She shrugged one slim shoulder. "Perhaps I do, perhaps I don't."

Jamie felt air rush back into his lungs and smiled in relief, then scowled at Daphne. "Not ladylike, Miss Hutchins."

She smirked up at him, her nails biting into his arm despite the layers between them. "Not sporting, you mean."

He hummed in satisfaction at hearing his words from the night of the ball. "I thought you weren't listening to me."

She looked away at once. "I wasn't."

Her reddened cheeks told him otherwise, and he allowed himself a small smile as he led her on. A group of finely dressed men and women blocked the way to the boxes, and they saw the approach of Daphne and her parents, their expressions clearly finding the approach less than pleasant.

"Well, someone has certainly learned to dress herself," Maria Wells commented with a sneer, looking over Daphne with her small eyes.

Jamie bristled and noticed his cousin Jonathan, who had been leaning against a wall nearby, suddenly stand upright, his eyes fixed on Miss Wells with a determined glint in his eye and a tight jaw that Jamie knew all too well.

He needed no other encouragement.

Jamie considered Miss Wells with a pitying smile. "Yes, Miss Wells, and we are all quite proud of you for managing the thing on your own, but perhaps a less obvious declaration of your success? Modesty is always more appreciated. If you will excuse us." He nodded to her, then pulled Daphne along as the crowd instantly moved for them, stunned into complete silence.

Jonathan caught Jamie's eye, fighting a grin, but only nodded at him, bowing to Daphne.

"I don't think your parents heard her," Jamie muttered, glancing behind at her parents, who were still wide-eyed and gawking at the theater itself.

Daphne suddenly exploded into a fit of giggles, and he looked down at her, surprised by the warmth that hit him at the sound. "Miss Hutchins?"

"Did you see her face?" she wheezed, covering her mouth with a pristine glove, very unlike the ones she had worn the other night. "Oh, I can't breathe . . . Oh my."

Jamie chuckled and pulled Daphne a touch closer to him. "I shouldn't have praised her so warmly. Someone should have told her that particular shade of yellow was popular last Season, but is not at all the fashion this time."

Daphne squeezed her eyes shut, laughing herself into silence now, her face growing red. "Stop, oh, stop, Jamie."

The sound of his name from her lips hit him squarely in the chest, and he was unprepared for the effort it took to breathe once more. He couldn't say anything as they walked to the box, Daphne eventually settling herself back into composure.

"Why would you do that?" she asked him, her voice equally composed once more. "You knew to what she was referring. You made a comment about it yourself."

"That was a joke, Daphne," he insisted with a scolding look. "I would never have truly said anything of the kind."

"I know that. But we both know there was truth in it, as there should have been."

Jamie considered his answer carefully, then sighed as he held the curtain for her to enter the box. "I could joke with you about it, Daphne, because there was no malice intended and you knew that. She intended nothing but malice, and I could not have that. I would not."

Daphne's brow furrowed, and she glanced at her parents, still too far away to hear them. "But you didn't have to throw it back at her, Jamie," she hissed. "I am a spectacle; you do not have to be."

Was she concerned about his reputation if he continued to stand by her? It was a touching thought, though he doubted she had considered anything so serious where he was concerned. She would most likely even regret saying such a thing later in the evening when she recollected it, knowing how it must have sounded.

But, perhaps, *this* was Daphne, stripped of the restraint and stripped of her own agenda.

What a puzzle she was.

He leaned closer, smiling warmly. "I never mind being a spectacle when the cause is just. And in case it escaped your notice, my cousin was ready to act as well."

She reared back a little, her full lips parting. Then she frowned. "Oh, I doubt that very much. I saw him, of course, but surely it would have been in defense of you, should anything have arisen. You already told me he disapproves."

Jamie was shaking his head before she finished. "He doesn't disapprove. He thinks I'm mad."

"That makes two of us."

"There is a marked difference. He would have left me to

the wolves had it been only me," Jamie went on, ignoring her completely. "But you? He would have thrashed someone for you, purely because it is right. Maybe not Maria Wells, he draws the line at thrashing women, but someone would have bled, certainly, just for you. And because I have a vested interest in you, which Jonathan cannot resist interfering in."

Daphne seemed stunned into silence as she stared at him, processing what he had told her. Clearly, she had not expected anything of the kind to be said, and she did not know what to do about it.

"Does that surprise you so?" he murmured, reaching out a finger to touch her gloved hand.

She nodded slowly, her eyes unfocused. "I didn't expect . . . I don't . . ."

Jamie smiled gently at her, taking pity on her confusion. "I'll explain everything in a moment, once your parents are settled. Take your seat, Daphne. I'll be there shortly."

Again, she nodded, then turned to take her seat, sitting stiffly for a moment. Then she seemed to shake herself, looking around the crowded theater, and yawned dramatically before slouching in her seat.

The effect was instantaneous. Those nearest the box began frowning and whispering, looking at Daphne with disapproval.

Jamie shook his head, unable to keep from grinning.

Whatever Daphne was playing at, she was very good at it, and he was thrilled he had taken the chance to court her early on—far earlier than he would have otherwise. He just could not risk missing a single moment of her antics and was desperate to see what she would do next. Even Jonathan had agreed it would be entertaining, though he questioned the wisdom of such close proximity and could not discern the reason for Jamie's interest.

He would see it shortly. They would all see it shortly.

He nodded politely to the Hutchinses as they entered the box, Mrs. Hutchins still all in raptures over the grandeur of the theater and having a box to flutter over him at all. It was a wonder that the sedate Mr. Hutchins had a wife who was so excitable, but Jamie had never professed to understand the bonds that existed between a married couple. Not everyone married for affection, and years of marriage surely built up a tolerance for some things.

They sat in the seats Jamie indicated and began whispering to each other, while he took his seat next to Daphne, who still maintained her sluggish pose, which her parents had yet to notice.

"Nobody yawns at the theater," Jamie scolded with a smile.

She looked at him for a moment, then gave another pointed yawn while saying, "I do." She shook herself after the yawn and smirked at him. "And I am willing to bet several others do as well."

She was undoubtedly right, but he couldn't give in so easily. "Well then, none look as fetching as you while they do so."

Daphne gave him a disbelieving look, then turned her attention to the stage, where the play was beginning. "Don't flatter me, Mr. Woodbridge. It won't work."

"Don't be proper now," Jamie scolded, smiling. "You were doing so well."

He saw her lips quirk, but she maintained her cool composure. "Don't pretend you know me, Mr. Woodbridge."

"I would never," he assured her. "I enjoy being taken by surprise, and I know I am in for a great many surprises with you."

Now she did smile, but it was smug. "If you manage to survive being near me long enough to witness any more."

"I may surprise you myself, Daphne." She glanced at him with a superior expression, doubt rife in every facet of her features. Jamie nodded once, smirking. "Vested interest, remember?"

Daphne sighed and rolled her eyes dramatically. "I refuse to be your own personal spectacle, Mr. Woodbridge. Find your entertainment elsewhere."

"And miss the great diversion you present?" He snorted softly. "I think not. I determined from the moment I first saw you in Bond Street that this would be the most amusing Season I've ever spent, and I set my mind on enjoying every part of it."

"Then you're an even greater fool than I took you for," she hissed, her cheeks coloring. "Greater than your cousin thinks, too, I daresay."

Jamie chuckled and watched the play before them, though he could still see Daphne clearly in the corner of his eye. "Then you don't know my cousin very well. He's determined to enjoy this Season as well, but not at your expense."

Daphne heaved a great sigh as if the effort of conversing with him was simply too much to endure. "Then at whose?" she asked, though her voice clearly indicated she really would rather have not.

"At mine."

She jerked a little beside him, but he pointedly kept his gaze on the stage. "What? Why?"

He smiled. "Disappointed that someone won't be paying attention to you?"

"No," she muttered petulantly, settling back. "I just find the idea of paying attention to you a rather boring concept."

He suppressed a laugh at her wit. "So does everyone else, most of the time," he allowed. "I'm really a very boring person."

On cue, Daphne yawned once more, this time quite loudly. Her mother turned around and gave her the sort of scolding look that all mothers possess in great potency. Daphne reluctantly straightened up, scowling and looking more miserable than anything Jamie had ever seen a person at the theater.

The moment her mother turned back, Daphne slouched once more.

"He's watching me," Jamie murmured low, leaning closer, "because he knows that I'll be enjoying whatever it is you have planned. He wants to see how you affect me."

Daphne glanced at him again, brow furrowed. "That's not particularly nice. Why would your cousin care?"

"Because he is an interfering busybody, despite his polite facade." Jamie smiled fondly, shaking his head. "Jonathan and I are only months apart, and we were raised together. I was raised with all of his siblings, and as there are a great many of them, I seem to have inherited the nuisance of siblings without the trouble of the true relationship."

"Siblings are a trial," Daphne countered in a surprisingly dark tone. "I've not found much they are good for."

That drew Jamie's gaze away from the stage to her face, and he was surprised to find a raw anguish there, her eyes burning with pain and anger. He looked away quickly, knowing she would hate being so exposed and vulnerable to him.

What had been in Daphne's past to render such an expression and such words?

"Well," he said quickly, desperate to move away from whatever pain was there, "they are remarkably good at hiding evidence of mischief when all could be punished for the deeds.

I can recall at least a dozen instances where we ought to have been severely punished, but we were so skilled at covering up our ways that they were never discovered."

He counted Daphne's twitching lips a great victory. "So you would be praised for your villainy?"

"For our cunning, surely," he corrected. "But we are long past such deeds."

"So you say."

The actors did or said something that brought laughter from the audience to a new level, but neither he nor Daphne joined in, as neither had been paying attention. Jamie managed a smile; Daphne looked supremely bored.

"I don't know anything about the Woodbridges," Daphne said thoughtfully, her tone contrasting with her expression.

"Would you like to?" Jamie inquired, keeping a teasing smile on his face. He would love nothing more than to tell her all about them, about him, about the kind of life they'd had, but if he knew her, and he was beginning to think he just might, he doubted she would allow such a long-winded explanation of something so personal.

She shook her head slowly, her jaw tight. "No, that was not an invitation. It was simply a statement. I've never heard of the lot of you, so why should anyone care?"

He exhaled sharply, the sting of her words real despite the amusement he found in them. She was trying so hard to be callous and unfeeling, but anyone with eyes could see the fire within her, and if they paid close enough attention, they would also see the passion she possessed for a great many things. Dancing, for one, and unless he was very much mistaken, the theater as well.

She was a witty one and proud. She also seemed to have a passion for sparring with him, which he would exploit whenever he had the chance.

"I've never heard of you either," he told her, "yet I care. Perhaps more for not knowing."

"Then you are a very great idiot, Jamie Woodbridge," she replied easily, a smile now on her face.

Jamie grinned and settled himself in to enjoy the rest of the evening. "Yes, so I have been told. My cousin Ross said as much not two weeks ago, but that had nothing to do with you. Ross is the second son, you know, and feels the strain of that unfortunate business on a daily basis."

"I don't care."

"Neither do I, to be sure, but Ross does, so the rest of us must feel it."

"Please stop talking."

"Now Ethan, on the other hand, thrives upon being a younger son," Jamie went on, keeping his voice low so that no one but Daphne would hear, "but he is a twin, so Emma would never let him get too far out of line. She's a bit of a snob, compared to the rest of us, but still too wild for convention."

"Are you going to go through the entire family?"

He nodded once. "It is a very long show, I am told, so there will be plenty of time to give you the full scope of Woodbridge madness."

"Oh, Lord."

"Grace is the quiet one," he went on, emboldened by her apparent misery. "Quite the mystery. Scares me to death."

"I will throw myself out of this box if you don't stop," Daphne warned.

Jamie shrugged once. "It's not that far. You won't be too injured. Your mother would bodily restrain you, at any rate, so for your own sake, don't attempt it."

Daphne snorted in surprise, covering her mouth at once.

"Leo is an infant, though he refuses to accept it, but puppies of fourteen never see themselves clearly . . ."

Five

aphne was in a right mess of things, and there was absolutely no indication that anything would change in the near future.

She had done everything she could possibly think of to deter Jamie from his courtship of her, and he was not budging. Worse than that, he seemed to enjoy her efforts, viewing them as a challenge and not an obstacle.

He rambled on happily when she blatantly ignored him, took absolutely no offense with anything she said or did, and smiled at her every moody response. He was unfailingly cheerful, which ought to have been irritating to her, and surprised her regularly with his quick wit. Her sarcasm was rewarded in equal measure, her barbed insults provoking a repartee of teasing that only encouraged them both.

It had been two weeks since the night at the theater, where he had detailed so much about his family throughout the first act that Daphne could have recited all of the pertinent details of every Woodbridge sibling and half a dozen stories from their childhood. She hadn't thought he really would go into all of that, but he seemed to enjoy testing her the way she did him.

Worst of all, she was beginning to enjoy it.

She was beginning to enjoy *him*.

It was the most horrifying result that could have come from all of this.

She enjoyed the wicked glint in his eye. She enjoyed the anticipation of his response, knowing it would be something clever and would make her bristle and laugh at the same time. She had actually enjoyed hearing him talk about his family—the way his tone warmed when he spoke of the girls and how he smiled when he considered the boys. She had protested repeatedly throughout the telling and had even risen on one occasion to leave, only to be hushed back down by her mother.

She had been secretly pleased to have been forced to remain. She wanted to ask him questions about the family, prod for more details on them all, but she could not give in to interest. She could not be eager.

She could not enjoy him or his stories or his attentions.

And she could *not* enjoy the way he touched her without seeming to notice.

The second act of the play that night at the theater might have been worse than the first, but for entirely different reasons. At the interval, he had taken her for a turn about the theater, her parents in tow again, and she had ignored him in every way she could. Her hand was on his arm, as it had to be, but she kept her expression lifeless and did not respond to a single word he said. She had been so convincing that she had heard whispers about it and about him. It ought to have bothered him, but it did not dampen him at all.

When they had returned to the box and to their seats, he'd been as silent as she had been, sitting side-by-side. Daphne had just been able to focus on the show at hand when she felt something grazing along her forearm and wrist. She glanced down quickly to see Jamie's fingers running up and down her glove, but in an absent fashion. His hand was opening and closing, his fingers dragging along the fabric, the feeling sinking into her skin beneath. She watched his fingers move for a moment, waiting for them to shift higher or lower to get more of a reaction from her.

They never did.

She frowned. She did not know much about men or the art of flirtation or seduction, but she suspected that someone with certain designs, whether innocent or nefarious, would have pressed his advantage to its limits, whatever they happened to be. Yet Jamie didn't. Over and over, his fingers moved in exactly the same pattern, at exactly the same speed, and with exactly the same absence of intent.

Daphne had glanced up at Jamie and found him intent on the stage, for once not seeming to be aware of her. He wore a small smile, but not the teasing one he used when provoking her. There was absolutely no indication that he was intentionally teasing her now, nor that he was even aware of what he was doing.

She returned her attention to the stage, but nothing there could draw her like Jamie's fingers on her arm. The more she tried to focus on the stage, the more she felt the slow drag of his fingers. There was an odd comfort in them, and she felt herself growing warm with it. She tried everything she could to ignore it, to shut off all feeling to that particular limb, but her resistance only seemed to increase its effect.

Finally, she jerked her hand away and folded it in her lap, her cheeks burning and her breathing unsettled.

Jamie looked at her, whether in surprise or amusement she could not have said, and then his hand rested too comfortably on the back of her chair, where it safely remained the rest of the evening.

Daphne's arm burned for the rest of the night, even after the maddening man left her presence.

No scolding of her mother's could ever have matched the

scolding she gave herself that night, and she determined to double her efforts, not only to scandalize society, but to shake Jamie Woodbridge loose from this inane courtship.

Having gained the trust of her mother once more, after a week of mostly proper behavior, as far as she knew, and having met all of the stricter requirements as far as invitations and behavior went, Daphne had now earned the right to attend events in the company of her aunt alone, so long as her mother oversaw her dressing before she left.

Of course, her mother had no way of knowing that Daphne managed to hide a gown of her own choosing in the carriage so that she could change into it once they were safely away from the house. It was a bit awkward to accomplish, but traveling with a willing chaperone made that much easier. Well, perhaps not willing so much as indifferent. Aunt Josephine, her father's sister, was perfectly content to let Daphne do whatever she wished—a worthless chaperone as far as propriety went, but rather convenient for Daphne's purposes.

Her mother had no idea Josephine was not nearly as proper as Daphne had led her to believe.

The change in ensembles brought more attention to Daphne and more whispers, more rumors and disapproval, and she reveled in it. Jamie had been surprised—she could see it in his eyes—but he escorted her and stayed as close as she would let him. Which, most of the time, was not particularly close.

She shocked roomfuls of people by refusing to dance at all, turning down what limited requests were made of her, even from Jamie.

She had considered scandalizing a group of guests, most of whom she had not been introduced to, by asking the one person she knew whether his wife's lover was in attendance this evening. The other half of the room had been whispering about it, and everybody in London knew of it. But that reminded her too painfully of the comments made about her at home, and she could not let herself go that far. Besides, she was doing well enough without actually causing anyone true humiliation.

In any conversation, she was too blunt, too honest, too rude, and while never outright offensive, she certainly danced with the line. She took comfort in the fact that her conversations were limited and interest in her was kept to a minimum. She was not particularly keen on being infamous, as she had no intention of returning to London for anyone to continue discussing her. She had no doubt she would be talked about, but as she was not truly shocking, it should not last long.

But if Jamie did not give up on her soon, she might have to be more drastic. She had tried to be downright cruel to him, but as she could find nothing of significance to target in his person, her barbs fell harmlessly by the wayside.

It did not help that she did not truly wish to hurt him.

In fact, she found herself wanting to confide in him about a great many things.

She could not allow that. She would never trust any man with her personal thoughts and feelings, and she would certainly never take an interest in a man her parents approved of so highly. That was what had gotten her into trouble before, and she refused to make the same mistake.

The trouble here was that Jamie was just the sort of man that she would have wished for herself, had the Incident never occurred. He was charming, he was polite, he was clever, and he could make her laugh so easily it seemed unnatural. He was devoted to family, did not particularly care about fortune, though he had a decent one, and surprised her at every turn, despite her best efforts.

And he was handsome. The sort of handsome that makes one smile, and then the smile fades as one gets more acquainted with him and the handsomeness grows and grows until the sight of him steals breath and weakens knees.

She was not claiming to have stolen breath or weakened knees, nor would she admit to the beginnings of any such feelings or stirrings. She simply acknowledged that he was that sort of handsome.

If she were interested.

Which she was not.

Definitely not.

Just because her stays seemed a bit tighter at seeing him walk toward her in his pristine eveningwear with his dark hair perfectly in place, the hint of a smirk on his flawless lips, and his eyes an indistinguishable color as they warmed upon seeing her didn't mean anything.

"Good heavens," Daphne breathed, grateful Mary had had the foresight to give her a fan, as she needed to use it quite rapidly now.

Jamie bowed before her with absolute precision, and not even Daphne's repeated reminders of cool composure could ring in her head over the buzzing that James Woodbridge brought to it.

"Lovely, Miss Hutchins," he murmured as he straightened. "As always."

Daphne bit her lip on a short laugh. Lovely. Her dress was orange. Not a warm and sunset glow sort of orange, but the sort of orange that made one cringe and was really quite obnoxious. She'd already decided not to look at herself for the rest of the night. There was nothing lovely about it or her. Except maybe the cut of the dress, which was really quite slimming, but no one was going to notice that.

Jamie offered her an arm, smiling fondly. "May I?"

Daphne looked at him dubiously, then exhaled noisily as she haphazardly tossed her arm through his. "Oh, why not?"

He nodded his gratitude impertinently, and then proceeded to take her about the room. "That is an exquisite gown," he told her, tilting his head for a better look. "I haven't seen that shade outside of the Indies."

Daphne looked up at him in surprise. "You've been to the Indies?"

He shook his head quickly. "No, I only saw an exhibition once."

She tsked and looked away, making a face. "Pity. For a moment, you were almost interesting." A lady nearby tittered at her words, and Daphne rolled her eyes again. "I may not stay long this evening, if the company does not improve."

"I shall endeavor to improve matters for you," Jamie pledged in the teasing voice that made her want to smile, "though you already made an indelible impression simply by attending at all."

Daphne raised a shoulder in a careless shrug, although her lips lifted in amusement. She swore the other day that she would not come, and let that be known, though she never sent an official refusal. "I changed my mind."

"Ah, a woman's prerogative." He leaned closer to murmur, "What were you wearing when you left the house, Daph?"

She jerked her head away, glaring at him. "Don't call me Daph!" she hissed.

"I thought you wanted them to talk," he countered, taunting her with a brow lift.

She snorted and tried to tug her hand away, but he held it fast. "About me, not about you."

Jamie frowned and continued to promenade her around the room like some prized pony. "Well, that's a bit selfish, I must say. Especially when I'm courting you."

Daphne did not bother to hide a snarl. "Against my will."

He gave her a scolding look and squeezed her hand tightly. "No one is forcing you to talk to me, and yet . . ."

She opened her mouth to reply, then turned away with a scowl.

He had a point. The trouble was that she enjoyed talking to him.

Too much.

She was saved the trouble of responding when his cousin, Mr. Jonathan Woodbridge, approached them and bowed. "Jamie, would you be so good as to introduce me?"

Daphne was delighted by Jamie's scowl as he did so. "Miss Daphne Hutchins, may I present my cousin, Mr. Jonathan Woodbridge? Jonathan, this is Miss Hutchins."

Mr. Woodbridge bowed again, and Daphne most likely stunned the entire room when she curtseyed rather perfectly before him. "A pleasure, Miss Hutchins."

She gave him a fond smile. "And mine as well, sir."

Jamie looked between the two of them with suspicion. "What is this? What are you doing?"

"Is he speaking to you or to me, Miss Hutchins?" Mr. Woodbridge asked in mock confusion.

"I cannot say, sir," Daphne replied innocently. "Surely he would never be so informal with a young woman, whether or not his cousin was courting her."

Mr. Woodbridge nodded soberly, his blue eyes dancing the same way Jamie's did. "Quite so, very poor manners. Might I redeem our family name with a dance, Miss Hutchins?"

Oh, this was going to be rich. Daphne beamed up at him and placed her hand in his. "It would be an honor to allow you the attempt, Mr. Woodbridge."

After two full weeks of refusing every dance, the room seemed to still in stunned response to her being led out to the dance floor, and Jamie may have squawked in distress when his cousin yanked her hand out of his.

The music started up, and Daphne and Mr. Woodbridge joined the rest of the couples in the first movements of the dance.

"That was entirely too much fun, Mr. Woodbridge," Daphne praised as they took hands to circle around.

He chuckled softly. "Yes, I thought you might enjoy that."

"How did you know?"

He gave her a knowing look. "You think Jamie doesn't confide in me? I know all about you, Miss Hutchins. I know what sort of spectacle you make, and how much you want Jamie to leave you be."

Daphne blanched at being so exposed and lowered her eyes to his cravat, grateful when they were able to be part of the next movement, saving her from having to answer.

"It is nothing personal," she confessed when they were back together. "Your cousin is a fine man, and there is nothing untoward about him."

"Oh, Miss Hutchins," Mr. Woodbridge broke in, shaking his head. "Don't think for a moment that you need to defend my cousin, or that I am in some way criticizing you for anything. I know Jamie very well, and you won't find a better man in England, except perhaps myself."

Daphne released a short laugh at that and clamped down on her lips again.

"I'm enjoying this process very much," Mr. Woodbridge continued, sounding more serious than his words were. "You are proving quite a challenge for Jamie, and it is rare that I get to witness such a thing. It is good for him to have to work for what he wants. It is what makes him who he is."

The urge to laugh faded, and she peered up at this somehow wiser version of Jamie, though they were only months apart. "And you think that I am something he wants?"

She received a rather sardonic look that held a very serious tone behind it. "You don't think so? My dear Miss Hutchins, aren't you paying attention at all?"

Daphne sputtered softly, then glanced over at Jamie, who was watching them both with a somewhat conflicted expression. He seemed pleased and yet also thunderous, his eyes fixed on them with a curious intensity, his arms folded across his chest.

That was not the Jamie she had expected to find.

But it was quite an attractive Jamie to behold.

"Good heavens," she muttered under her breath.

Mr. Woodbridge laughed to himself and lifted his chin a bit more. "Come, Miss Hutchins, let us show off this brilliant dress of yours to the other side of the room, just in case anyone here has not been blinded by it."

Daphne laughed loudly in response, which made the room titter once more. "You know all my antics, then," she stated, looking closely at this cousin of Jamie's, noting their similarities, which were many, and their differences, which were few.

"I do," he replied with a nod.

"And which has been your favorite?"

He smirked down at her. "I was rather fond of the tartan and Scottish accent at Lady Raeburn's garden party two days ago."

Daphne grinned with great pride and delight. "Yes, that really was quite a good one. I was quite proud of my brogue. Do you know which has been Jamie's?"

Mr. Woodbridge shook his head, still smiling. "He doesn't have one. Jamie likes them all."

She hadn't expected that, and it quite occupied her mind for the rest of the dance.

"Who is that?" Mr. Woodbridge asked suddenly, indicating a man across the room who was staring at them.

Daphne looked, then rolled her eyes dramatically. "It's my brother," she told him drily. She glared at Ned fiercely from her spot. "He probably wonders what I'm doing."

On cue, Ned raised a brow at her.

"I imagine many other people have that same question," Mr. Woodbridge mused.

She looked up at him with a quick smile. "Not you?"

He shook his head easily, looking bemused. "You seem to have a plan, and it would be ungentlemanly to question it."

Despite her aversion to liking Jamie Woodbridge, and all that he wanted from her, Daphne found herself growing quite fond of this particular cousin, and that was something she did not mind anyone else knowing.

After she had been turned over to Aunt Josephine, she witnessed the wordless argument between the cousins as Jamie made his way across the room to her. Aunt Josephine watched in bemusement as Jamie turned Daphne back toward a corner of the room where he fetched her some punch and glared at her.

"That was not at all sporting, Daphne," he scolded quite plainly. "You can't dance with Jonathan anymore."

She shrugged as she sipped. "I don't need your approval to dance with Jonathan, Mr. Woodbridge."

Jamie shook his head repeatedly, swinging back and forth firmly. "No, no, I draw the line at you calling him Jonathan while I remain Mr. Woodbridge. Did he tell you to call him that?"

"He might have done." She sipped her drink slowly, then smacked her lips together just to shock the older woman sitting nearby, who quickly moved to another seat.

"He would never," Jamie vowed. "Not even the Mothers call him Jonathan unless he is in a very fine mood."

"The Mothers?" she repeated, giving him an odd look. "That sounds ominous. What is it?"

Jamie reared back slightly. "Are you asking me a personal question, Daphne? Out of real interest?"

All of Mr. Woodbridge's words about Jamie came flooding into Daphne's mind, and she exhaled slowly, letting a genuine smile form on her face as she looked at him now. "Don't make me regret it, Jamie. Tell me now before I change my mind and ignore you again."

He looked so pleased by her response that she completely forgot to be indifferent and enjoyed every moment that he spent talking about his mother and his aunt, both of whom were as mothers to him, and then they spoke of his family home in Oxfordshire, as well as his own estate in Norfolk. Before she knew it, Daphne was falling in love with both houses and quite desperate to be rid of London to see them both.

When she decided it would be better for her to leave, Jamie escorted her back to Aunt Josephine and her brother, who had apparently grown bored as well.

"Why did it bother you so to have me dance with Jonathan?" Daphne asked Jamie as they approached them. "Tell me the truth."

Jamie looked sheepish, but he held Daphne's hand tighter. "As a general rule," he told her quietly, "and apart from pitying wallflowers, Jonathan only dances with women he considers to be potential and suitable candidates for marriage." He wrinkled his nose and shrugged helplessly. "I didn't want him putting you in either category."

Daphne tilted her head, her heart warming. "I am no wallflower, Jamie. So why fear the other?"

His hold tightened. "Because I don't want to risk him taking you from me. And there it is."

Oh.

His eyes searched hers, waiting for a response of some kind, and Daphne stared right back, barely able to breathe.

Slowly, she brought her worn glove up to his face and caressed his cheek gently. His eyes widened, and his grip on her other hand suddenly clenched.

"I'm not choosing Jonathan," Daphne whispered before she could stop herself. Then she dropped her hand and swept away, fighting warring emotions of relief, embarrassment, excitement, and horror within herself.

What was she doing? What was she about? She wasn't choosing Jamie either; she wasn't choosing anyone. She was here to ruin herself, to ensure she never came back to London, to live out her life in peace and alone, in her own company. She should not be excited to see Jamie. She should not want to kiss him for his sweet words, nor laugh at his wit, nor wish to dance in his arms by the light of the moon.

Those were silly wishes for silly girls, and she refused to be one of them.

Ned walked her to the coach and frowned when there was only room for her and their aunt within. "Aren't you for-getting something?" he asked, scolding her a little, sounding too pompous for her taste.

Daphne glared down at him from her carriage seat, then pretended to recollect something. "Oh, that's right, I forgot to get a husband today. I knew I had forgotten something."

She slammed the door in his face and called to the driver, who sent them racing for home, leaving her brother to find his own way there.

Six

He was going to marry Daphne Hutchins. There was no doubt in his mind about that anymore—not that there had ever been much doubt at all.

Even Jonathan was insisting that he do so, which was a shocking revelation in and of itself.

Granted, Jonathan had been laughing when he'd said so, which ought to have been warning enough, as his cousin understood how difficult it would be to convince Daphne to consent to any such thing, as she was still so resistant to their courtship.

A full month of courting her, and she still scowled when he got too close.

He knew it was only halfhearted, though. He could see the way she looked at him when she forgot to have those walls of hers up. When she was not pretending to hate him, she actually liked him.

And as she was not seeking out attention from any other man to spite him or make him jealous, he thought he might have had a fair chance of eventually convincing her to give up her charade and like him in earnest.

He liked her in earnest.

He loved her.

And not many people would believe that, seeing her the way they did.

Jamie loved her more for being harder to understand. It made every glimpse into her true self more precious to him.

And now that he could sense her resistance weakening, he was willing to be patient, knowing it may reap the reward he so desired in the end.

But knowing Daphne, she had more secrets up her sleeves. She was always surprising him, and while he did not know the reasons for her behavior this Season, he did not doubt that there was an excellent reason for it.

She was always better behaved if her parents were around, but he did not believe it was any sort of deference to them. Oh, he had no doubt she loved her parents, but there was some very strong resentment there, and he suspected her being in London was chief among that resentment. She seemed more herself when he called upon her at home, dressed in more comfortable clothing and usually with a book in her possession. More than once he had wondered if she might beat him with the book, but after getting to know Daphne more, he wagered she valued the book in question too much to be so cruel to it.

He knew she was trying to force him to cease his courtship, though he didn't understand why. And she didn't seem to understand that nothing she was attempting was remotely terrifying for him and certainly nothing that was going to send him running from her. She was a bold and engaging woman with a sharp wit and lively spirit. Too brash, perhaps, but she had not as yet done anything that could possibly ruin a reputation. For all her shocking behaviors, nothing ever could be considered breaches of morality, and her gowns, while either hideous or simply out of fashion, were never daring in cut or inappropriate for the setting.

Even Daphne Hutchins had boundaries, and he enjoyed seeing what she would do within them.

He was determined to dance with her tonight, despite having not succeeded thus far. She could not hold him off forever, and he had seen how she had danced with his cousin. She was graceful and elegant and had enjoyed every moment of it. He'd tried to inform her that he was a much better dancer than Jonathan, but she did not seem to care.

He hadn't been able to speak with her yet this evening, but he had seen her enter with her parents and brother, and as she was in the company of her family, she was quite properly dressed. Quite fetchingly, too, in the simplest of white muslins. She looked ethereal, and he wanted to tell her so. He wanted her to know what she made him feel. He wanted . . .

Well, he wanted a great deal, but patience was a virtue he was growing quite good at.

Mostly.

He started in the direction of Daphne, whose parents had moved on to another group while she remained behind with a few others, none of whom looked displeased with her, so she must be behaving.

A small commotion near the front of the ballroom drew his attention, as well as that of others. A striking man was entering the room with a petite blonde woman on his arm, and suddenly the room seemed to buzz a little more.

Daphne's face had gone as white as her dress, and her gloved hand clenched her fan so tightly it was likely to break.

The man, whoever he was, entered the room completely and smiled at the gathering, then saw Daphne and brightened. "Ah, my little friend," he said loudly enough for anyone nearby to hear. "I hadn't heard you would be in London. You finally came out of hiding, eh?"

Daphne's chin clenched tightly, as if she wanted to give it

an impertinent lift but could not manage it. She barely resembled the fiery woman he had come to know. She looked more like a frightened child than anything else.

Jamie looked around for her parents and brother. They watched the exchange with wide eyes, almost fearful. Well, if they would not go to her, he would, and he made his way through the curious guests towards her.

What was going on here? He didn't like anything that made Daphne look so small. Whoever this man was, Jamie wished him far, far away.

"I heard it was quite a long time before anyone saw you, Daphne," he continued, patting the hand of the girl next to him, who obviously had no idea what was going on. "I do hope you've gotten over it."

Anybody watching this interaction could see that Daphne had not gotten over it—whatever *it* happened to be. She was trembling where she stood, and the whispers reaching Jamie's ears spoke of broken hearts, broken engagements, and possibly a loss of virtue. Whether any of that was true remained to be seen, but there was nothing that society loved as much as gossip, and this was certainly a story.

Daphne swallowed, but said nothing as she stared at this man, betrayal and anger etched in her features.

The man nodded at her and pulled the girl on his arm away, gliding on to the next group.

Daphne remained where she was, still staring at where he had been, her face no longer white, but a rapidly darkening shade of pink. She was, no doubt, hearing the whispers now—the judgment, scorn, and pity of those around her.

Jamie moved as quickly as he could, nodding at Jonathan, who also began to move. Daphne's family seemed to be in shock where they stood.

Jamie reached Daphne first and took her arm gently, but

firmly in his hold. "Come, Miss Hutchins," he murmured with a warm smile. "I must claim the dance you promised me before my cousin claims one for himself." His words had the exact effect he'd intended, those around her now gossiping on the Woodbridges associating with her and what that could mean.

Daphne looked at him with watery eyes, no hint of indignation or fire in them.

He smiled further at her. "Come, I must have this dance."

She nodded absently and came without resistance—another indication that all was not well. "Jamie," she whispered when they were away. "I cannot dance at this moment, not even with you."

"I know, Daph," he replied gently, rubbing her arm discreetly. "We're going outside."

She nearly sagged in relief and nodded, one tear making its way down her cheek.

Jamie held his breath that no one would see that, and he could not wipe it away without causing more gossip, which was the last thing she needed. He hurried her outside and down off the terrace into the garden, which was lit well enough for anyone to stroll in. The night was cooler than he expected, and he rubbed Daphne's arms gently as he led her farther from the house, keeping to the best lit paths should her family wish to seek them out.

A small bench rested near a large tree, and he settled Daphne there, not sure if he ought to sit beside her or stand before her. He settled for taking her hands and rubbing his thumbs over her fingers. "Are you all right?"

She looked up at him and slowly shook her head before dissolving into tears, effectively breaking his heart in two.

"Oh, Daphne," he murmured, moving to sit beside her.

"I'm fine," she said through her tears. "I'm fine."

"Yes, so your tears express," he teased, wiping a few from her cheeks.

She managed to smile a little. "I'm just so . . . so angry! And hurt and confused and embarrassed."

He nodded sympathetically, holding her hands tightly. "I could see that. I brought you out here so that you could cry or yell or hide for a while—whatever you need to do, away from all of that."

"Thank you," she managed, her head dropping as more tears fell.

Jamie was beside himself, wanting to hold her, but not entirely certain she wanted him to, or that he would be able to stop if he did hold her. All he knew was that he would give a fortune to see her smile again. "I will even let you slap me, if you think it will help," he suggested with a smile.

Daphne released a watery laugh, squeezing his hands. "It must seem very silly to you," she told him, "finding me flustered and embarrassed by such a thing when I am clearly prone to embarrassing myself."

"Not at all silly," he replied, shaking his head. "It makes perfect sense to me."

She looked at him in confusion, her eyes still luminous with tears.

He smiled, rubbing her hands again. "You've spent this entire Season thus far making a spectacle of yourself without the slightest bit of embarrassment because you know exactly what you are doing, whatever it is. It is always on your terms. You can embarrass yourself because it is your plan, but you have no intention of *being* embarrassed. This man's coming, whoever he is, was unexpected and embarrassing and painful, and it distressed you, as it probably should have." He shook his head slowly once more. "Not at all silly."

Daphne looked at him for a long moment, then smiled softly. "Oh, Jamie. You are too clever for your own good."

That drew a swift smile from him. "I know."

She sighed and wiped at a tear on her cheek. "My reaction may not be silly," she said in a low voice, "but I was." She sniffed and tossed her elegantly coiffed hair. "I'm going to tell you something I've never told anyone else. My family knows, but they were there."

"You don't have to tell me anything, Daphne," Jamie insisted.

She gave him a gentle smile that turned his insides upside down. "I know. But you deserve to know."

Over the next several minutes, she told him about something that she and her family had only referred to as the Incident since its occurrence two years ago. The man was Miles Watson, a neighbor of theirs, who had been a sort of sweetheart to Daphne for most of their childhood. As they had grown older, Miles had taken more of a personal interest in her, and she had the same for him. They had an understanding of an engagement, but no formal arrangements had been undertaken.

During a house party celebrating the birthday of Daphne's sister, Phoebe, Daphne had gone in search of Miles, only to discover him in a most compromising situation with her sister. It did not help matters that both Phoebe and Miles had laughed about it, even when the families had been told. They did not deny it, and nor, they claimed, had it been the first time.

Hasty engagements had been arranged between Miles and Phoebe, but the marriage never took place, as both insisted they had no desire to marry. Phoebe had been sent away to live with an aunt in Shropshire, cast off from her family, but Daphne had been the one to feel the effects of the betrayal.

Miles's family had done all that they could to hush things up, and the relationship between the two families was now strained, but the way of the world made it possible for Miles to lead a relatively untarnished life once it had been clear there would be no children from what had taken place.

"I was only recently brave enough to go into Reading," Daphne confessed, her voice slightly hoarse from her tale. "It was nothing to go into the village nearby; they all have moved on with their lives. But in Reading, I'm a living reminder of what happened, and it all comes crashing back down. My parents insisted on this ridiculous Season so that I might make a good match to redeem our family name, but they seem to forget that I was the one injured in all of this. And I was not ready. How can I trust anyone after that? Any man? We had known him all of our lives, my parents practically worshiped him, and yet we were so mistaken. I was so mistaken. So silly. So naive."

Jamie sat back against the bench, reeling from the revelations. It was a terrible story, and he wished to heaven that Daphne had never had to endure it. No one so sweet and trusting should have had such a betrayal, especially not within her own family. It was no wonder she held herself so guarded; he could hardly blame her.

"So your plan for the Season . . .?" he asked, looking at her with new interest.

She smiled, though she was close to tears again. "Ruin myself without actually ruining myself. Ensure that I can stay safely in Berkshire and do exactly as I please for the rest of my days. If I am a great embarrassment, no one will make me come back and truly embarrass myself by being inadequate for another man."

It was a brilliant scheme, it truly was, if a heartbreaking one. There was simply one flaw in it.

"You could never be inadequate for anyone worth having," Jamie told her with raw honesty, reaching up to smooth away another tear. "You deserve everything you once wanted, everything you want now, and so much more. You deserve to stand up for yourself and repair the damage inflicted upon you through your own strength. You deserve to live, not to hide, Daphne."

Her face crumpled again, and she shook her head. "Don't make me cry, Jamie. Don't."

"I can't help it," he admitted, smiling at her, though she couldn't see it. "I make everybody cry. But you can cry on me, if you like. I am more than willing to hold you, in a purely supportive manner."

Daphne laughed through her tears and reached up to stroke his jaw, shaking her head.

"I'm serious, Daph."

She smiled at him. "I know you are, Jamie. That's why I can laugh."

He returned her smile and took her hand from his jaw, though he loved having it there, and kissed the back of her glove, then turned her hand over to kiss her palm.

He caught her brief intake of breath and smiled at it, lowering her hand to their laps, still holding it.

Daphne stared at him for a long moment, tears still lingering, her lips curved in a delicate smile.

At the risk of appearing anxious, Jamie cleared his throat. "So am I going to get to hold you, or . . .?"

Daphne laughed again, this time far more merrily, and wiped at her eyes with her free hand. "Yes, Jamie, you can hold me," she laughed. "But first . . ."

Before he could inhale, her lips were on his, soft and inquiring, and he responded instinctively. One of his hands suddenly pulled at her waist while the other cupped her jaw, his thumb absently stroking against the skin. She was sweet, so sweet and so lovely, and her lips pulled at his with a delicacy that drove him wild. He brushed his lips over hers gently, over and over, knowing it would never be enough, but content for this small taste at last.

He let her break away when she was ready, though his breathing was far too unsettled for his taste. Hers was only slightly more controlled, and she eyed him with curiosity, a smirk on her lips.

Jamie sat back, then lifted his brows at her. "Now I can hold you?"

Daphne giggled and leaned against him, resting her head against his shoulder. "Only for a moment. No ruination here, remember?"

"Right, I remember," he told her, wrapping his arms around her to cradle her, but not too tightly. "I shall hold you in a most gentlemanly fashion, I can assure you."

She snorted softly in his hold. "Is there such a thing?"

"Of course," he protested with mock offense. "There is a gentlemanly way of doing everything."

"I don't want to know."

"You really do not. It is quite tedious, very boring."

"So are gentlemen."

He coughed in mock distress. "Oh, that hurts! Boring? Tedious? I have never been so insulted!"

She laughed shortly, nuzzling against him. "I doubt that very much. Knowing you as I do now, and hearing about your family, I would wager they have given you far worse. I know I have recently."

"True," he sighed, rubbing his hands up and down her back as he felt her shiver. "You have tested my gentlemanly limits, and I do not know how I shall bear it."

She looked up at him with interest. "Then you'll release me from our courtship?"

He frowned at her immediately. "Not a chance, Daph."

Daphne scowled. "It was worth a try."

He smiled and seized the opportunity, leaning down to kiss her just once. "Not a chance," he whispered against her lips.

She shivered again, but he suspected for a different reason. Then she shifted away from him and rose from the bench. "We had better return," she said, averting her eyes. "I wouldn't want us to be missed."

Jamie remained on the bench, looking up at her. "Daphne."

She turned to face him, trying for her usual demeanor with him. "Yes?"

He could see right through the facade and gave her a slow smile that made her eyes widen. "Please tell me I can kiss you again. You cannot give me a taste and then forbid me from ever having it again. That would not be kind."

"Not sporting, you mean," she whispered, folding her arms.

He shook his head. "Not sporting."

Daphne stared at him for a long moment, then lifted her chin, and gave him a firm nod. "You may earn your kisses through very good behavior."

"According to you or to me?" he asked suspiciously, rising to his feet.

"Probably both," she admitted. "But you may not steal them. Understood?"

Jamie nodded obediently. "Understood." He held out his hand. "And if you are comforted, Miss Hutchins, I believe I claimed a dance."

She smiled and placed her hand in his. "Thank you for your comfort, Mr. Woodbridge. It was very gentlemanly."

He squeezed her hand tightly, winking at her. "Thank you for the compliment, Miss Hutchins. Might that be worthy of a kiss?"

She immediately went on tiptoe and kissed his cheek. "Just enough."

He narrowed his eyes at her, then offered his arm to her. "Not quite what I meant, Daph."

She took his arm, and he led her back toward the house. "You didn't think I was going to make this particularly easy, did you, Jamie?"

"Of course not," he scoffed as they ascended the terrace stairs. "When have you made anything easy for me?"

Daphne slapped his chest, laughing, and they caught sight of Jonathan leaning on the terrace railing.

He nodded at them both. "This is me playing chaperone," he informed them. "Don't tell anyone, but I could neither see nor hear you, and while I trust that you were well-behaved, I will properly perjure myself if there is speculation of anything untoward."

Daphne looked at Jonathan with a smile, then turned to Jamie, tilting her head. "I don't suppose your cousin could earn a kiss."

"No," Jamie said flatly, glaring at her. "Absolutely not."

"I don't see why not," Jonathan mused, considering the idea.

"No."

Daphne laughed and shook her head. "Come on, Jamie. I want that dance you said I promised. But I am pointedly ignoring you the entire time."

Jamie looked down at her with a wolfish smile. "You think you are, Daph. But just you wait."

Seven

aphne was beside herself. Falling apart at the seams. In a whole heap of trouble. In over her head.

All because of Jamie.

Ever since that night with Miles, whose name she could now think or say without pain, he had been more fixed by her side, no matter what she said or did. Two more parties with horrendous dresses, loud laughter, and ruining at least six card games where they were partnered, and he never appeared even the slightest bit irritated with her.

She had been asked her opinion on country living as opposed to London, and her response had made several others cough in surprise, but Jamie had only smiled at it. He told her later that he quite agreed.

Agreed? She was intentionally being difficult, saying things for reactions, and he agreed?

What was it going to take to get this man away from her?

She chewed on the inside of her lip while she sat in the theater box, the same one from weeks before, the same man beside her, and the same agitation rising within her as his fingers dragged over the same spot they had before.

She would probably have to actually want him to be away from her for any of her ideas to work, and she had never wanted anything less than to be away from Jamie.

Except coming to London at all.

And even that was up for debate.

Without coming to London, she would never have met Jamie, and he had changed everything for her. She would never forget his sweetness and understanding when Miles had shown up, and she could not get their kiss out of her head. Despite saying that he could earn kisses, they had yet to share another one. She had been keeping him at a distance, which was the hardest thing she had ever done. More and more she just wanted to wrap his arms around her and throw away all of her efforts for the Season.

She couldn't.

She had come too far. She had spent the last two years not talking about the Incident. About what Miles and Phoebe did. About how she felt. How she hurt. About anything at all.

She had not talked in such a long time, and now she was talking. She was acting.

She couldn't give in now.

And he needed to stop distracting her with the gentle strokes on her arm.

"Stop," she hissed.

The stroking stopped. "What?" he replied in a very low tone. "What's wrong?"

"You're stroking my arm," she informed him, as if he didn't know. "Stop."

Jamie was staring at her, but she kept her eyes on the stage, desperate to focus on the opera and still her pulse.

Halfway through a stunning trio, the stroking started up again. She did not react, knowing he would be looking for a reaction, and increased her focusing efforts on the stage. When it was once more driving her crazy, she plucked his fingers from her arm and settled them in his lap.

He chuckled softly, which sent a warm ripple down her spine, rather like the stroking on her arm did.

Twice more he did the same thing, and she responded the same way.

The third time, she huffed a sigh. "I will tie your hand to your chair," she whispered, smiling in spite of herself.

"I'll risk it," he said, his mouth too close to her ear.

Why did that sound so appealing? Why couldn't it sound like the worst idea in the world? Why didn't his touch make her skin crawl instead of sing?

Why?

The stroking resumed, slower and more pointed, even through the material of the glove she could feel its fiery trail along her forearm and down to her wrist.

It was incredible; no one looking into the box and seeing them would have any idea that Jamie was doing anything at all. They would not be able to see that Daphne was slowly being driven wild by this impossibly attractive, charming, good-hearted man with a sharp wit. Every pass of his fingers sent her pulse ricocheting, and if the glove weren't in place, he would feel it for himself.

She glanced at him and saw a small smirk on his lips.

That maddening fool knew exactly what he was doing to her.

Well, two could play at that game.

Daphne sat as still as she could, her eyes fixed on the stage. She knew Jamie was as attuned to her as she was to him, and if she reacted at all, he would know. She forced her expression to be perfectly bland and ignored every passing stroke of his fingers.

Every. Slow. Brush.

It was worse than before, knowing he was paying attention, hiding how she loved it . . .

He was watching her now, pointedly and without shame.

She was not pulling her hand away. She was not moving his hand.

She was not tying his hand to the chair.

She took pity on the poor, deluded man who was bent on courting her and gave him the smallest, slightest smirk.

His faint exhalation was all she needed to hear. She closed her eyes and let down her resistance for just this moment, just for him. She let herself feel and enjoy being so tenderly touched, barely anything at all, and yet she could feel it down to her bones. It was so easy, so natural, so comfortable, yet it made her feel alive.

Just as Jamie did.

Slowly, so she wouldn't alter his pattern, Daphne rotated her hand so that her palm faced upward. On cue, Jamie's fingers passed up toward her wrist once, twice, and on the third pass he moved farther down and laced his fingers with hers.

If she hadn't been focused on controlling her expression and pretending to be unaffected, she would have smiled enough to make her cheeks ache. As it was, she would strain the muscles in her face containing the smirk she wore, and she curved her fingers around his.

"Daph," he whispered, and her heart lifted within her.

The sudden hum of voices broke the moment as the first act ended and the interval began. They both sat for a moment, fingers entwined, before her parents and aunt moved from their seats in front of them, and they released hands quickly.

"Shall we take a turn?" her mother asked with a warm smile.

"Of course," Jamie said politely, rising. "After you, Mrs. Hutchins. Mr. Hutchins. Mrs. Ansley."

They made their way out of the box, and Daphne was grateful for the interval and a more public setting where she might collect her thoughts and find sense once more. Jamie would behave with others around, and Daphne would . . .

Well, she would be very, very quiet until she could untangle her own thoughts.

Her parents and Josephine stopped to speak with some acquaintances of theirs, while Daphne and Jamie waited nearby, watching other guests meander by.

"Too many feathers," Jamie commented after a group of ladies passed.

Daphne giggled. "And too much fragrance. I can barely breathe."

"I hope you aren't taking notes. I couldn't bear that as well."

"It did cross my mind."

Jamie groaned softly, and then silenced himself as her parents returned to them. They only walked on a moment or two more before her mother expressed a desire to return to the box once more.

Once inside, before they could return to their seats, her mother turned to face her, looking downright murderous.

Daphne reared back in surprise. "Mama?"

"What is this I have been hearing, Daphne?" she demanded in a dangerous hiss, hands on her hips. "What have you been doing with the opportunities I have given you this Season?"

"I . . ." Daphne tried, feeling anxious and wishing Jamie wasn't here for this.

"Changing your gowns after you leave the house?" her mother barked, her voice cracking sharply. "Speaking harshly? Poor posture and poor manners?"

"Mama," Daphne pleaded, her face beginning to flame.

"Darling," her father murmured, but he received a sharp rap to the chest. Even Aunt Josephine was paying rapt attention, and she looked bewildered by it all.

"How could you, Daphne?" her mother whispered. "How could you embarrass us in such a way? It is no wonder that Miles Watson jilted you for your sister, and I have no idea what is possibly persuading Mr. Woodbridge here to court you when there is not much to recommend you."

Daphne stared at her mother in horror, then shot out of her seat and fled the box, barreling down the corridor until she found an alcove behind some heavy curtains. She sank against the wall and covered her mouth to stifle the sobs that threatened to escape.

Before her panic could reach its full strength, the curtain was pulled aside, and Jamie was in the alcove with her.

"You can't be in here with me," she protested, waving him out. "It's not proper."

"I don't care, Daphne," he retorted, folding his arms across his chest. "Try to make me leave."

"I am going to cry, and it's not going to be pleasant," she warned him.

He gave her a scolding look that made her heart soften. "I figured as much, Daph. It's all right."

Daphne shook her head. "No, it's not. It's not all right." Her face crumpled, and she pressed her wrists to her eyes. "My mother is right. She is right. What in the world possessed me to do something so mad as to intentionally ruin myself just to spite them? I was never a disobedient or willful child. Despite my stubbornness, I always behaved and did as I was told." She lowered her hands and shook her head, her breath hitching. "I never spoke out of turn, I never said what I was really thinking, and I minded my manners." She looked up at the too ornate ceiling for the alcove, tears rolling down her cheeks.

"This was such a mistake. I am only being petulant and juvenile, acting out to prove a point. What is the point of any of this when I am only going to live in the misery of my apparently deserved loneliness for the rest of my life?"

There was silence in the alcove, and she looked over at Jamie expectantly.

He was watching her with a startling intensity that surprised her. His arms were tighter across his chest, and his eyes filled with a new light as he considered her. He slowly shook his head, taking a step toward her. "There are so many errors in what you just said that it would take me far too long to explain and correct you. I am a patient man, but I would rather hold you for an inappropriately long period of time until you simply don't believe a single word that just came from your lips."

Daphne stared at him, a pair of tears rolling down her cheeks, wondering how this man could possibly have a true interest in her or anything she was. She had tried everything to push him away, and there was plenty to dissuade him without her help, yet here he was.

"Why won't you just leave?" she rasped, her voice choking with tears yet to be shed.

Jamie's stance softened, and he came to her, taking her face in his hands. "Don't you understand? I am not going anywhere. Ever."

"Jamie," Daphne whispered, gripping his wrists.

"I will always be here for you," Jamie insisted, his thumbs smoothing away her tears. "I will always stand beside you. I will always smile when you're around, laugh for no particular reason, be drawn to your side, want to carry you away, and crave the touch of your lips. Because I am always going to be as in love with you as I am right now. The only thing keeping me from asking you to marry me right this moment is you."

Daphne released a soft sob, and Jamie kissed her gently, touching his forehead to hers.

"What if I'm not ready?" Daphne asked with a sniffle.

Jamie stroked her cheek again, smiling. "Then I'll ask you next year. And the year after. And the year after that. It could be twenty years from now, and I would still be asking you."

That made her smile. "Really?"

"Well, at some point, people would begin to talk, and we'd probably be forced to marry just to keep us both in polite society, so to save us both that agony, you might as well accept me while society still considers us foolish but relatively innocent."

Daphne chuckled, her heart swelling with a love for this man that took her breath away. She might not be quite ready to accept his non-proposal, but she was not going to pretend this wasn't the sort of love that she had dreamed about her entire life.

Jamie grinned at her laugh, then kissed her again, wringing pleasure from her that she had never imagined. "I won't ask until you're ready," he whispered, nuzzling her gently. "Only tell me when, and I won't hesitate."

She rubbed her thumbs over his wrists. "Is it enough that I want to say yes, even if I can't let you ask yet?"

"That is everything," Jamie told her, nodding against her.

Daphne sighed, still gripping his wrists. "We'd better go back to the box. My parents will be missing us."

Jamie stepped back, sliding his hands down to hers. "I think we've had enough theater for one evening. Your aunt is willing to leave, if you wish."

"I just want to go home," Daphne murmured, nodding her head.

Jamie brought her hands to his lips and kissed them. "I thought you might. Come on, I'll take you both home."

"Can we just leave everyone?" she muttered as Jamie checked the corridor outside of the alcove to ensure they were safe from prying eyes. "Aunt Josephine isn't exactly observant, despite her recent use to me."

Jamie laughed quietly and waved Josephine out of the box. "I'm not quite that improper as to see you home myself or to send you alone, so we really must take her along."

Daphne rolled her eyes, looping her hand through his arm with a groan. "The trouble with gentlemen . . ."

Two days and no proposals from Jamie later, Daphne found herself walking into another ballroom with another elegant dress her mother had picked out, and this time she did not pay any attention to the whispers of those around her. She'd had far too much time to think since that night at the theater. She had a long conversation with her parents, wherein several apologies were made on both sides, and Daphne settled on a course both she and her parents could live with.

Tonight, she had intentionally arrived late to this party, but not for the usual reasons.

This time she needed to ensure that someone had arrived before her and would already be here.

She had one more bold and shocking thing to do before this madness was ended.

And as she surveyed the room, she caught sight of the person in question, fixed a cool smile on her face, and moved across the ballroom directly to him.

"Miles," she said warmly, catching both him and his female companion off guard.

They both looked at her in surprise. "Daphne," Miles replied, recovering quickly. "What a pleasant surprise."

"Yes, isn't it?" she answered with a less than pleased tone. "Will you introduce me to your friend?"

Miles turned to indicate her. "Miss Jane Fairview, this is

Miss Daphne Hutchins. Miss Fairview has kindly consented to let me pay courtship to her, Daphne."

Miss Fairview smiled hesitantly and curtseyed to Daphne, which she returned. "Miss Hutchins."

"Miss Fairview, a pleasure." Daphne forced a false smile, feeling nothing but pity for this girl, who could know nothing about this man she was allowing near her.

That was all about to change.

"Mr. Watson and I are old friends," Daphne began, sparing another false smile for Miles, who watched her warily. "Neighbors in Berkshire. We were even childhood sweethearts before we grew up."

"Daphne . . ." Miles warned, which earned him a look.

She returned to Miss Fairview, not bothering to keep her voice down. "I could tell you all sorts of things about Mr. Watson, my dear, but let me suffice with giving you this bit of advice: if you do not mind having for a husband a man who has broken promises to a girl he had pledged matrimony to, then please allow his courtship to continue. If you do not object to the idea that the promises were broken because of a marked degree of infidelity and that he was caught in the most compromising of situations, then yes, continue to allow him your better acquaintance."

The room was rapidly growing abuzz with her revelations, though several patrons shushed the others to better hear what Daphne was setting down. Miles looked pale, while Miss Fairview seemed to grow more and more horrified by the moment.

"In fact, Miss Fairview," Daphne continued, taking the girl's hand, "the only reason why Mr. Watson is available to be courting you is that he and my sister were too stupid to marry when the arrangements were made to salvage their reputations. If you, or anyone, wishes to confirm my story, you may rely upon the testimonies of my family, as well as that of his. And, though I don't know you or your situation, I suspect he is after your fortune, whatever it may be. I have it on great authority that he has been cut off with only enough to live on and that the entire Watson family estate and fortune has been settled upon his younger brother, who is a delightful man, and I would be happy to introduce you, should you prefer a more suitable candidate. Otherwise, my dear girl, I do suggest that you look elsewhere for settling your future happiness." Daphne squeezed her hand. "No one deserves to be tied to such a man, and as one who was spared that pain, I can certainly attest to that." She smiled tightly, giving Miss Fairview an encouraging nod, and then turned from their group without sparing a single look for Miles Watson or the past they had shared.

The path before her cleared as she moved away from them, and she felt as though she could breathe freely for the first time in nearly two years.

Daphne smiled with real pleasure, one of the first of these smiles that many of the people present would have seen on her, and while they whispered as she approached and passed, she could not tell if they were disapproving or admiring. She looked the part now; a lovely green muslin with proper cut and styling would do that for a girl with her complexion and coloring, and she would undoubtedly be asked to dance later.

She anticipated she would be otherwise engaged and must disappoint those offers.

If the look in Jamie Woodbridge's eyes as she approached him were any indication, every dance would be otherwise engaged for quite some time.

"I am so in love with you at this moment," he said with unabashed pride as she reached him.

Daphne smiled at him with all of the love she had never

allowed herself before. "That is all I needed to know," she replied. Then she went up on tiptoe and pressed her lips to his, reaching one hand up to curl around his neck and pull him as close as she could.

He responded with the proper enthusiasm, and she felt further passion simmering beneath the surface, sighing when his hands cradled her face and took control of the kiss.

Amidst the shocked and startled gasps and squeals of those around them, Jamie broke off, laughing in disbelief and touching his nose to hers. "You do realize that you have ruined yourself."

Daphne laughed in response. "I imagined it might, yes. But that was the plan, was it not?"

Jamie pulled back, still holding her face in his hands, his eyes growing serious. "You have to marry me now."

She nodded soberly. "An appropriate consequence for my actions. Especially given my speech to Miss Fairview just now."

"Daph," Jamie murmured uncertainly, his smile gentle, but hesitant.

She gripped the back of his neck tightly, forcing him to pay attention. "I knew what I was doing, Jamie." She pulled back to give him a daring smirk. "Will you dare to ask me now?"

At last, Jamie grinned in outright delight. "Are you asking me to ask you?"

"I might be," she countered with a light shrug. "If you can ask me after all of this, I would be a fool to refuse."

Jamie shook his head, stroking her cheeks. "Will you marry me, Daphne Hutchins?"

Daphne tilted her head. "Do you love me?"

"With all of my heart," he replied fervently.

"Then I accept." She found herself unaccountably emotional and fought the rise of tears. "Because I love you, too, and I don't want to spend another moment pretending otherwise."

Jamie was quick to kiss her again, dissolving any hint of tears. This time, they drew scattered applause from those not shocked by a surprise engagement and displays of affection in the middle of the ballroom.

He released her with one more teasing pass of his lips, then held her close for a long moment. Daphne inhaled the warm, comfortable scent of him, sighing at the relief of being in his arms.

There was so much ahead of them, and she was eager to begin it all.

Becoming aware of the attention surrounding them, Daphne eased out of Jamie's hold reluctantly. "We should probably get out of this ballroom," she murmured with a laugh. "People are staring."

Jamie looked around, considered the effect they had had, and grinned devilishly. "Let them stare," he proclaimed boldly, kissing her again, and pulling her onto the dance floor.

"Not gentlemanly," Daphne laughed, lacing her fingers with his as they took their positions.

Jamie winked at her, still grinning. "But rather sporting, wouldn't you say?"

She shook her head, thrilled with his response. "Yes, my love. Very sporting, indeed."

Epiloque

Four weeks later, the wedding of the Season took place in St. George's, Hanover Square, as all fashionable marriages must. The guests were a variety of people, all family and friends, but most only came for the promise of a spectacle, and they were disappointed by the rather sedate nature of the ceremony.

Not a single shocking thing occurred.

Unless one considered an overenthusiastic kiss between the bride and groom after the ceremony to be shocking—which some undoubtedly did.

Mr. and Mrs. Woodbridge settled into life easily at the estate in Norfolk, reviving the house and its lands into a thriving estate worthy of the Woodbridge name.

Daphne was easily adopted into the Woodbridge family, instantly a great favorite with them all, and a particular confidante of the Mothers, which terrified the rest to no end.

Her shocking days behind her, and under Jamie's gentlemanly tutelage, Daphne ran the household at their newly christened Milsbury House, formerly known as Brimley, with precision and kindness, and a great deal of laughter, as was the nature of the family.

And when she and her sister eventually reunited years

later at Phoebe's wedding to a handsome and congenial clergyman with two young children, Daphne managed to keep a civil tongue in her head and even offered profound congratulations. They were followed privately by more sincere condolences to her new brother-in-law, who accepted them with a smile and good graces. Jamie only had to remind Daphne to behave six times, which was only two more than he gave their daughter, and one more than he gave their infant son, who conveniently cried during the ceremony to provide a much needed escape.

There were no tears at that wedding, only excessive laughter, and it continued for days following between Jamie and Daphne, who were, by then, well on their way to a third child.

And the next time they were in London for the Season, both Daphne and Jamie were better behaved.

But only just.

About the Author

Rebecca Connolly writes romances, both period and contemporary, because she absolutely loves a good love story. She has been creating stories since childhood, and there are home videos to prove it! She started writing them down in elementary school and has never looked back. She currently lives in Minnesota, spends every spare moment away from her day job absorbed in her writing, and is a hot cocoa addict.

Visit her online: RebeccaConnolly.com

Made in United States
North Haven, CT
24 October 2023

43159213R00173